I0580153

OTHER WORKS BY RENEE LEAR

Circumstantial

The Divorce Diet

My Friend Gavin

TIMES THREE

RENEE LEAR

To order additional copies of this book, contact:
Bookwhip
1-855-339-3589
https://www.bookwhip.com

DEDICATIONS

This book is for my inspirations,
my children: Brooklyn, Stefan, Bodee & Gavin,
and for their father Ronnie, who was the first to read this
book. We love you, miss you, and think of you every day.
Also for my biggest fan and supporter, my Mom.

PART I

"THE INTRODUCTION"

CHAPTER ONE

Sweat poured down Vahn's face as she crouched behind the late model Buick. Her right thigh felt like it was on fire. She looked down to see how bad it was. There was a lot of blood but it was only a flesh wound. A bullet had grazed her as she dove for cover behind the car.

She knew he was waiting for her. She checked her clip not sure of how many shots she'd fired off. Only two left. She quickly slid in a new clip, took a deep breath and jumped up firing in his direction using the car for as much of a shield as possible.

Vahn had squeezed off two rounds when he rushed out from behind the dumpster firing at her. She hit the ground and saw his feet running out in front of the car. She brought her gun up in front of her and locked in on his ankle then squeezed the trigger.

Blood and bone exploded as he fell to the ground and she heard him giggle…what the hell, was that a giggle? She had just blown his damn foot off.

He wasn't moving so she crawled toward the front of the car keeping her gun on him. She looked around the tire to see his face. He was motionless, staring at the sky.

Suddenly he reached up, touched his chest in a flirtatious way, and giggled again. What the hell? Then the smell of stale sheets, incense, and marijuana filled the air. She blinked twice and the man faded as an old beat up dresser came into view.

Raynor stood under the hot steamy water hoping it would relieve his aching muscles. He tilted his face up towards the showerhead, feeling the rhythmic beat of the water on his temple.

As he closed his eyes, he suddenly felt a sharp burning sensation in his right thigh. He whirled around and looked down at his leg wiping water from his eyes. At first he saw only his skin, untouched. Then it seemed to transform into denim covered with blood. He reached down to touch it, then fixed his vision on his hand. It was a woman's hand. He quickly buried the heals of his hands into his eyes rubbing as hard as he could. Trying to erase the image from his mind, he wondered if this was the result of too many long hours or if he was just losing it.

When he opened his eyes again his shower had transformed into a street. He seemed to be lying on the ground looking out from under a car. He watched as feet ran out in front of the car. A woman's hand holding a gun came into view, seemed to aim at one of the feet that were running, and pulled the trigger. He watched with intensity as the bullet exploded the ankle of the person running. Then as quickly as the image had come, it left.

Raynor stared at the back of his tiled shower in disbelief. He could only feel the water trickling down his back as his ears rang from the sound of a gunshot.

"Damn, only dreaming," thought Vahn. But the sight of the man's ankle exploding had been so vivid, so real. And it had felt…so good.

"Okay Vahn, let's see if we can keep our sadistic side under wraps a little while longer," she said laughing to herself.

Then she heard another giggle. She threw back the covers and sat up. She sat there for a moment trying to fully wake up. Wearing only a T-shirt and a pair of panties, she looked down at her thigh. No blood. She thought that it was strange that in the dream, she had actually felt pain when she was looking at the flesh wound.

Getting out of bed Vahn walked through the beads strung in the doorway between the bedroom and the living room. Johnny, her so called fiance, was lying on the floor wearing only silk boxers, with a half naked girl who looked no more than seventeen years old.

He took a drag off the joint he was holding, put his lips to hers and exhaled into her mouth. He then looked up at Vahn and smiled.

"Hey Vahn baby. We were just havin' a little party."

Leaning against the doorframe and crossing her arms she smiled smugly at him saying, "That's great. And who the hell is she?"

The girl turned her head to look at Vahn and managed a smile though she was so stoned she could only raise one side of her mouth.

"I met her at The Pub. I thought we could all get together and let fate take its course. So what do you say? Why don't you come join us?" Johnny asked as he bent his head back down and began making circles around the girl's belly button with his tongue.

"It's real tempting, but I think I'll have to pass,"

Vahn said as she turned back into the bedroom. Shaking her head and cursing under her breath, more angry with herself than with him, she knew this was her queue to exit.

Vahn had wanted to leave Johnny for over a year, but she had first planned on saving some money. This little incident would just put her plan in motion a little prematurely. This wasn't the first time he had brought someone home with him, but she was going to make it the last time she had to put up with it. The only problem now was where to go.

Walking to the dresser, Vahn reached behind it and pulled two duffel bags from their hiding place. She then opened the drawers of the dresser, threw her clothes on the bed, then quickly stuffed them into the duffel bags.

Going into the bathroom that was adjacent to the bedroom, Vahn put her hands on either side of the sink and stared at herself in the mirror. She had a beautiful olive complexion, long flowing deep brown hair, and crystal blue eyes. There were times when she looked in the mirror and felt as if she were gazing at a stranger. Though she knew that she was very beautiful and very intelligent, the choices she had made in her life seemed to distance her from the person that was staring back at her.

Taking a deep breath, she quickly grabbed her deodorant, toothbrush, toothpaste, and hair essentials, then walked back to the bed and stuffed them in the bag as well.

Looking around and making sure she had all of the few items she owned, Vahn pulled on a pair of cut-offs and her Nikes. Instead of going back through the living room where heavy moaning was now coming from, she opened the window and stepped out onto the metal platform of the fire escape. She pushed down on the old rusty steps. They let out a loud creak before finally giving under their own weight.

Vahn descended the stairs feeling as if a weight had been lifted off her shoulders. But now what? She had followed Johnny there to Portland, Oregon, all the way from Ohio. She was clear across the country from anyone she knew.

Not sure of exactly what she was going to do, Vahn began walking in the direction of the Denny's she was a waitress at. It was about a thirty-minute drive from her apartment, so she knew that she wasn't going to make it there any time soon. The only thing she knew for certain was that she needed to be there for work the next day, so she figured that heading that way wasn't a bad idea.

"You really hit the jackpot this time didn't you," she thought to herself. "You follow an asshole to a place you know nothing about and for what?"

Vahn had been eighteen years old when she met Johnny and he had been the much wiser, so she thought, twenty-three. She had just graduated from high school and he had been at one of the after parties.

Though she had her fair share of boyfriends over her school years, she had managed not to become completely infatuated with one guy, until Johnny. He had come out of nowhere and swept her off her feet. He seemed to have all the answers. She instantly fell in love.

After being together for two years, Johnny came up with a brilliant plan. The next thing she knew they were living in Oregon. Johnny's idea of a stable job was running drugs for his cousin, Ian, who also lived in Portland.

Having a drug dealer for a boyfriend and living in the slums, she was too ashamed to call home for help. Her mother had thrown a fit when she told her where she was moving to. Vahn couldn't stand to hear the words 'I told you so' come from her mother's mouth. Shirley, her mother, had been married five times and was the last person she wanted advice on men from.

So, Vahn had decided to stay and tough it out.

She had been in Portland for three years and all she had seen were her apartment, her wonderful place of employment, and the mall a few times. What a great life.

Vahn, trying hard to be the opposite of Shirley, had latched onto the first Romeo that had presented himself. In spite of the man he was, she tried to stay with him vowing that she wouldn't start the ball rolling as her mother had and sleep with more men than she had fingers and toes before reaching the age of twentyfive.

After walking for about forty-five minutes, Vahn found herself standing in front of a hotel that looked like she might be able to have the bed all to herself instead of being pushed out by a monstrous roach in the middle of the night.

She checked in with the oversized and under maintenanced manager, received her room key, and headed for her room. The hotel was a one level stretch of rooms. She was thankful that she wouldn't have to climb any stairs. Her legs were tired of walking and her shoulders were tired of lugging around her bags.

Walking about half way down the row of doors Vahn came to her room. She unlocked her door and went inside bolting it back behind her. She threw her bags on the bed and looked around. The room was so small; it held only three pieces of furniture. A bed, a nightstand, and a dresser.

The bed looked to be about a queen size and had a gold and green flowered comforter on it. The headboard of the bed was against the left-hand wall, and the bed was pushed up into the far corner so that one side of the bed lined the far wall. Taking up what little space remained on the left-hand wall was a small nightstand. On it was a green oversized lamp with gold felt balls hanging off the lampshade. And to complete the ensemble, taking up the entire wall on the right hand side of the room, stood a four-drawer dresser.

The bathroom door began where the dresser ended. Vahn went in the bathroom and noticed it had a standing shower stall, toilet and a small sink with vanity mirror above it.

"Home sweet home," she said. She put her clothes in the dresser deciding that this was as good a place as any to stay until she could decide what she was going to do next.

On the floor next to the nightstand was a phone book, which she didn't quite understand since there was no phone. She looked on the city map wanting to see how far she was from the Denny's she worked at. Realizing that she had no clue as to the exact location she was in, she went outside to check the street signs.

Opening the door to her room, Vahn stepped out onto the sidewalk and started walking toward the street. She could see the sign facing her said Twentieth Street. Getting closer to the corner she was about to step off the curb to determine what intersection she was at when she heard a woman screaming. A young woman, probably in her early twenties, came into sight as she rounded the corner across the street.

"Help me! He's going to kill me!" She screamed as she stumbled but continued to run. She was wearing one black high heal and a strapless red leather dress.

Vahn started across the street to ask if she could help when a man came running around the corner behind her. He lifted his arm towards the woman and shots rang out. Vahn turned to look at the woman and saw her body being pitched forward. Everything looked as if it were in slow motion. Her body was raised off the ground. As she came down she looked like a rag doll. Her head bounced off the pavement and was still.

She was facing Vahn's direction and seemed to be looking right at Vahn, or through her. More shots rang out snapping Vahn out of her daze. She suddenly realized that she was standing in plain view. She quickly hid behind a car which was parked a couple of feet away.

She wanted desperately to do something, but what? There was no phone in sight and she knew if she went running for help she would get shot herself. Having no other choice she decided to stay where she was.

Looking through the passenger side window, she could see the man walk up to the woman. He put his legs on either side of her, straddling her body. He raised his gun and emptied the clip into her. With each shot she seemed to convulse as blood exploded onto the sidewalk. Her eyes, never changing stared straight at Vahn.

"You stupid bitch!" He yelled, his face twisted with rage. "Thought you could take my money. Thought you could outsmart me. Never!" He screamed stomping the back of her head. He walked to the front of her body and squatted down. He grabbed a handful of her hair and lifted her face up level with his own.

"You are my bitch, which means the money you make is my money. You wanted a way out. Well, I just gave it to you. I'm a fucking saint ain't I." He put his tongue out and licked her face from her lips to her forehead. Slamming her head back to the ground he stood up. Vahn could see blood dripping off his chin.

He began frantically going through his pockets. He pulled out something small.

She couldn't tell what it was at first. Then she saw him put his hand up to his nose and realized that he was snorting coke. After a few moments he put it back in his pocket, threw his head back, and walked around the corner out of sight.

Vahn's first instinct was to go check on the woman but she realized there was no way in hell that she could still be alive. Making sure that the street was still, she ran into the manager's office to see if he had called the police.

He was sitting in his chair with his head tilted backward, snoring. He had slept through the gunshots. Considering how loud his snoring was she decided it was possible. Leaning across the desk Vahn grabbed his phone and dialed 911.

Raynor sat on his couch eating pretzels and drinking a Corona, trying to concentrate on David Letterman's show. His mind kept wandering back to the incident in the shower. He wasn't sure if he had been hallucinating or if it was possibly real. Yet how could it have been?

Deciding he was ready to go to bed he clicked off the TV, rolled up the bag of pretzels and walked to the kitchen. He put his pretzels away and threw away his beer bottle then headed down the hall.

Walking to the bathroom he turned on the water and grabbed his toothbrush from its holder on the sink. He opened the medicine cabinet and pulled the toothpaste off of the shelf.

When he closed the mirror he was not looking at his reflection. The sound of running water faded as his bathroom turned into a street scene.

He watched as a woman's body was flown forward from gunshots then seemed to bounce off the pavement as she landed.

As more shots rang out he seemed to flinch and felt as if he was running toward a parked car. As he crouched behind the car he could see through the window that the man was now straddling the woman's body. But something else held his attention. He could see the reflection of a woman out of the corner of his eye in the passenger's side mirror of the car.

Each breath she took followed his own pattern of breathing. She was beautiful. She had dark flowing hair and he could see her amazing blue eyes perfectly. He wondered if he was seeing these things through her. He decided he must be. But why? Was she just a figment of his imagination, or was she an actual person?

Not wanting to lose the vision he tried to concentrate on staying with her. He felt his body rise and look out over the hood of the car. The woman across the street lay motionless and the street was deserted.

He then seemed to be running toward a building. He tried to look for any kind of sign to tell him the name of the place. He saw no signs but noticed that out of his right eye he could see consecutively numbered doors with cars parked outside of them. Guessing it was a hotel he tried desperately to move his vision toward the sky, thinking that there was probably a large sign above the building. Unable to shift his vision, he assumed that he was just along for the ride and in control of nothing.

As the woman opened a door and walked in, there was a large man snoring in a chair. She reached across the desk and grabbed the phone. As she dialed 911, Raynor read the numbers printed under the buttons, 555-9867.

He felt his hand reach up to rub his eyes, and when he brought it down he was staring at his own reflection in the mirror.

After giving the police her statement Vahn went back to her room. She looked on the map and noted that she was about six miles away from Denny's. She didn't have enough money to take a cab so she'd have to run. All through junior high and high school she had been a member of the track team, so the thought of pounding the pavement didn't bother her.

She took a quick shower then crawled into bed. All she could think about was the emptiness in the woman's eyes as she had lain dead with that blank stare on her face. Replaying the scene over and over in her head she wondered if there was something she could have done. She felt like she should have been able to do something.

Recalling the dream she had awoke from earlier, she remembered how in control she had felt. A far cry from the helpless way she had been hiding in the street. Finally she gave up and decided to try to get some sleep. She reached over and clicked off the light saying, "I guess it's just a fucked up ending to a fucked up day."

CHAPTER TWO

Apparently the manager was used to sleeping in and didn't want to be bothered with having to give wake up calls. Vahn had found an alarm clock in the drawer of the nightstand and had set it for 4:30a.m.

When it went off that morning she fumbled around trying to find the snooze button. She felt the long bar, which was usually how a snooze button was shaped, and pressed it. Nothing. She pressed it again this time holding it down. Still it continued to go off, each beep like a little explosion in her head. She opened one eye and turned the clock up so she could see what button she had been pushing. Sure enough it was the snooze button.

"Must be broken," she said, turning off the alarm.

If this clock had been through a life like the one she had left at Johnny's then the snooze button was definitely abused. The poor thing had taken a beating every morning.

Vahn slowly dragged herself out of bed and went to the bathroom. She took a quick shower. After drying off and wrapping the towel around her, she brushed her teeth then pulled her hair back. Walking to the dresser, she pulled her clothes out and slipped on a pair of sweatpants and a sweatshirt then pulled on her Nikes. She grabbed her duffel bag, put her waitress uniform in it, then left for work locking the door behind her.

As she jogged towards Denny's she tried to pace herself so she wouldn't be drenched with sweat by the time she got there. At 5:25 a.m. she arrived and walked through the doors. Since the restaurant stayed open twenty-four hours she didn't have to wait for anyone to let her in. Her shift was scheduled to start at 6:30 a.m. so she had plenty of time to eat and change.

Vahn walked into the kitchen area to ask Deke to make her an omelet. She put her bags down on the floor and jumped up on the stainless steel counter, which was used for cutting meats. Though this was a "health hazard" and she had been written up for it more than once, she had to sit there and talk to Deke every morning otherwise her day would always turn to shit.

"What'll it be little lady?" Deke asked doing his best John Wayne impersonation and flashing her a smile.

"Give me a Western Omelet Duke," she said laughing.

Deke noticed her sweats and running shoes and said, "What's the matter? You see a black man this morning and it spooked you so bad you had to run?" Being black himself Deke could never resist throwing comments like that into the conversation.

"You're hilarious Deke," said Vahn rolling her eyes.

"Hey I've got to give you a hard time," said Deke.

"Yeah you'd like to," she smirked.

"Hey now, it's way too early in the morning to be making comments like that. You'll get us both in trouble." Deke raised his eyebrows and smiled at her as he was chopping the ham for her omelet.

Returning the smile Vahn said, "Well, I'm gonna go change. Yell at me when it's ready please sir." She jumped down and grabbed her bag then headed toward the back.

"No problem darlin'," he said cracking two eggs simultaneously.

After changing and getting her omelet from Deke, Vahn took it to the break room and sat down at the table to eat. The morning paper had arrived and she instinctively took out the classified ads. It was a tradition there that the only part of the paper ever read was the classified ads. The goal of every employee was to find a better job.

Vahn had just turned the page when a big ad at the bottom right hand corner caught her eye. It read, "Portland Police Department now testing for new recruits. Highest scores will be placed into the Police Academy where room and board will be provided. Learn to serve your community in the law enforcement division. Graduates will be our newest members to the Portland Police Department. Join us to protect and serve the Portland area. Testing takes place at the Civic Center on May 20, from 3:30 p.m. to 6:30 p.m."

Vahn's blood raced as she read the ad. She had never really thought of herself as a police officer, but the thought of it now seemed perfect. If nothing else it would be free room and board. That had to be better than the dump she was now staying in. The thought of not having to pay for it made it sound even better.

May 20th. She suddenly realized she had no idea what the date was. Vahn got up and walked to the schedule. The day was now Tuesday May 16th. Saturday was the 20th. Four days away. Obviously they would have had to print that ad at least two weeks in advance. She wondered why she had overlooked it until now. Her mind wandered back to the night before and all she could see were the dark hollow eyes of that helpless woman staring straight through her.

As hard as he tried, Raynor could not keep his mind on his work. He had called the number he had seen thirty minutes after he had come out of "the vision". A burly voice had answered saying, "Yeah, Moonlight Motel."

Knowing that the motel in his vision was an actual place sent chills up his spine. He wasn't quite sure how to react to all this. He wanted to bolt from his house and drive to the motel hoping to see the woman, but he knew that she would be locked away in her room. He had no idea what room she was in or what her name was.

He looked at the clock on his desk; it read 2:30 p.m. He wondered if she had a job and what time she would get off work. For some reason he had a feeling that she would be going back to the motel and wasn't staying there for only one night.

Leaning back in his chair he closed his eyes. He pictured her reflection in the mirror. Her hair was so beautiful and her eyes…He remembered so clearly the wild look of terror on her face as she watched the woman being ripped to shreds by bullets. That look excited him more than anything.

Leaning forward, Raynor gathered the papers on his desk and put them back in their folder. He got up from his desk then headed for his car.

Fortunately he knew exactly where the motel was located. He didn't want to waste a lot of time driving around the city. For reasons he couldn't explain, he somehow knew that if he were to go to the motel and wait, then he would eventually see her.

As he pulled the car up to the motel he looked at his watch. It was 3:10 p.m. He parked in the same spot that the car, which the woman had hidden behind, was parked the night before. It gave him a perfect view of all the rooms.

Raynor's hands were shaking. His anticipation grew with every tick of his watch. Again he searched his mind for any kind of connection between the woman and himself. He could think of nothing. Maybe this was the late effect of an acid trip his mother had while pregnant with him.

His mind wandered back to when he was seven years old. He remembered being in the old shed out behind his house. In front of him sat a Ouija board surrounded by black candles. He had read that if you first sprinkled blood over the board you would get a clearer reading and be able to summon more spirits. He recalled holding the cat over the board, blood dripping from its neck…

Raynor blinked as a taxi pulled up in front of the office. The woman stepped out of the cab. She was wearing a waitress uniform. He couldn't quite tell which restaurant she worked at but from the looks of the uniform it was some type of diner. He despised anything less than a gourmet meal, with only the occasional exception of McDonald's.

He watched as she walked to the fourth door, pulled the key out of a bag she was carrying, and unlocked the door. She hadn't looked his way, and he hadn't been able to get an excellent look at her face, but he knew it was her. He could now see the rest of her body. He had only been able to see her face the previous night and had wondered what her build was like. She looked to be around 5'5" and she had a slim yet muscular figure that complimented her well.

He wanted to wait a while to see if she would go anywhere so that he could follow her and learn more about who she was and what type of woman she was. Though he knew that deep down, behind all the charades, all women were alike. Some women just have more talent at hiding things than others.

After two hours had gone by she appeared in the doorway wearing shorts and a T-shirt. She walked towards the office and went inside. There was a window facing Raynor's car so he was able to watch her pick up the phone and dial. He wondered whom she was calling. She wasn't exactly dressed for a night out on the town.

She put down the receiver after a few moments, said a few short words to the man at the desk, then walked back to her room. He wanted so much to walk to the room and talk to her, but what would he say? He knew that there was a special link between them and he had to determine what it was. Until then he knew he would have to keep his distance.

About thirty minutes later, a car with a Bob's Pizza sign on it pulled up in front of her room. The delivery boy stepped out of the car and walked up to her door.

She paid him, took the pizza then closed the door.

Assuming that it was safe to say she wasn't going anywhere for the evening, Raynor stepped out of the car and walked toward the office. He could see the manager sitting in his chair staring at the TV, which was bolted to the far wall. He wondered if the manager was going to be cooperative, or if he would have to help him cooperate.

Stepping inside the door he heard the man snoring. He walked up to the desk and leaned towards him. The man's eyes were open, but he was snoring. Shaking his head Raynor reached across the desk and picked up the logbook. He looked to room four. Vahn Carver was the name written next to the room number. He drew in a deep breath and exhaled, letting her name pass over his lips. Perfect. It was perfect.

To the right of her name it showed that she had the room reserved for the next three weeks. Smiling, he walked out of the office.

CHAPTER THREE

Saturday May 20th seemed like it took years instead of days to arrive. Vahn had become more excited every time she thought about becoming a police officer. She had always liked the idea of the rush that seemed to come with chasing down the "bad guys".

The only movies she watched were action movies. Love stories made her ill and Disney movies made her cry. It always seemed cruel to her that in most children's movies one loved character had to die.

As far as dramas were concerned, she looked at it this way, her life was depressing enough, she didn't need to pay seven dollars to sit in a dark place and feel depressed. Therefore, action movies were about all that interested her. They always left her feeling exhilarated and alive.

Vahn had also learned how to handle guns at an early age. Earl, her mother's boyfriend of one year, which was between her second and third husbands, had been a gun fanatic. You name it, he had it. He had always tried to get her mother to target practice with him but she would never do it, saying it would hurt her ears and possibly pull her arms out of socket.

Vahn on the other hand was fascinated. Earl had a .380 that he taught her to shoot with. She was only eleven years old at the time, but it was a small handgun that was easy for her to handle. He taught her how to load it, shoot it, and clean it.

Though he was a psycho anticipating the end of the world, he was very careful with all of his weapons. He taught her how to respect them and made sure she handled every weapon she touched with caution and full knowledge of its capabilities.

They had practiced every day when she got home from school. By the time her mother told him to hit the road, Vahn was able to empty a clip into the center of the target, squeezing off the first shot then closing her eyes for the next six.

When Earl left he let her keep the .380 but her mother had sold it saying that it tempted her to "put it to good use". Back then, Vahn couldn't figure out what she had meant by that because her mother had hated guns. Thinking about it now she realized that there probably were a few times after that when her mother may have bit the bullet if a gun would have been handy.

Here she was now, sitting in a huge auditorium attempting to pursue a career as a police officer. The ad didn't say how many cadets were going to be accepted. Looking around every seat seemed to be taken. She began to wonder why she had gotten her hopes up about this after all.

She wasn't really worried about the test. She had no idea what it was going to be like but she had always maintained a 4.0 GPA through school. Not because she had worked hard for it, but because it had come naturally.

It was now almost 4:00 p.m. They had said the testing would start at 3:30 p.m. If they were waiting for more people to show up she wondered where they were going to put them. Finally a man walked up on stage and went towards the microphone standing in the center.

"Ladies and gentlemen," he said pausing to cough. "I think we can begin now. First I would like to make some announcements. This was not stated in the ad in the paper but we're stating it now. If you do not have a high school diploma or GED you are now excused."

Many people around Vahn groaned and got up. She moved her legs to the side so two people could get by her to leave.

"If you are not a U.S. Citizen or are not legally able to work in the U.S. you are excused." She couldn't tell how many people this applied to because there were still many people filing out that didn't have diplomas.

"If you are physically or mentally incapable of performing the duties of a police officer, such as running, maybe arresting someone twice your size and even possibly shooting another human being, you are now excused."

A few people looked around at each other as if having doubts. Some stayed seated, others rose and left.

"And finally, if you have been convicted of a crime, or have been in trouble with the law, other than traffic violations you are now excused."

To Vahn's surprise many people got up after this statement. The man waited patiently until everyone that intended to leave was out of the auditorium before he proceeded.

"Now that we've done some weeding, let's get on with the test. The tests are now being passed out. You will also be handed two pencils. If one lead breaks, use the other, if its lead breaks, either use your teeth to sharpen it or you're out of luck," he smiled as if amused with himself after this comment.

Looking around Vahn felt a little more at ease. The auditorium had thinned out slightly. A man walked up beside her and counted out six tests. He asked her to pass them down. She was also handed a can full of pencils. She picked out two, making sure they both had sharp points, then passed down the can that held them.

"When you finish the test, bring it down and place it on the table in front of the stage. You are then excused. They will be graded and the results will be posted two weeks from today outside this very auditorium. Be sure to keep your eyes to yourselves, boys and girls, and good luck." He smiled, rocked back on his heels, then turned around and walked off.

Vahn was glad she didn't have any questions since he didn't bother to ask if there were any.

"Well, here's to the future," she said as she turned the first page.

Raynor closed the door to the Civic Center after watching Vahn open her booklet and begin her test.

He couldn't remember ever feeling so alive.

He walked outside and headed toward his car putting on his sunglasses. He knew that he would be wearing a smile for at least the next week. As he opened the door and slid into the driver's seat, he fastened his seatbelt and decided to take a long drive to help him think things through.

He still had no idea what the link between himself and Vahn actually was, but he knew now that she was the sign he had been waiting for. He knew without a doubt that she would pass that test and enter into the academy. Their paths were destined to cross before the vision ever had taken place.

As a child, his only escape from his home life had been the library. For reasons unknown to himself he was never interested in Jack and Jill, Rip Van Winkle, or any kind of cute cuddly children's story.

When he was four years old, one of his mother's "male friends" as she had called them, had left three journal type books on the coffee table while escorting his mother into her bedroom to have "grown up talk". He couldn't read yet but the pictures had fascinated him.

There had been several cloaked men around a square stone table. A naked woman was bound to it and a man, wearing what he thought was a cow's head, held a dagger over the woman. As Raynor had run his fingers over the many pictures they had become warm. The pictures seemed to be radiating some kind of energy and gave him a yearning that he could not yet understand.

The pictures never left his mind. He thought about them daily. As he got older he took advantage of every chance he could to read more and fill himself with knowledge and power. He stole the Satanic Bible from the library when he was seven and hid it out in the shed behind his house. The more he read, the more he believed.

After coming to the realization that he had visions of or through, Vahn twice, he recalled something that he had read from the book. To be one of the dark god's chosen "angels" one had to make several sacrifices in a certain time period, and in a certain way. The first step was to pray and perform several rituals. If you were found worthy, you would be shown a sign. Raynor used to dream about the day he would be shown his sign. As he thought about it now he laughed to himself. The thought now seemed so ridiculous.

He was taken away from his mother at the age of twelve and put into a boy's school. It was actually more like a militarized orphanage rather than a school. At first he longed for his bible and other books. He felt that he was helpless without them. Then after completing his aptitude tests, they showed him to be overly intelligent for his age. He quickly forgot about the demons and Ouija boards. He became convinced that all the power he had known had come from within himself and not from some fictitious God.

Many of the boys hated the place, but Raynor actually became quite fond of it.

When you've never known any kind of order, order tends to be welcomed whether it be lenient or extremely strict.

The only luxury the boys were allowed was stationary and any kind of sticker they liked to seal the envelopes with. Raynor chose plain white stationary with his name printed at the top in bold black letters. He then chose the yellow happy face stickers that read, "Have a Nice Day" on them.

Having no one outside of the orphanage to write to, he amused himself and everyone else with little riddles and notes that showed his sick sense of humor. Before long, the stickers became Raynor's trademark.

Not exactly aware that he had driven all the way to the beach, he pulled up to an overlook and stepped out of the car. He climbed over the logs, which were enclosing the small parking area and climbed down to a huge rock, which would give him a beautiful view of the ocean.

Sitting on the rock his thoughts shifted back to Vahn. He no longer believed in any kind of God. Except for himself. It was an invigorating feeling to look someone deep in their eyes and try to express to them that at any moment he could pass judgment and decide that it was time for their life to succumb to him.

He learned many valuable lessons from being placed in the school. The one he cherished the most was to do things right the first time. Which also meant that you must always have patience, and take your time. This thought brought a smile to his face. Knowing that Vahn would be in the academy for six months gave him more than ample time to plan things perfectly.

CHAPTER FOUR

For two weeks Vahn continued to stay at the motel wondering what she was going to do if she was not accepted into the academy. Johnny had come into Denny's twice proclaiming his love for her. Each time asking her to let him charge a meal to her tab. What a prince.

She had managed to finally get rid of him the second time after informing him that there was a possibility she would become a police officer. This bit of news made him choke on the bite he had taken, act as if he was going to vomit, and graciously excuse himself by running out the front door never to be seen again.

Deke had a perfect view of the bar where Johnny had been sitting and had seen Johnny's spectacular performance.

"You didn't tell him what I've been putting in his food every time he orders something did you?" He asked laughing. Deke always managed to "spice up" the food Johnny ordered in one way or another, which seemed to pick up Vahn's spirits no matter how bad of a day she'd been having.

The morning the scores were to be posted Vahn woke up early anticipating the outcome of not only her test, but also her life. When she arrived at the Civic Center there were already several people waiting in line to see their scores.

To the left of the bulletin board was a desk where two people were sitting. She watched the line ahead of her. After looking at their scores some people went to the desk, others left the building.

When she reached the front of the line she found her name and beside it was printed 92.7. There was a bulletin posted beside the scores, which read, "If you have received a score of 85 or above please step to the desk for an interview appointment time."

Relieved and anxious Vahn stepped to the desk. The man on the right looked up and said, "Name please."

"Jovahna Carver," she said hoping he would pass on making any comments about her first name. He looked on his list of names, spotted hers, and told the woman next to him her score.

"Your appointment time is 3:00 p.m. Monday," she said writing Vahn's appointment time first in her log then on a small card. The woman looked as if her face would crack if she were to smile.

"Your interview will be in the main office of the Police Academy. Thank you."

She tossed the card to the edge of the table without so much as an upward glance.

Vahn's shift ended every day at 3:00 p.m. so she had to take off an hour early so she could make it to the Police Academy for her interview on time. As her cab pulled up in front of the academy she was surprised by its size. She knew it would be big but this building was really outstanding.

Vahn paid the cab driver and got out. There were many people walking around in blue uniforms. They didn't have badges. The uniform was decorated with only a circular patch on the right shoulder, which had PPA in the middle of the two leaf vines, which outlined the inner circle of the patch. As far as the rest of the uniform went, it was just your basic blue button down shirt and straight leg pants. These were complimented by nothing less than black patent leather shoes.

Walking through the massive oak doors of the academy Vahn looked around not sure of which way to go. The only options were left or right. She noticed some people coming out of a door down the right side of the hall. When it was fully opened she could see that "Main Office" was printed on the door.

Once inside she gave the receptionist her name then took a seat in one of the many chairs lining the wall. There were two offices along the far wall. A man emerged from one of them looking like he'd just come out of the interrogation room after twenty-four hours of questioning.

The receptionist picked up the phone and was apparently letting the staff know that she was there. When she put down the receiver she looked at Vahn and said, "go ahead in Ms. Carver. It'll be the left door on the far wall."

Vahn felt a rush of anxiety, as that was the door the other "interviewee" had come from. After slowly walking to the door, she opened it to reveal an extremely muscular man sitting behind what he made look like a kindergartener's desk. He rose and extended his hand.

"Miss Jovahna Carver, correct?"

"Yes sir," she replied shaking his hand.

"Good afternoon. My name is Darren Torrel. I'm the Director here at the academy. Please sit down and make yourself comfortable." He settled into his chair and began shuffling paperwork.

"Well, let's see here. This little piece of paper tells me that you received a 92.7 as an overall grade on your exam."

"Yes sir." She felt so small in the presence of this giant. He had to be about 6'6" and weighed at least 250lbs. He looked as though he was in his early forties but she guessed he could be older and possibly just look outstanding for his age. Though he was a big man his facial features were soft and pleasant. He had olive colored skin, coal black hair with a few gray strands here and there, and deep brown eyes. His voice was soft yet still very forward and masculine.

"Our procedure is that we first have you take the test. We look at your scores, and then we interview you to see what type of person you are. Just because someone makes a high score on a piece of paper doesn't mean that they are ready to become a police officer. If you pass this interview you will be enrolled into the academy and you will take classes here for six months. Upon graduation you will be placed into a precinct, which is chosen by the Portland Police Department."

Darren leaned back in his chair turning it slightly to the right and crossed his legs, resting his hands on his left knee.

"The first question I have for you is why do you want to be a police officer?"

Oh shit, thought Vahn. Here we go, character analysis. Of course she understood that this was important but she wasn't really prepared for questions like this. On top of that who was this guy to judge her anyway. She had assumed that she would be sitting in a room looking at several individuals. She had been told that she would have to pass an oral board, which she assumed was where several people ask you a series of questions about police scenarios.

Though having to deal with only one person made the situation a little less tense, this also narrowed her chances of being accepted. This one man could simply decide he didn't like her for whatever reason and she wouldn't stand a chance.

She hadn't thought about answering any questions that would allow him to probe her psyche. She had also made the mistake of assuming that the psychological testing would take place at a later time.

Before she realized what she was doing her mouth opened, "well, sir, could I ask you one question before we begin?"

"Certainly," he said giving her a small nod and a smile.

"Well, since my fate lies in your hands, I would like to know what kind of experience you have analyzing personality traits." Vahn clamped her mouth shut as hard as she could. She couldn't believe she had said that once it came out of her mouth. She expected him to stand in a rage and throw her out of his office for insulting his ability to do his job. Instead, he smiled, uncrossed his legs and leaned forward on his desk with his hands clasped together.

"Well, I have my Masters degree in Psychology and a Bachelor's in sociology. I was also on the police force for fifteen years. That's just the rough details. If you need more in depth details I'll be more than happy to give them to you."

More than embarrassed Vahn felt herself blushing slightly and said, "No sir, that's fine I apologize."

"No need to apologize. That's an excellent question. You know in all the interviews I've done over the years you're the first person ever to ask me that." He smiled at her and leaned back in his chair once more. "Now, the first question was why do you want to be a police officer?"

So much for stalling, Vahn thought. She couldn't decide whether or not to take the honest approach, or the tell him what he wants to hear approach. So she just opened her mouth and decided to let whatever happened to jump out be her answer.

"Well, I've always been interested in law enforcement. I feel like I would be a good asset to the force and that I would be helpful to my community."

"Mm, hmm," he murmured, obviously not impressed by her answer. "And what is the most appealing aspect of law enforcement to you?"

Donuts were the first thing that popped into her mind. She struggled to keep a straight face, try not to laugh hysterically, and think of an actual answer all at once.

"Protecting the people and stopping injustice." Damn that sounded corny as hell, she thought.

"And do you think that you can stop all injustice?" He asked narrowing his eyes at her.

"Of course not. I'm not a super hero, just a possible police officer doing my duty." Vahn felt as if she was having one of those terrible dreams where you find yourself naked in a large crowd.

"What exactly is a police officer's duty?"

"To protect and serve?"

"Why are you putting your answer in the form of a question?" He asked. He seemed to be looming above her now.

"Did I?" She suddenly felt extremely hot and was trying to remember if she had put deodorant on that morning.

"I'll tell you what," he said. "I'll give you a chance to start over with every one of these questions. What I want you to do is take three deep breaths and clear your mind of everything."

When she hesitated he raised his eyebrows which quickly made her start taking in her first breath.

"You have been giving me answers that you think I want to hear. Trust me, I've heard those answers before. Unless you want to become Barney Fife after you graduate I doubt those are the answers you're really feeling. Becoming a police officer isn't something you just decide to try. You have to be a part of it and it has to be a part of you. Otherwise, you'd be putting your life in jeopardy, setting yourself up for a fall. Now do you feel better? More relaxed?" He asked after she finished her third breath.

"Yes, much better," she lied.

"Okay then, my first question was why do you want to be a police officer?"

Vahn felt words begin pouring out of her mouth about how she had always felt there was an emptiness about her. A void which needed to be filled. When she had read the ad for the academy she felt great anticipation about it. It seemed like the right thing to do. Darren sat back nodding at her periodically. She continued on telling him about Earl and her love of firearms, to her dreams she always seemed to have; which she didn't know if that was a very good idea since she usually shot someone in them. Finally she ended with the murder she had seen take place only weeks earlier, which left her feeling that she should have been able to do something.

"I hope you realize that you did the right thing by staying out of it. There was no need for you to be killed too." He looked at her with concern in his eyes.

He could obviously tell how it had bothered her.

"I know you're right, I just wish I could have done something."

"Well, Miss Carver, I think you're mentally competent to handle being a police officer. Usually we give the polygraph and do your background check before we start you in the academy. This year, unfortunately, we are pressed for time. Therefore you will receive your polygraph and your background check will be conducted while you are here. If either of these proves you to be insufficient for the department, you will be let go. As for now, see Ms. Robbins at the desk where you signed in and she will give you more details on your acceptance." He pushed his chair back and extended his hand again.

"Congratulations Miss Carver. I wish you the best of luck here at the academy."

Half surprised that it was over Vahn got up, shook his hand, and thanked him.

After getting the specifics from the desk clerk, Vahn walked out of the office and out of the building not thinking that a chapter of her life had ended, but that the heart of it had just begun.

—◦◦◦❈◦◦◦—

Raynor picked up the binoculars that had been lying beside him. He watched as Vahn sat on the stairs to the academy. From the look on her face he knew that she was in. Knowing that he would have a hard time seeing her over the next six months he wanted to memorize every curve, every detail, everything about her. With each day to come he knew that he would be closer to fulfilling his destiny.

As a cab pulled up in front of the academy he watched as Vahn rose and started toward the door. He pinched his lower lip between his teeth, holding his breath while she moved. When the cab drove out of sight he laid the binoculars beside him and closed his eyes. The anticipation he felt was almost more than he could bear.

CHAPTER FIVE

Vahn woke the next morning actually excited and anticipating the days ahead. It felt strange to have something to look forward to. She had been told that she could move into her room at the academy as soon as she liked, and she thought the sooner the better.

After taking a shower and getting dressed, she packed her things, checked out of the motel and took a cab to the academy.

Vahn's assigned room was in the west wing of the building on the second floor. Once inside she was astounded by its size. Each side of the room had a twin size bed, desk with reading lamp, and a tall metal cabinet with double doors.

In the backleft hand corner of the room was a wooden door. She walked to it and pushed it open. The bathroom. Nothing fancy, just your basic bath and shower combination, vanity sink with a mirrored medicine cabinet, and a toilet.

Turning back into the main room Vahn wondered which side of the room she should take. There were a few pencils and some folders strung across the desk on the left side of the room. She also noticed some shoes under the bed. So since the left side already appeared to be occupied she walked over to the right and opened the metal cabinet. There were two drawers in the bottom of it and bars across the top to hang clothes from.

Vahn had received a combination along with her room number. After the numbers for the combination was the number twenty-nine. Turning the padlock over, she saw the number twenty-nine was carved into the metal. Not in the mood to unpack just then, she stuffed her bags into the cabinet then shut and locked it.

Sitting on the bed Vahn was not sure of what to do next. There were a lot of people walking through the halls, but classes didn't start until the next week. Finally she decided to go into Denny's and quit her job. She knew the right thing to do would be to give a two weeks notice, but she had worked there for almost two years and they had never done her any favors.

Walking to some payphones located in the main entranceway, she called another cab to take her to the restaurant.

When Vahn had returned the previous night, her room had been empty with still no sign of her roommate. As she woke that morning she was greeted with the sound of someone vomiting. Her first instinct was to go in the bathroom and see if she could help, but who knew what her roommate was like. She may be completely offended that Vahn had invaded her privacy.

After a few minutes she decided to knock on the door to see if everything was all right. "You okay in there?" She asked tapping quietly.

"Fine, fine," a voice answered trying to choke back another round. Feeling her own stomach start to churn, Vahn walked back to her bed and sat down.

After about ten minutes of more vomiting, then what sounded like gargling, a 6'1" blonde appeared in the bathroom doorway. In spite of her height she did not look lanky in any way. She had good posture. Her arms and legs looked like they were in great shape with just the right amount of muscle tone, and she possessed the perfect hourglass figure.

"Sorry," she said pointing back towards the door. "I had to party last night." She walked towards Vahn extending her hand. Vahn stood up to shake her hand and noticed her head was even with the other woman's chin.

"I'm Ricki Kile. I take it we're roommates."

"It looks that way," she said shaking her hand.

"Vahn Carver, nice to meet you."

Ricki grabbed her stomach then walked over to her own bed and flopped down. "All right, I'm gonna cut to the chase. This is a straightforward question and I'd appreciate it if you'd answer yes or no. Any kind of 'maybe' qualifies as a yes in my book."

Vahn wondered what the question could possibly be.

"Are you a lesbian?" Ricki asked with a questioning look.

Vahn laughed and said, "Unfortunately I'm about as heterosexual as they come.

I'm not sure that men are worth the trouble though."

Ricki let out a sigh of relief. "Hey don't think that I have homophobia or anything. What people decide to do is their own business. I had a roommate in college who was into females and we got along great, but I also didn't undress in front of her. People are only human, and hey let's face it, I have an awesome body." She smiled proudly as she pointed to her breasts.

"Main point being that I have an addiction to the nightlife, and I would love it if we could go together. I only asked because I wouldn't want to take you into some place that had a bunch of slobbery men if you weren't into that, know what I mean?" She asked rolling over onto her back. "Anyway, this is great maybe you can keep me out of trouble. So, since you like men do you have one?"

"Absolutely not, and I'm not planning on it," said Vahn.

"Great! As soon as I recuperate we will have to go shake our asses," said Ricki.

"I haven't been out in a long time, but maybe I'll let you drag me out," Vahn said smiling. "So where are you from?"

"Born and raised right here in Portland. I'd like to say that I'm from, or have even been to for that matter, some exotic place, but nope this is it. Heaven on earth huh?" She smiled, "What about you?"

"I was dragged here from Ohio. I was brilliant enough to follow a loser who I thought was my Romeo."

"Ohio? A Yankee huh? Interesting. Hey have you ever been through West Virginia?"

"Quite a few times, why?"

"Is the entire state filled with barefooted in breeders?"

Vahn couldn't keep from laughing. "Kinda like Texans still ride horses through town?"

"You're right, sorry. It's hard to be open-minded when all you've seen is one place. You tend to believe that everywhere else is some foreign land where you wouldn't understand what was going on and nobody would understand you." She rolled back onto her side and looked at Vahn.

"Damn I need to travel! That'll be second on my list after I win the lottery. First is to completely spoil myself with anything and everything imaginable."

The two women talked for a while longer then decided to go out for breakfast.

Before she knew it, it was the first day of class. Vahn found herself in a drab blue uniform sitting in a cramped classroom listening to lectures of what was going to be expected from everyone, and a rundown of what the students could expect in the upcoming months.

Much to Vahn's anticipation, they finally made their way to the shooting range. From the outside it looked like a huge storage building. Once inside, Vahn was awe struck. She had never been in an indoor shooting range. It was actually set up similar to that of a bowling alley. There were lanes on either side of the building. In the middle was an enclosed room with bulletproof glass extending to its ceiling. The building's low ceiling made it look like a small area when it was actually huge.

The side of the enclosed area facing the entrance had a secured door and in the center it was set up like a bank teller's booth. There was a metal circular speaker used to talk through, and a big drawer which passed between the wall so nothing had to be handed out through an open space.

The inside of the area contained rows and rows of floor to ceiling shelves. Most of them were sectioned off into numbered cubicles each containing black pouches. On others she noticed shotguns and high powered rifles.

"Whoa," she said to herself. "Big boy toys."

Vahn's class lined up to receive their guns. When she came to the window, the drawer slid out to reveal one of the black pouches. It had number twenty-seven on the bag. The man behind the glass smiled at her.

"Your lane number is twenty-seven. Put on your headgear and goggles and wait for an instructor before you begin," he said.

Vahn walked until she came to her lane then set the bag on the counter. There were walls on either side of her making a private cubicle and her lane looked to extend about fifty yards back.

There was a switch on her right side that controlled the electric arm that held the target. There wasn't a target up so she backed up and looked under the counter. Sure enough there was a huge stack of them. They were the same kind she used to practice on. The image of a head and torso. Now that she thought about it, she could understand why her mother had freaked out over her target shooting as a child. The targets had never been that of a hunter's bulls eye, but always the image of a person.

Vahn unzipped the pouch. In it was a set of headgear, or ear protection, which she put on and adjusted to her head. Also inside were a pair of yellow goggles, and a 9mm handgun. It didn't have a clip in it and she didn't find one in the bag. She pulled back the chamber to make sure it was empty.

"You ever handle a gun?" Asked a gray haired man of average size, who looked to be in his mid fifties, as he limped around the corner.

"Yes sir," she replied laying the gun down on the counter.

"Oh yeah? Was it a handgun or a rifle?" He asked taking a clip and two boxes of bullets out of a bag he was carrying.

"It was a .380. It's been a long time though."

"Well, that's excellent. I take it you know what you're doing but I have to go over it with you anyway." He looked at her and smiled. His smile was merely a movement of his mouth. Vahn could see how empty his expression was. She wondered if his limp was caused by something that happened in the line of duty. From the emptiness in his eyes, it seemed like he probably lost a lot more than mobility in the incident.

He opened the first box of bullets and picked up the clip. He tilted it up so she could see what he was doing. "You put the back part of the bullet in first, and slide it in. This clip holds sixteen bullets."

Once he had the clip full he set it on the counter and picked up the gun and pointed at the side. "This button is the safety. When not firing you must immediately put the gun on safety. This also has a second safety feature. This long part running down the handle of the gun must be pushed in, otherwise the gun won't go off. In other words, you could sit here all day with it lying on the counter and keep pulling the trigger. Nothing would happen. You have to be gripping the gun while pulling the trigger, which pushes in the safety on the handle." He looked up at Vahn. "You follow me so far?" He asked.

"Yes sir," she said nodding her head.

"To begin shooting you slide the clip in and pop it into place with the palm of your hand. Take the safety off. Put your hand on the top of the gun and pull back the chamber. After doing this your gun will be cocked and ready to go. Do you have any questions?" He asked.

Vahn shook her head no. He bent down and grabbed a target. He then reached across her and pushed the button up bringing the arm to the counter.

"Place a target in like this, then position it wherever you want. Today we're just free shooting so it's your call." He pushed the button down taking the target away from them. When it was about fifty feet out he motioned for her to step aside and he centered himself to the target.

"Okay," he said taking his headgear from around his neck and putting it over his ears. "Watch what I'm doing. When you're ready, like I said, pop the clip in like this. Then take off the safety and cock the gun. Place the gun in your right hand if you're right handed, left if you're not. Place the hand that's holding your gun in the palm of your opposite hand. Keep your arms steady when shooting. This is not a motion of the arm. This is simply a motion of your index finger. Don't jerk your wrist or your arm. You'll be off your mark."

He turned from her and faced the target, took aim and fired twice. Both shots hit center mast. "All right," he said putting the safety on and handing the gun to her. "Your turn."

Vahn took position, took the safety off, and fired. Though it had been years since she had shot a gun, she was only pulling a little to the left. The instructor seemed satisfied. He patted her on the shoulder and limped to the next lane.

Vahn lost all consciousness of the world around her. She quickly lost herself in that isle. With every shot she fired she became more relaxed and more on target.

The next day after more of what seemed like endless hours of lectures, Vahn's class was taken to the gym to get suited up for a five-mile jog.

"Running," said Ricki. "I don't see why we have to run. I hate running. My height and the force of gravity don't mix. Every time I run I feel like the top part of my body is steel and the ground is a magnet pulling me down. Besides what ever happened to 'Stop or I'll shoot!' That command doesn't say anything about us having to run." She continued mumbling to herself as she tied her shoes.

Vahn was becoming very fond of Ricki. She had never been the type to make friends easily. Mostly because she had always been on the shy side, but Ricki was outgoing enough for both of them.

"We're going to Randy's tonight right?" Ricki asked with a huge smile and a 'please, please, please' look.

"What's so great about this place again?" Asked Vahn.

"What the hell do you mean what's so great? There's alcohol, there's men, there's testosterone in the air. What more could you ask for?"

"How about free drinks, clean sex, and not having to wake up next to a slob who you thought looked like Brett Favre the night before."

"Don't worry honey. No matter how blitzed you get I won't let Joe Gunn drag you off anywhere.

Besides I've promised myself that I'd be a good girl for the rest of the week so you can keep me in line too, okay?"

Vahn finished tying her shoe, got up, and gave Ricki a hand up off the floor. "I guess you talked me into it."

After a couple of miles Vahn was starting to feel more relaxed. She had a set pace, her breathing was excellent, and the trail through the woods was gorgeous. Ricki on the other hand was wheezing beside her.

"I'm on my deathbed! I'm running to my death."

"Breathe in through your nose and out your mouth. You're breathing like an ox in heat," said Vahn.

"Thanks for the encouragement. I feel much better now," panted Ricki stumbling over a rock. She took a deep breath in through her nose then exhaled. After several times her posture improved and she turned to Vahn smiling.

"Hey, this is great! It works. Where've you been all my life?"

Vahn laughed. The fresh air and the smell of pine were exhilarating.

"Hey Carver, did you notice that red head with the outstanding ass?" Asked Ricki licking her lips.

"What red head? I didn't see anyone with red hair."

"Okay maybe not red, red, but an awesome strawberry blonde color. I think he was checking you out before the run. Come to think of it, I noticed him in class and he was checking you out then. I meant to tell you about it yesterday."

"Did you get his name?" Vahn asked just for the sake of conversation. The last thing she wanted was to be bothered by a man.

"No I didn't get his name, but I think you should." Ricki looked back over her shoulder. "Here he comes."

"Hey!" A male voice yelled from behind them.

Vahn instantly began to pick up the pace.

"Hey ladies, wait up!" He had to sprint to catch up to them. "I thought you jumped the trail, I've been trying to catch up to you for three miles now."

"Well, Vahn here is trying to kill us both. So far it's working pretty well," smiled Ricki.

Vahn continued to look straight ahead and kept running. The man came up on her right, in between her and Ricki, and was trying to stay even with her. "I won't be able to keep up this pace for long," he said. "I was just wondering if you might want to go out and get a drink or something tonight?"

Vahn acted like she thought he was talking to Ricki and kept running not giving any expression.

"Vahn right?" He asked pacing himself beside of her.

"Oh sorry. Yeah that's right," she said trying to manage a slight fake smile. Looking his way a little she did notice he wasn't bad.

"Well, what do you say Vahn? Will you let me buy you a drink?" He asked almost out of breath.

"Hmm, that's really sweet of you, but you know, I don't drink. Sorry." Vahn said stretching her legs out even more and pulling away from him.

"Well how about dinner?" He yelled falling behind and finally bending over to catch his breath.

"Maybe some other time," yelled Vahn back at him.

Ricki was panting beside her. "I can't believe you! Did you not see the body on that? Did you not see the sweat? Damn girl, I was breakin' out in hives over here!" Said Ricki shaking her head.

"It's bad enough he only wants one thing, but it'd be worse to have to look at him for the next six months while he passed me and moved on to his next victim. Now give me a break would ya," said Vahn.

"Only because I know talking to brick walls results in your words bouncing right back at you," wheezed Ricki still shaking her head.

That night both women got ready for a night out. Ricki wore short frayed cut-offs, a black V-neck shirt that was sleeveless, and black cowboy boots. Vahn decided to wear a knit skirt that clung to her every curve, and a shirt that was made of soft sweater material. It had short sleeves and a scooped neck. It was also short enough to show half of her belly button. The ends of her hair were pulled back but she left a few strands hanging in the front.

"Ah oh, you have 'Take me home' written all over you!" Said Ricki laughing. "Let's hope you don't get drooled on too much."

"I can see half your ass, thank you very much," said Vahn smiling. "Oh no. It just hit me that you're wearing boots. Please tell me we're not going to have to listen to honey tonk all night long."

"There is a great mixture of music and people there. Trust me I can only take so much of that myself.

These boots just happen to attract mostly cowboys which are much sweeter and feed you much better lies on one night stands than your average jock," said Ricki putting her arm around Vahn as they walked out.

Once inside of Randy's Vahn was overwhelmed with anxiety. She suddenly would have killed for a huge black trench coat. The bar was so crowded that Vahn couldn't even see three feet in front of her. As soon as they had walked in the door, men were turning around and looking at them both from head to toe. Vahn stared straight at the floor afraid to lock eyes with anyone.

"Loosen up sweetie. Let's go to the bar and scope things out." Ricki guided her over to the bar.

Besides the fact that the music was so loud she couldn't hear herself think, it smelled like a locker room and the smoke was so thick she was waiting for someone to scream 'Fire'. There were so many people that they could hardly move.

When they reached the bar there were actually two stools free. Ricki hopped onto one and Vahn sat down beside her. She was looking in the mirror behind the bar at the huge crowd behind them.

"What'll it be ladies?" Yelled the bartender.

"Give us two Miller Lite's," said Ricki.

"No!" Vahn yelled looking up. "Give me a double Tequila Sunrise."

"Damn girl. You're more nervous than I thought," said Ricki.

"No, I'll be fine after about ten of those," Vahn said managing a slight smile.

The bartender slid the drinks across the counter. Vahn took the straw out of the glass and gulped down half of hers.

"You gonna be okay?" Asked Ricki.

"Well, it's like this. We partied constantly in school but it was always in the woods or at someone's house. Johnny and I really didn't go anyplace but this little whole in the wall Pub, so yeah, come to think of it, this would be my first time in a place like this. I'm a bar virgin I guess."

"We'll sure take care of that tonight," winked Ricki tipping up her beer.

About that time a 6'5" stud in a black cowboy hat with an astounding belt buckle walked up to Ricki. "Can I take you for a spin?" He asked holding out his hand and grinning from ear to ear.

"Great! Let's go." Ricki turned around as they walked off toward the dance floor. "He's even taller than me," she whispered, giving Vahn a thumbs up.

Vahn watched Ricki who looked so at ease on the dance floor, spinning around and turning every which way. Vahn would have no clue how to even begin to dance to country music.

Finishing her drink, Vahn ordered another. After taking the first drink of it she felt a tap on her left shoulder. She turned around to notice the strawberry blonde guy from the academy. He was sitting on the stool beside her leaning against the bar with his lips pursed together and his eyebrows raised.

"Well, hello there," he said not even showing a hint of a smile. All Vahn could do was stare at him.

"I forgot to introduce myself before. I'm Chase Hawkins," he said coldly.

Great, thought Vahn, a man with a grudge.

"So, why don't you drink? Against your religion? Oh, what have we got here?" He asked pointing to her glass. "It looks like a drink. Can't have alcohol in it though, right? Bartender!" He yelled.

The bartender walked over to Chase and leaned forward so he could hear him.

"What's the lady drinking?"

"Double Tequila Sunrise."

"A double?" Chase raised his eyebrows so high Vahn thought they might jump straight over his forehead. He pushed the stool back as he stood up and pulled out his wallet. "Well, I'd like to buy her two more," he said throwing money down on the bar.

Bending over he whispered in her ear, "I'm a big boy. I can handle rejection. Just next time try 'no' instead of feeding me your bullshit stories." He stood back up and walked off.

Vahn was shocked. She hadn't known what to say. Her tongue was tied. It was like he had just slapped her in the face. What a prick! He acted as if they had been engaged once. What she did was none of his damn business. She didn't have to explain anything to him. That was the first time a total stranger had been able to completely infuriate her.

"Tell, tell, tell!" Said Ricki plopping down on the stool beside Vahn trying to catch her breath. "I saw him over here what did he say?"

"Not much," said Vahn still pissed beyond belief.

"Well what did you find out about him?" Ricki asked.

"His name is Chase and he can't handle rejection."

CHAPTER SEVEN

The following week self-defense classes were scheduled to start and Vahn became more nervous the closer they came.

"I have no idea how to do any type of martial arts," complained Vahn working on a paper for class while Ricki laid on her back and painted her toe nails as she held them above her.

"Don't worry. It's great. You'll love it."

"That's what you say about everything. 'It's great you'll love it'," said Vahn mocking her.

"Okay, so you're nervous. Haven't you ever fought before?" Asked Ricki sitting up and carefully placing her feet on the floor.

"Well, I've gotten in plenty of boxing matches with Johnny and a few of his little flings, but never like breaking anyone's neck or bending their elbows back the wrong way or kicking someone in the eye."

Ricki laughed and shook her head. "You watch way too many movies. All forms of self-defense are an art. You'll get the hang of it. Promise."

Much to her regret Vahn found herself sitting with her classmates in a white uniform with a shirt that looked like a robe and white loose pants. She saw the instructor's mouth moving but she was so nervous that she was blocking out his voice. For a moment she panicked. She thought the instructor was pointing right at her until the man next to her got up and walked to a white line on the mat.

The instructor stood opposite of him. He yelled some strange noise then blocked the cadet's punch with his right then flipped him over his left leg onto the mat making him land on his back. Once the cadet rose to his feet, they faced each other and bowed.

After that cadet sat back down beside Vahn the instructor began to randomly select cadets to spar with him. She felt like a schoolgirl that didn't know the answer to an important question and didn't want to be called on.

The instructor demonstrated three more moves then paired people off to practice on each other. He had his list of names and was calling off pairs with mat numbers.

"Harper and Dean, mat #3. Clark and Walker, mat #4. Hawkins and Carver, mat #5."

"Oh no," mumbled Vahn closing her eyes. She had been trying to avoid Mr. Chase Hawkins since the incident in the bar. She kept her eyes closed hoping she had heard the instructor wrong.

"Hmm, mm. I promise I won't bite."

Vahn looked up to see Chase standing in front of her extending his hand to help her up. Reluctantly, she held out her hand and let him pull her up.

"Mat #5," he said pointing to the left. "That's us."

As they walked toward their mat Chase said, "so, did you have much of a hang over the other night?"

"Look I'd appreciate it if we could just concentrate on what we're supposed to be doing, okay," she said stepping onto the mat then stepping to the white line on the right.

"Sure, no problem," he scowled. He stood opposite of her and put his hands up getting in the defense position. Vahn stood there not quite sure of what to do since she hadn't been listening.

"Well, do you want to be the attacker or what?" He asked.

"Yeah, this is fine," she said. Besides it would feel good to nail him in the jaw. Vahn looked at how he was standing. He was leaning a little to his right, so she thought if she threw her right it would throw him off balance and she might be able to nail him with her left.

"Here goes nothin," she thought throwing her right. She went from looking at his face to looking at the ceiling. She tried not to wince at the paid in her lower back.

"Okay," she said to herself, "maybe that wasn't the best approach."

His face came into view over hers. "Shall we try that again?" He pulled her up to her feet.

This time she threw her left, which was blocked, then quickly threw her right, which was also blocked, and once again, she was staring at the rafters, with the wind slightly knocked out of her.

"Let's switch," said Chase, obviously enjoying himself.

Vahn tried to stand like he had been standing before. He threw his right fist. She wasn't ready and it surprised her. Her first reaction was to duck. When she did, he put his foot on her hip and pushed her over.

Each time they switched rolls or she tried something new he always came out on top. Finally, the instructor blew his whistle and told them to hit the showers. Vahn couldn't remember the last time she had so much "fun".

That afternoon Vahn went down to the shooting range to try and regain some of her self-esteem. She checked in, got a black bag, two boxes of bullets, and went to lane thirty-eight. She loaded the gun, put on her headgear and goggles, and put up a target.

After emptying her clip the first time, she reloaded and put up a new target. A week and a half had gone by. Only five and a half more months to go. She put the target sixty feet out. So many thoughts swam around in her head. Her childhood. Her mother. Going to school. Graduation. Johnny. Moving to Portland.

She then thought back to her junior year. That year she had decided that she was going to be a zookeeper at the Columbus Zoo and take care of the big cats. The tigers, lions, leopards, etc. Everything seemed so simple and perfect and planned out then. And now here she was. There's no way in hell she would have believed someone if they would have told her she'd wind up in Portland, Oregon with no clue as to what the future would hold.

While reloading for the third time, Vahn remembered a challenge Earl, her mother's boyfriend, had given her. It took her several months to perfect it back then. She wanted to see how good she'd be at it now. Pushing the button up she put the target back about seventy-five feet.

She had to reload four times before she was finished. She smiled satisfied with herself for still being able to do her "trick", as she had called it. She decided to get everything ready to go before she brought in the target. She made sure the gun was empty, then put everything back in the bag.

Before she could bring it in all the way she heard, "Howdy, neighbor!" Chase had poked his head around the corner to her left. Vahn stared at him not saying anything, just thinking she had seen enough of him for one day.

"Would you like to take a look at my handy work?" He asked smiling. Still with only his head visible.

"Why not," she said slightly curious as to how good of a shot he was.

Stepping around the corner, he held out the target. There were seven holes in the area of the heart, and seven holes in the middle area of the head.

"Not bad, huh," he smiled. "This was my best one.

Let's see yours."

Stepping back to her cubicle Vahn smiled and pushed the button down bringing in the target. When it came to the counter Chase leaned towards it and whispered, "Oh shit."

Vahn walked off and turned in her bag.

Chase stared at the target. There was a hole the size of a baseball dead in the center of the head. She had apparently started with one shot in the center, then shot around it so close that you couldn't distinguish how many shots she had fired. Each shot had taken away part of the target. Never leaving paper between any of the shots. So when she was finished all that was left was a single hole.

After Vahn left the shooting range she went to her room and took a scalding hot shower. Deciding a bath sounded even better she put the plug in and sat down while the water filled around her. She had just turned off the water and lay back to soak every aching muscle in her body when Ricki knocked and stuck her head in the door.

"You've got a visitor," she said smiling and winking. Instantly Vahn knew it was Chase.

"Please just tell him that I'm in the cafeteria or something," moaned Vahn. He was really beginning to annoy her. He was why she needed to relax in the bath in the first place.

"Yeah right, so I just explain how I've been carrying on a conversation with the shower curtain because I was mistaken and thought it was you? He's standing in the doorway watching me as we speak."

"All right, tell him I'll be out in two hours and he can come back then."

"Damn, try not to make it too obvious you're blowing him off," said Ricki closing the door.

Vahn laid a wash cloth over her eyes and relaxed in a half-conscious state until the water started to turn cold. She looked at her hands, it looked as if she had been put into one of those machines that suck fruit dry so it can be used as trail mix.

She put on her robe and opened the bathroom door. Chase was lying on her bed reading a magazine. He looked up at her then looked at his watch. "An hour and forty five minutes. You're fifteen minutes early," he said smirking at her.

"What the hell do you think you're doing? I could've walked out here naked if I had forgotten my robe."

"I think I'd be able to handle that," he said smiling.

Vahn clenched her fists and felt her face and neck turn red. She was so mad she couldn't say anything.

"Look, I don't know what's up your ass but I think you need to get over it," he said throwing down the magazine and sitting up.

"I want you to get off my bed and get the hell out, now!" Vahn screamed ready to kill him.

"You can't be serious. You do know that the only way to resolve problems between two people is to put them in the same room until they work it out. Therefore, sorry but I can't go until we've settled our differences."

Vahn was dumbstruck. Never in her life had she ever met anyone so annoying. Johnny was a total asshole but at least he knew when to leave her alone.

"Now, I'm not a psychologist or anything but if I were to guess I'd say that you had a troublesome childhood," he said narrowing his eyes and cocking his head to the side.

"And if I had to guess I'd say that you were a spoiled fucking brat that always got everything his way," said Vahn.

Instead of getting him pissed off like she had hoped he just laughed. Seeing that she wasn't going to win Vahn looked at her clock. It was 6:30 in the evening and she was starving.

"Okay, fine. If you're going to insist on giving me a hard time the least you can do is take me out for the dinner you offered."

"Great. You get dressed and I'll meet you by the payphones in the parking lot." Chase got up, winked at her and walked out shutting the door behind him.

"Unbelievable," she said as she opened her cabinet to get her clothes.

They ended up going to Gardetto's. It was a very loud sports bar that only served pizza and beer. Beer by the pitcher was cheaper then individual bottles. She wanted Miller Lite and he wanted Bud Light. After arguing about it they decided to get individual bottles.

When they went to order the pizza, they couldn't agree on what kind to get. She liked everything and he only liked pepperoni. She told him he could pick off all the extra items, he didn't want and he told her that by the time he did that his pizza would be cold and he refused.

Finally, the girl taking the order settled it, "Excuse me," she said. "Did you ever think of getting half-and-half?" She looked like she was on the edge. Vahn and Chase looked at each other then reluctantly agreed.

"It's called compromise kids," she said rolling her eyes, putting her pencil behind her ear and walking to the back to put in their order.

Amazingly enough, they actually agreed on where to sit. There was a second level that was quieter than the downstairs area, which was centered around two big screen TV's that were currently showing a basketball game.

"So, tell me," said Chase. "Is Vahn your full name or what?"

Not wanting to tell him her actual name she tried to mumble it under her breath.

"Come on, it can't be that bad," he said taking a bite of his pizza.

"Jovahna," she said looking to see if he was going to bust a gut.

"Jovahna? Who came up with that?"

"Well, from what I understand my father's name was Jonah and my mother was just infatuated with him. I happen to be the result of a class they skipped together." She looked at Chase to see if she was boring him and he actually looked interested.

"Anyway," she continued, "she thought that if she named me after him he would maybe come around and be interested. Since I was a girl she settled on Jovahna."

"So did it work? Did he come around?" Chase asked.

"No, he said I wasn't his and he didn't want anything to do with me."

"I can't imagine what that could feel like. I'm sorry."

Whoa, Vahn thought, he actually looks sincere. She wondered if she should let him have any more beer.

"Yeah, well, I can't say that I blame him. My mother's sex life hasn't exactly been a secret. I don't know whether she was always promiscuous or if she just decided she might as well start since that's what everyone thought anyway. But she's been getting more than her fair share ever since I can remember." Vahn grabbed another piece of pizza and took a drink of her beer.

"What about you?" Asked Vahn. "Why Chase?"

"It's actually kind of a funny story," he said blushing. "My father swears up and down that all through high school my mother used to chase him. Always asked him out and followed him around. My mother denies it saying that it was the other way around. Friends of the family tell me it was more of a mutual thing. Well, they ended up getting married and when my mom found out she was pregnant they couldn't agree on a name.

My father was positive she was having a girl and my mother was positive she was having a boy. So from the start they argued about everything."

"Did this bickering back and forth continue all through their marriage?" Vahn asked smiling.

"Still goes on daily. It seems like that's their way of flirting and showing affection."

"Hmm, that's strange, you'd think growing up around all that it would rub off on you." Vahn flashed a big smile at him. "So far I don't see anything like that in you."

Chase looked at her, then realizing she was being sarcastic he threw a piece of crust at her. She laughed.

"Anyway, when I was born they finally agreed to call me Chase since it seemed to fit because I came about from them chasing each other."

"That's sweet," said Vahn feeling a true smile on her face for the first time in ages.

"Yeah, I've got great parents."

After they finished their pizza they went to an arcade and played games until the manager had to run them out so he could close.

Back at the academy Chase walked Vahn to her room. He leaned over to kiss her and she put his head in her hands and pulled it down so she could kiss his forehead.

"Thanks a lot," said Vahn. "I really had a great time."

"Yeah, me too," Chase said smiling at her. "I'll see you tomorrow."

She watched him walk down the hall and descend the steps. She smiled and said, "Ricki's right, he does have a great ass."

CHAPTER EIGHT

Vahn woke up to Ricki tapping on her head.

"Wake up sweetie. It's Saturday. Let's go shopping!"

The two women decided to go to the mall. They drove around until Ricki found a parking spot she thought was close enough to the doors. They walked inside and first went into a leather store.

"How do you think I'd look as a biker bitch?" Asked Ricki holding a very short leather dress up to her.

"Perfect. Get a couple of tattoos and you'd be all set."

"Yikes," said Ricki looking at the price tag. "Three hundred and eighty dollars for that piece of cowhide. I think we can move on now," said Ricki hanging the dress back up.

As they went out into the main part of the mall Ricki looked slyly at Vahn. "Well, let's see here. If I remember right, when I left last night Chase was lying on your bed, and when I got back no one was around, and when I went to bed about eleven-thirty or so I was still alone in the room. Did you finally give in or what?" Ricki asked smiling.

"Since he was annoying the hell out of me I made him take me to get some pizza. He actually turned out to be an okay guy. So far anyway."

"Well, what all did you talk about? Do you have anything in common?"

Vahn looked at all of the couples walking in the mall and felt herself blush a little. Being drilled by Ricki and having a good time with him the night before had her emotions a little off balance.

"We talked about a lot of things. School mostly. I basically made him do all the talking. My life is so depressing it's not the kind of thing you want to tell to make any kind of an impression."

"So what do you think? Is there any hope of getting a relationship out of this?" asked Ricki.

"I don't know. He's hard to figure out. One minute I was ready to chop off his head and use it for target practice and the next we're playing NBA jam in the arcade. Strange."

"Yeah, that's a little on the strange side. But hey, ordinary is just that, ordinary, boring, blah." Ricki took Vahn's arm and walked over to a shoe store.

"Guess who I met last night?"

"Who?" Asked Vahn picking up a pair of strange shoes that had a huge buckle on them and looked like Rumple Stiltskin once wore them.

"This guy named Andrew. He's 6'2", only one inch taller than I am but I can't be too picky. Anyway he's an accountant and a financial advisor, and he drives a Lexus. Very sheik. I was just taking a walk last night and he almost hit me because he was talking on his phone and wasn't paying attention to where he was going." Ricki paused long enough to hold up a sandal and ask the clerk if she had it in a size ten. The clerk went to the back to check.

"Anyway, he got out and apologized and it was like love at first sight! I mean I know that sounds like bullshit, I used to think so myself, but all we could do was just stand in the middle of the road and we kept shaking hands while everyone around us beeped and yelled."

Vahn had never seen Ricki like this before. It was kind of cute. "Sounds really romantic Ricki," she said.

"Oh, you have no idea. I just can't put it into words." She slipped on the sandals and looked in the mirror. "Do these make me look like Cleopatra or the fifty-foot woman?"

"Neither, they look great. Now buy them and finish your story."

Ricki paid for the sandals then they went to the Food Court and each got a giant pretzel and a Dr. Pepper. They sat down at a small table in front of the pretzel place to continue Ricki's story.

"Well," said Ricki, "I know it was a crazy thing to do, and under most circumstances I never would have done it but, I got into his car and we drove to Sonic," she laughed. "Can you believe it! Sonic. We pulled in between a Pinto and an old beat up Chevy truck. He ordered two foot-long chili cheese dogs and he was in a three-piece pin striped suit."

"Wait, wait, wait. Are you out of your mind? What if he would have driven you to Canada and chopped you into pieces between here and there? You didn't know anything about this guy!" Vahn knew that people sitting close by were staring but she didn't care.

"Shh," said Ricki, smiling at their nosy on lookers. "I know it was dumb but it just seemed like the right thing to do. He didn't act like a big hot shot dick or anything. He was kind of stuttering and he was just adorable. I actually wasn't trying to figure out the size of his dick while I was looking at him."

"Oh, shut up!" Yelled Vahn laughing and turning red. "You're crazy, you know that. But hey, I guess that is strange for you isn't it."

"Yeah, I mean I can't remember the last time a guy actually made me nervous you know. Well, it turns out that he grew up in a little city on the border of Oregon and Washington. His father was a farmer and that's how he was raised. They helped put him through school, and here he is.

He says he feels awkward in his clothes and his car. I could tell before he even said anything. He's the cute clumsy type." Ricki sighed and stirred her ice with her straw.

"I can't believe what I'm seeing." Vahn reached up and felt Ricki's forehead. "You're not delirious. Don't tell me you're actually that into this guy."

"I don't know. I've never felt this way before." Ricki leaned in close so she could whisper, "You know what else is strange. I don't even have the urge to go to Randy's tonight."

Vahn laughed and shook her head. "He must be something special for you to not want to go shake your ass. Does this mean you're considering the word 'monogamy'?

You do know what that word means don't you?"

Ricki slapped Vahn on the arm. "Of course I know what it means. What's weird is that I always viewed it as a bad word. Now it sounds. I don't know…meaningful?"

Vahn smiled happy to see Ricki like this, though it was definitely going to be a change.

When they were done with all their shopping they were making their way to the end where they had parked when Vahn grabbed Ricki's arm and pointed towards the exit. There was a man practically dragging a pregnant woman out the doors.

"Come on," said Ricki pulling Vahn in their direction.

By the time they reached the doors and ran outside to look for them, they saw him pushing her towards the door of a beat up Nova. They heard her scream as he backhanded her and she fell out of sight.

Ricki sprinted towards the car and Vahn was right behind her. When they rounded the car he was pulling her up by her hair and trying to get the passenger door open. Ricki kicked his hand into the door, slamming it shut.

He let go of the woman's hair and whirled around. "You want some too bitch! I've got plenty to go around!" He pulled a knife out of his pocket and started waving it at Ricki.

Vahn went around to the right, she was in total shock. Everything was happening so fast she didn't know if they were about to be stabbed to death or what was going to happen.

The man lunged. Ricki kicked his hand sending the knife flying.

"Oh, you think you're bad huh. You're gonna wish you never got into my fucking business." The man was wearing combat boots, holy jeans, and a shirt with a nazi swastika. And of course the finishing touch was a baldhead.

"Fucking skinheads," Vahn said. She then looked towards the woman who was still lying on the ground.

She was looking at Ricki and the man wild-eyed. Vahn went over to her and helped her to her feet, then quickly led her around to the front of the car.

The man ran at Ricki trying to tackle her. She grabbed his back and fell with him throwing him over her shoulder with her knees as they fell. Ricki popped back up while he slowly rose to his feet.

"Come on asshole!" Screamed Ricki.

He came at her again throwing a right. She blocked it, nailed him in the nose then kicked him backward. He stumbled and reached up touching his nose. He looked at the blood on his fingers and smiled.

Again he came at her throwing a right. She blocked it, grabbed her wrist and threw her elbow into his right eye. He limped backward and bent over holding it.

This time when he stood up he wasn't laughing.

"I'm gonna kill you bitch."

He came after her one last time, again throwing his right. Ricki blocked it, punched him in his mouth, grabbed the back of his head, kneed him in the stomach as hard as she could, then backed up and kicked him square in the face.

When he fell, Ricki ran over, threw her knee into his chest and wrapped her hands around his throat. "You think you're a tough bastard don't you. Did you not see that she was pregnant? Pregnant you stupid fuck!" She squeezed his throat even harder. His hands flew to his throat clawing at Ricki, trying to get air.

Talking through clenched teeth she continued, "But pregnant or not you don't hit women. Did your mamma not teach you that? Huh? Or maybe you just don't give a shit. Maybe your daddy used to hit your mamma and you think it's all right. Is that it?"

The man's legs began to shake as his bloody face turned from red to purple. Vahn couldn't believe what she was seeing.

"Here's a news flash you piece of shit, it's not polite to hit women."

Vahn looked at Ricki. She had specks of the man's blood on her face. The veins in her forehead and on the sides of her neck were bulging out. She was blood red and tears were streaming down her face. She was spitting while she talked and her lips were quivering.

"How about if I just kill you right now so I don't have to go home tonight wondering if you're gonna do it again. How would that be muther fucker!" The man's eyes were starting to roll up in the back of his head. Vahn ran over behind Ricki and tried to get her off of him but she wouldn't budge.

"My daddy used to hit me, and my mamma, and my baby sister, and you know what? I swore to myself. Swore! That if I ever saw a man hit a woman I'd rip his fucking throat out!"

"Ricki!" Screamed Vahn. "Let him go! You're going to kill him, now let him go!" Vahn had both of her hands wrapped around Ricki's arm and was trying to yank it off of his throat, but she was too strong. She was transfixed on killing him. His tongue was hanging partly out of his mouth and it was turning blue.

Vahn knew he was only seconds away from being choked to death. She ran around the man's body so she could face Ricki. Her whole face was distorted in an angry rage. Vahn slapped her as hard as she could. Nothing. She slapped her again. Nothing. She grabbed Ricki's face in her hands and started screaming.

"Ricki you're scaring the fuck out of me! Let go of his fucking neck now! He's not worth it! He's not your father damn it, let him go!"

Finally this seemed to trigger something. She blinked twice and let go of his neck. Several people had begun to surround them. When Ricki let go of his neck, he laid still. Vahn pushed her off of him and looked at two men standing close by.

"Somebody give him mouth to mouth!" Screamed Vahn not really worried about him, but if he died, Ricki's life could be over.

Ricki had a blank stare on her face. She seemed to be in shock.

"Ricki, talk to me," said Vahn trying to get her to snap out of her daze. Suddenly Ricki looked at Vahn, then the man, and started crying hysterically. Vahn felt tears pouring from her own eyes. She wrapped her arms around Ricki and rocked her back and forth.

The police came out and took Ricki, Vahn, and the pregnant woman to the police department. An ambulance was called for the man. The pregnant woman stated that she had just told the man that she had gotten a sonogram and their baby was a girl. He had wanted a boy. He had threatened the woman's life saying he was going to kill her and the baby and find someone else to give him a son.

No charges of assault were brought against Ricki even though she almost killed the man. They said that since she had been acting in the other woman's defense, and since he pulled a knife on her, she was also acting in her own defense. Therefore the man would be unable to press any charges against her. The woman and Ricki both pressed charges against the man, and the woman was taken to a safe house for women and children.

Vahn went back and got Ricki's car then drove them both back to the academy. On the ride back, Ricki stared out the window and cried. Vahn didn't feel like it was the best time to talk about things. She knew Ricki would bring it up when she was ready.

That night Vahn sat in Ricki's bed holding her head in her lap and stroking her hair. Ricki finally cried herself to sleep. Knowing she didn't want to be alone, Vahn propped a pillow behind her head and slept there sitting up and holding Ricki.

Ricki stayed in bed all day Sunday. Vahn brought her food and made her eat at meal times. They talked all day. Ricki told her what it was like growing up in an abusive home. Vahn had no idea that Ricki had such a traumatic past. She was such a cheerful person.

So outgoing. Vahn never would have guessed.

Ricki explained that her past was the reason why she never settled down with a man. She would much rather be the heart breaker herself. When the incident of the day before was brought up, Ricki could barely remember what had happened. The last thing she remembered was kicking his knife away. She had no recollection of almost killing him.

"I've blocked out more things in my life than most people remember," said Ricki. "That's how I made it through my childhood. I guess I'm still pretty good at it."

In class on Monday, Chase asked Vahn if she wanted to go eat lunch with him. She agreed.

Since they didn't have a whole lot of time they decided on McDonald's. When they sat down Chase had a huge smile on his face.

"What?" Asked Vahn, afraid of what was coming next.

"Well, I just thought that since you seem to need a little extra help in the self- defense department, and I could use some improvement on my shot, that we could help each other out," he said smiling.

"Oh, you did, did you?" She asked. "First, what makes you think I want you to be the one to help me out. And second, why would I want to help you out?"

"Well," he replied, "first because there's no better teacher than myself, and I'm sure you're tired of lying on your back all the time. You could get a reputation you know," he said laughing. "And second, I would be willing to wager that you'd love showing me up on a regular basis."

"I must admit you have a point," she said smiling.

Chase and Vahn had decided to meet in the gym at 7:00 p.m. Meanwhile, Vahn was working on a paper while Ricki was in the bathroom getting ready to go to dinner with Andrew. There was a knock at the door and Vahn got up to answer it. She opened the door to a six-foot tall white teddy bear.

"Ahh, hello," said Vahn wondering if there was someone behind all that fur.

"Yeah, ah, hi," said Andrew dropping the bear. "Is Ricki ready yet?" He was trying to pick up the bear while holding flowers in one hand and candy in the other.

"Do you need any help?" Asked Vahn smiling.

He was making her nervous.

"Oh, no thanks. I think I got it."

"Well, come on in. She's almost ready." Vahn watched him struggle trying to get through the doorway. She remembered Ricki saying he was cute and clumsy.

"That's her bed if you want to set those down," said Vahn as she went back to her desk and sat down. She propped up her elbow and rested her head on her hand, almost curious as to what Andrew would do next.

He began trying to position the bear just right for Ricki. A pillow propped up the bear, which was almost bigger than her bed. He then put the flowers and candy in its lap. Vahn watched as he kept fiddling with it, and rearranging it. She wanted to tell him it looked great, but she didn't think it would matter much, and she wasn't sure she could do it without laughing.

Ricki cracked the bathroom door and poked her head out. She looked at Andrew and smiled and blushed at the same time. She opened the door and walked out toward him.

"Hi," said Ricki standing at the foot of the bed. There was a long silence as they simply stood, staring at each other.

"This is different," Vahn said to herself. She was used to seeing Ricki control a room full of men with her slyness and good looks and now she looked so nervous it was almost funny.

Fidgeting with her fingers she finally said, "Is that for me or are they just kicking me out and this is my replacement?"

"That's more like it," said Vahn. She turned back to her paper as the two laughed and walked out together arm in arm, so infatuated with each other they completely forgot about Vahn being there. She smiled and shook her head still shocked by the change Andrew made in Ricki.

At 7:00 p.m. Vahn went to the gym and found Chase kicking a punching bag.

"The man definitely has good form," she thought. As she walked over to him, he stopped and smiled at her.

"Okay," she said. "I'm ready for today's dose of embarrassment."

"Great," said Chase. "I'm ready to give it to you." He laughed and grabbed her hand pulling her to the mat.

He positioned her on one white line then walked to the other opposite of her.

"Now, I'm going to show you a couple of simple block techniques, then I want you to try them, all right?" Vahn shook her head yes.

"First of all, your defense position is this." Chase pointed to his feet as he explained. "Keep your feet about shoulder width apart and put one out in front of the other so that you have a good stance and can't be thrown off balance easily. Put both your hands up.

Make fists but keep your thumbs towards your face."

Chase stopped and looked at her. "You're supposed to be doing this along with me Vahn."

"Oh, sorry," she snapped out of her daze and stood as he was demonstrating.

"Now, when someone throws a punch at you, to block it you use your forearm. Don't block the punch out. Always block it to the inside making their arm come down in front of their body."

"I'm lost. Tell me why you have to block it to the inside."

"All right, I'm going to throw a punch at you and I want you to block it however you feel comfortable."

Chase let her get into position then he threw his right at her. Vahn threw her left forearm up blocking his punch by making his arm go above her head. As soon as she did, he threw his left and let his knuckles rest against her jaw.

"Ah, okay, I guess that explains it," she said knowing that if this were an actual fight she would be out cold.

"Let's try it again this time block down, or to the inside." He let her get into position then threw his right again. She used her left forearm again, this time crossing over in front of her body, making his fist and arm go down in front of him instead of up. He was unable to use his left because his body was turned slightly to the right and because his right arm was in front of him.

"That was great! You did it." He said smiling.

"Now let's do that again and once you block with your left, that leaves your right hand free and my face open, so take advantage."

Again he threw his right, Vahn blocked it in and put her fist on his nose. The scene from Saturday flashed back into her mind. She had watched Ricki do this exact same thing. At the time Vahn was impressed but more caught up in the moment and worried. Now that she knew that there was a method that Ricki had been following and that there was a reason behind every move she made, Vahn was even more in awe of what Ricki had done. She knew that there was no way in hell that she could have handled the guy the way Ricki had. She hoped that soon everything would come to her naturally as it had Ricki.

After about an hour of practicing Vahn noticed great improvement and she was grateful to Chase for giving her important pointers. They each took showers then met back in the gym after putting their regular clothes back on.

"Did you eat dinner?" Asked Chase.

"No, I was trying to get a paper done. I didn't even think about it really," Vahn said shrugging her shoulders.

"Do you like Chinese?" He asked looking at her hopefully.

"Yeah, I love Chinese."

Chase let out a sigh of relief. "You don't know how glad I am to hear that. I usually have to go by myself because everyone else I know hates it."

Chase picked a restaurant called Little China. Vahn ordered Garlic Chicken and Chase ordered Sweet and Sour Pork. They each gave the other a taste of what they had ordered and decided to split everything so they could each have some of both.

"Who gave you your interview into the academy?" Asked Chase.

"Darren Torrel I think it was," said Vahn wiping sweet and sour sauce from her chin.

"Big, huge guy?" He asked.

"Mm, hmm," Vahn muttered, she had a mouthful of food. She was trying not to look like a total pig but it was delicious and she was starving.

"Did he ask you why you wanted to become a police officer?"

Vahn finished chewing and wiped her mouth. "Yes he did. Did you give him as dumb of a first answer as I did?"

Chase laughed and said, "Yeah, I told him it was because 'Chips' was the only thing I ever watched on TV. What was your answer?"

"I told him I wanted to help my community," she said embarrassed.

He laughed saying, "I bet he loved that. Seriously though, what was your real reason?"

"I don't really know to be honest with you. I just saw the ad in the paper and it seemed like the right thing to do."

"Well from the way you shoot there must be something in your background that led you toward law enforcement."

"Not exactly," said Vahn smiling at the thought of Earl. She told him about Earl and how they used to practice.

"So, did he teach you how to do that hole in one thing?"

"Hole in one thing? Oh, oh that," said Vahn remembering him seeing her target from the other day. "Well, Earl had never actually been able to do it. He always came close but he could never do it without having a stray shot here or there. I think that was probably because his right eye was crossed. But anyway, he gave me the challenge and after about three months of practicing every day after school until bedtime and almost every waking hour on the weekends, I finally did it."

"That is really amazing. I've never seen anything like it."

"What's your story?" Vahn asked. "Was the urge to be Paunch more than you could stand?"

Chase laughed. "No. I actually just grew up around it. My dad and my uncle are firemen. My mom is a paramedic. My aunt and uncle on my mom's side are police officers, and the list could go on forever. I originally tried to be a rebel. I went to school to be an architect."

"Too much pressure from your family made you change your mind?"

"No. They were actually real supportive. It's just that over the few years that I went to school I realized more and more that architecture wasn't what I wanted to do." Chase took a bite of rice then continued.

"On family holidays, like Thanksgiving, Christmas, Easter and the Fourth of July, most families play cards or Scrabble or something. Well, since I can remember my family has always had shooting competitions, and kickboxing matches. We also had a tower in our backyard with six flights of stairs that everybody would use to have timed races where you had to carry a fire hose up it."

"I think I saw that in the movie Backdraft," said Vahn remembering how she'd loved that movie.

"Our whole family got together to watch that movie the day it opened. We bought our tickets in advance. There were about thirty-five of us in the movie theatre. It was great. When that part came on everybody started laughing and joking with my cousin because the holiday before the movie came out, he fell down two flights of stairs while trying to beat my dad's record. All the other people in the theatre didn't think it was so funny that we were making so much noise though." Chase laughed remembering the moment.

After they returned to the academy he again walked her to her room, and this time she graciously accepted his kiss.

As the next month went by, Vahn and Chase spent more and more time together. Vahn had never really felt so much for any one person before. She wasn't quite sure how to deal with it.

Ricki, of course, had an opinion on everything. "What do you mean you don't know how to deal with it?" She asked. They were both lying in their beds talking across the room with each other.

"I mean, what if I'm thinking it's more than it's not. Maybe I'm reading more into this thing than there actually is."

"Hah! I've seen the way he looks at you. You two haven't even had sex yet so what does that tell ya?"

"My point exactly. I'm probably just a challenge to him. Once he gets it maybe things won't be quite so interesting anymore."

"Vahn, you're nutty. Just plain nutty." Ricki shook her head back and forth. "Why do you always assume that every guy is going to end up being like Johnny?"

"Because in the beginning he was 'it'. I mean he was perfect. He said the right things, he did the right things. He gave me no clues as to the man he actually was. And yes, looking back now it scares the hell out of me. I don't want to make that mistake again."

"You won't. Trust me. Now that you're older and everything is in a different perspective you'd be able to see another Johnny coming from a mile away."

"And would you be saying the same thing if you were still the old Ricki and thought men were only good for one thing? Now that you're in love you seem to have turned soft."

"If I was the old me I would still be saying Chase could be Mr. Right. I would just constantly be bitching you out for not having sex with him yet," she said laughing.

The next night Chase had asked Vahn to meet him in the gym at 9:30 p.m. She couldn't figure out why he wanted to go so late but she agreed to meet him anyway. Once she got there she found him in just the bottoms to their self-defense uniforms doing push-ups.

She could see the sweat glistening off his back.

"Control, control, control," she said to herself. She had held out for a month and a half now, wanting to make sure things were possibly going to last.

"Hey, great, you made it," he said jumping up and jogging in place.

"Yeah, I did." He looked so hot she didn't know if she was going to be able to stay in the same room with him for much longer. He walked to the end of the mat, picked up a towel, and started drying himself off.

"I thought we could work on kicks a little more if that's okay with you," he said.

"That's fine. Sure."

Chase walked over and put a red pad on each hand. Vahn walked in front of him, stretched her legs a little bit, then proceeded to practice kicking the pads. They usually talked the whole time they practiced but tonight neither one of them said anything.

His blue eyes seemed to be undressing her every time she looked at him. She knew that if they made eye contact it would be all over.

"Can we switch now?" Asked Vahn.

"Sure." He slipped the pad off his right hand, then his left. He took Vahn's right hand into his, intending to put it on for her. She looked up at him and their eyes locked. She didn't know if he made the first move or if she did, but the next thing she knew they were lying on the mat. He was on top of her with her head between his hands kissing her.

His lips and tongue felt so hot. She knew there was no turning back now. He pressed his body against hers and she felt her back arch to meet him. He rolled over so she was on top of him. She moved her lips to his neck. His skin tasted so sweet. She moved from one side of his neck to the other deepening her kisses.

He groaned and put her lips back to his.

Untying the top of her uniform, he quickly pulled it off and threw it to the side.

Finding the bottom of the tank top she was wearing underneath, he slid his hands under it. Moving his hands up, and bringing her shirt with them, she shivered. He put her breasts in his hands and pulled them towards his mouth. His tongue caressed each one with small circles, making her feel as if she was going to explode.

He pulled the tank top up over her head and flipped her over onto her back. His lips and tongue went from the top of her neck to her breasts, lingered once more then moved to her belly. He ran his tongue along the top of her pants. She then felt his hands slide up and pull them off.

He kissed the inside of her thighs. Her legs began to quiver. Hooking his fingers around the narrow strings of her panties he slowly pulled them off. He looked deep into Vahn's eyes, he knew she wanted him. She felt his tongue against her and she let out a low moan. She couldn't believe this was happening. After several minutes, he rose up and left a trail of kisses back up her body.

She ran her hands down his sides. Finding the top of his pants she pushed them down over his hips. He rested on one arm, reached back and pulled them the rest of the way off. He ran his hand up her thigh, then up her waist. She felt her body melt as they went from being two people to one entity.

After they had both taken showers, they met back in the gym. Vahn was so nervous she couldn't meet his eyes. Chase walked over to her and picked her up wrapping her legs around his waist.

"Tongue-tied are ya?" He asked giving her a huge smile.

Not quite sure of what to say she finally had to smile and say, "I can't believe you seduced me like that!"

"Seduced you?" He said laughing. "You were the one that kept looking me over, making it clear you were ready to attack at any second."

"You're so full of shit," Vahn laughed. "What if someone would've walked in! That would've looked real great."

"No one was going to walk in," he said putting her down and giving her a deep kiss.

"You can't know that for sure."

"Well, since I made it so the door would lock behind you and I was the only one in here to begin with, it was pretty definite that we'd be alone. Besides that I didn't hear any complaints from you then now did I?"

Vahn slapped him on his backside as they walked out together.

Sitting in his car looking through binoculars, Raynor watched as the two walked out of the gym, arm in arm. He was having mixed feelings about this man and about Vahn. He knew that she was special, and in knowing that she was special he had been under the impression that she was not full of the lust and greed that most women were consumed with.

Although, after seeing her with this man he knew that it was naive of him to even assume the possibility that she would have been a virgin. Of course her role in his plan would be the same, and her outcome in his plot would also remain the same regardless of her sexual status.

The few times Raynor had seen her leave the academy she had been with this man. His curiosity had gotten the best of him, and he had decided to find out the man's name and anything else he could. He had discovered that the man's name was Chase Hawkins. He seemed to have a respectable background. Solid parents, solid scores in high school, went to college briefly, then entered into the academy.

All of his scores, as of the past week, were high, which proved intelligence and competence.

Raynor's only concern was what his intentions were with Vahn. If he were just using her then he would be long gone before he would interfere with things to come. Though, on the other hand, Raynor knew that he couldn't let Chase get too comfortable with the situation. He couldn't afford having Vahn fall in love and get married, having kids, etc. She was to be only his and all of these extras could not be tolerated.

Knowing that being patient, and wise was the only thing to do, Raynor decided to sit back and let the story between the two unfold. If he didn't need to interfere, then that would be one less thing to worry about. If it so happened that he would need to interfere, he had the feeling that Chase Hawkins would not be a problem.

Walking back in her room, Vahn tried to keep Ricki from seeing the huge smile on her face.

"Hey girl. Can you come back from La La Land long enough to say hi?" Asked Ricki.

Vahn sat down at her desk and waved without turning around.

"Don't tell me," yelled Ricki hopping out of bed and running towards her. "Turn around and look at me."

Vahn could tell Ricki was smiling just as big as she was even though she couldn't see her face. Vahn tried to put on a straight face, then turned around. As soon as she looked at Ricki she just died laughing.

"You finally did it! I can't believe it! You know you're not getting out of this without details, so don't even try it!"

"Okay, okay. You got me," Vahn smiled. "It was nice."

"Nice? Nice. Nice is when your grandmother gets her corns removed. With his body it had to be better than just nice or something is definitely wrong with the picture."

"I'll put it this way. However good you think it was, it was better."

When Vahn went to her room after classes the next day, on her desk were a dozen roses. Six red and six white. The card read, "Just a Thank You for the best workout I've ever had. Love, Me."

Love. Did he have to use that word? The 'L' word had always been viewed as a bad word by her. "Well," she said. "At least he didn't say it." But deep down she knew that hearing him say it would actually sound pretty nice.

Vahn and Chase had agreed to meet in the shooting range that evening. She walked in and saw him waving at her from the other end. She got a set of headgear from the window, then walked over to him and looked at his target. There were a lot of scattered shots in the head area.

"I'm trying to do your little trick," he said. "As you can see, it's not working."

Vahn pulled his target in, took it down and put up a new one. "The roses are gorgeous. Thanks." She so badly wanted to kiss him, but she knew she couldn't. "I'm glad you like them," he said. The look in his eyes told her he felt the same.

"All right. First of all, I want you to just try to empty a clip center mast and I want to see how much your form has improved."

Chase took the clip out of the gun and started loading it. "Have you realized that we only have barely over four months left?"

"Time seems to be passing a lot faster than I thought it would," said Vahn.

Chase popped the clip into the gun. Took the safety off, and squeezed off three rounds. Vahn put her hand on his shoulder.

"You're jerking your wrist again," she said mocking how he had moved his wrist.

"Keep your wrists straight. Grip your gun a little tighter and only move your index finger to pull the trigger."

Chase shot the remaining four bullets. This time they all hit only a half-inch from one another. "So, is anybody coming to watch you graduate?" He asked reloading again.

"I called my uncle the other day to ask him if he knew where Mom was. He says she's in Bermuda or somewhere like that. He wasn't sure. She had met a travel agent I guess and took off with him not letting anyone know how long she'd be gone or anything. My uncle and aunt said they might come."

"Do they live in Ohio too?" "No, South Carolina." Chase put the loaded clip in and aimed at the head of the target. He was able to put on two eyes, a nose, and a mouth.

"Cute," said Vahn.

Reloading again, Chase asked, "What are you going to do after you graduate?"

"The same as everyone else I guess. Get assigned to a precinct and go from there."

"So you are planning to stay here in Portland?" He started bringing in the old target to put up a new one.

"Why wouldn't I?" She asked confused by the question.

"I didn't know if you were going back to Ohio or what. I don't know. I guess I was just hoping that we could see a lot more of each other in the future."

"Hmm, I'd have to think about that one," she said smiling.

CHAPTER TEN

As the months went by Vahn excelled in school and became more confident in herself. She had never before felt at ease with what was happening in her life. She had always felt like she was struggling with everyone and everything around her. Though at the academy she had chosen her own path and she felt as if she had finally set her life in the right direction.

One afternoon Vahn and Ricki decided to eat lunch together at Burger King. Vahn could tell by Ricki's face that she had been itching to tell her something.

"Guess what?" Asked Ricki taking a bite of her Whopper.

"Do I need to guess?" Vahn asked eating a fry.

"No, I'll just tell," said Ricki clapping her hands together. "Andy told me that he wants lots of kids."

"Was that a proposal or just a suggestion of wedlock?"

"I'm hoping it was a hint of a proposal."

Vahn took a drink of her Coke. "Are you telling me that you're actually ready to marry Andy?"

"If I had the money, I'd go buy him a ring and propose to him myself," said Ricki. "Do you think I'm crazy?" She asked blushing a little.

"Not really. I mean, you two look great together and you've actually done each other a lot of good. You've calmed down and fell in love, and he's gotten less clumsy and more sure of himself with the love he's found in you. I think it's great. I always thought you'd get married I just didn't think it'd be so soon."

"I figure, why wait? If you love someone, why should there be a chart of how to do things?"

"You're right," said Vahn. "Now are you going to wait for him or are you going to propose first?"

"I don't know. I'll have to see how brave I feel," she replied smiling.

Four months had gone by since Vahn and Chase had first been together. In that time they had dinner together every night and Vahn knew that things between them were becoming more serious with each passing day. She noticed a change in the way he looked at her. Though it hadn't been said she knew they loved each other. The way he touched her became more loving every time they were together.

Vahn had tried so hard not to let herself fall in love with him, but he made her feel things she had never known possible. She often thought about where their relationship would lead. She felt extremely childish when she would catch herself trying to imagine them growing old together.

Saturday afternoon Vahn had decided to go see a movie with Ricki. She had forgotten her purse, so she ran back up to the room to get it while Ricki waited in the car. When she opened the door she saw Chase leaning over her desk.

"Chase?" She asked. "What are you doing?"

He whirled around to look at her. "Nothing, nothing," he said turning red.

Vahn walked over to the desk and looked down to see that the little glass heart she kept her jewelry in was open and her favorite sapphire ring was in it.

"Did you find that somewhere?" She asked. "I've been looking for that for three days."

"Yeah, I found it in my room. It was under the bed in the corner. I guess that's why I didn't see it when you asked me if I had seen it the first time." Chase was putting his hands in and out of his pockets, and fidgeting with his watch.

"Well, I better go. We still having dinner tonight?" He asked.

"You're picking me up at seven o'clock right?"

"Yep, seven. See ya later," he answered practically sprinting out of the room.

'Well, he was acting strange enough," said Vahn.

Sitting in his car, which was parked at a remote gas station, Raynor felt his face turn red as his informant told him that he had followed Chase to a local jeweler where he had purchased an engagement ring. He had also overheard Chase telling the jeweler that he had made reservations for Portland Place that evening and he would be proposing to her over dinner.

"Break any plans you've made for this evening. I want you in that restaurant. Do you know what time the reservations are for?" Asked Raynor.

"Yeah. I called and confirmed they're for seven forty-five."

Getting his wallet out of his pocket Raynor handed his informant several one hundred-dollar bills. "Fine. I want you to go to Aldolpho's and get a suit. Then meet me here at six o'clock."

"No problem."

As his informant got out and shut the door Raynor gripped his steering wheel as tight as he could. He had known this was coming.

At 7:00 p.m. Chase knocked on Vahn's door. He had told her that they were going to a nice restaurant but he hadn't told her where. She had to borrow a nice evening dress from Ricki. Luckily they were about the same size in the chest and waist. She borrowed a slinky black dress with spaghetti straps. It hit Ricki right underneath her behind but on Vahn it came to a couple of inches above her knees. Luckily Vahn had black heels to match since she wore a seven and a half and Ricki wore a ten.

Chase was wearing a pair of Cavaricci slacks and a button down silk shirt. "Wow, you look great," he said looking just as nervous as he had been earlier.

"You look good yourself," she said smiling and taking his arm.

He had made reservations for them at Portland Place. Vahn had never been there before but she knew that this was the restaurant where the Governor and other big names of the city always dined. A small part of her wondered if this would be more than just dinner.

It was such a nice place.

"Just maybe," she hoped, "this will be a night to remember."

They pulled up to the front doors where a valet helped Vahn out of the car. They walked up carpeted stairs to the main entrance. Once they walked through the doors, the host asked Chase what name the reservation was under. He then took them to their table.

The whole restaurant was full with the buzzing sounds of hushed voices. The lights were low, and the tables were spaced apart so that conversations could not be easily overheard. As they walked towards their table Vahn noticed the many dinner parties with people laughing and toasting. She couldn't help but wonder how many of the men were sitting with women other than their wives, and how many businessmen were contemplating, or celebrating, illegal activities.

Their table was in the back corner of the restaurant. The host pulled her chair out for her, and handed them their menus. Vahn looked at Chase and noticed beads of sweat across his brow.

"Are you okay?" She asked.

"Okay? Oh, yeah, I'm fine. What about you? Is this okay? I know I didn't ask you where you wanted to go. I just thought this would be kind of a surprise."

"Are you nervous about something?" Asked Vahn trying to figure out why this strange behavior had suddenly come about.

"Nervous?" He laughed shakily. "Why would I be nervous?"

"I don't know. I'm sorry. This is wonderful. I've always wanted to come here."

Chase smiled at her, then buried his face in the menu. Vahn ordered Mostacciolli, and Chase decided on a twelve ounce Prime Rib. When the waiter asked if they'd like any wine, Chase replied that they would prefer Champagne. Vahn's heart fluttered a little but she quickly got angry with herself for getting excited over nothing. How could she even start to think that he was going to propose to her? Just because Ricki and Andy were on the verge of marriage, a house, and kids, didn't mean that she should get things between her and Chase confused.

Conversation through dinner was small talk. They never really focused on any one subject. Chase played with his food more than he ate it. After they had finished the main course, the waiter brought the dessert tray. Vahn selected a piece of caramel cheesecake and Chase settled on a piece of chocolate mousse.

Half way through dessert he let his fork fall with a clang and looked at Vahn.

"I...," he looked as if he had seen a ghost, he was so pale and shaky. "I...ahh. I was wondering,...well, I've been thinking that maybe we," he looked into her eyes, stood up, and rushed off in the direction of the restroom.

Vahn didn't know what to think. He had been acting so strange. She didn't know whether he had caught a bug or if he had just went plain nuts.

She couldn't help but wonder what he was going to ask her, and why whatever it was made him rush off to the restroom. Deep down she knew what she wanted the question to be, but the instant thoughts of marriage popped into her head she struggled to push them out of her mind.

Marriage was a big step, maybe he just wanted to ask her to get a place with him or something like that. She tried telling herself that she shouldn't get in a rush and get things confused, and she also didn't want to build herself up for a fall.

Inside the bathroom Chase splashes water on his face then stares at his reflection in the mirror. "Fucking coward," he says trying to regain his composure. He stands up and takes a rolled towel from the basket beside the sink and begins drying his face.

A man walks in the bathroom and stands behind him staring at him. Chase notices that the man is making it clear that he has a problem, so he puts the towel down and turns to face him.

"Can I help you?" Chase asked.

Raynor's informant smirks at Chase knowing that he will get the upper hand quickly. "I hope so! I'm Neil Carver and I'd like to know why you're having dinner with my wife."

Chase is immediately thrown off by the man's words and he tilts his head to the side wondering if he heard him correctly.

Jumping at his hesitation the informant continues, "I'm here with clients on an important acquisition. I look over and see you toasting with my wife. What the fuck? Who the fuck are you and what the fuck is going on?"

Chase tries to regain his composure as the man's voice raises and Chase knows he needs to be on the defense. "I think you may be confused. I'm having dinner with my girlfriend who is not married."

"So Vahn is telling you that she's not married? Not fucking surprising. Is she done playing cop yet? This fucking fantasy she has that she is going to run away from real life to play cops and robbers is complete bullshit and needs to stop," said the informant enjoying Chase's reaction to his words.

Chase reaches in his pocket and feels the ring box holding the ring he had been about to present her with. He becomes instantly embarrassed and enraged at the same time. "I didn't know she was married. She's never mentioned you before and I've never seen you before. So you tell me what the fuck?"

The informant laughs out loud and paces back and forth knowing he only has a few more minutes to piss Chase off enough to get him to leave. "Vahn and I started having problems last year. She comes from nothing, which I'm sure she told you, and my family owns three Fortune 500 companies. Every now and then she'll wig the fuck out and decide she wants to slum it and will go on some wild escapade and every time she suckers in a fucking fool such as yourself to top off the story. Too many fucking romance novels if you ask me!"

Chase feels his embarrassment turn to anger. He thinks of Vahn sitting at the table and about the time they had spent together. Everything had seemed so real and so genuine, but this man in his face pissing him off seemed extremely fucking real. He felt his rage rising.

"So you're telling me that Vahn is still married to you? You must be a great fucking husband for her to start a new life where you don't exist in it," said Chase struggling to keep his emotions in check.

The informant laughs in Chase's face knowing that he's gotten the best of him, "I have a table full of clients and don't want to cause a scene, but I'll be damned if you think your fucking ass is going to finish your dinner with my wife. I suggest you walk out the front door while you can still fucking walk. I'll make sure she gets back to the academy safely. I suggest you cease to exist in her life. Fade the fuck out!"

Chase looks at the man with a hatred that he had never felt before. The coldness of betrayal rushed over his body and he felt solid as a rock. He had nothing left to say.

"I'm going to let her finish out her stay at the academy, but this little love story is ending now. If I fucking see you with my wife again her pretty face will never be pretty again. You understand what the fuck I'm saying? I don't give a fuck that you're about to be a cop. You're the bottom of the fucking food chain. You're nothing," said the informant spitting at Chase's feet.

Chase wanted to destroy the man in front of him but his devastation and the fear of what the man would do to Vahn made him turn towards the door and almost rip it off its hinges as he exited the bathroom.

Vahn looked at her watch. It had been almost fifteen minutes since Chase had gotten up. She was worried but she knew that she couldn't go into the men's restroom to check on him. She contemplated asking the waiter to go in and see if he was okay, but she thought that might embarrass him. She decided to wait a little longer.

After half an hour had gone by, she knew that something was wrong. She waived the waiter over to the table. "Could you do me a favor?" She asked.

"Certainly, ma'am," he said.

"The gentleman that was with me seems to have been a little ill. I was just wondering if you could peek into the restroom and check on him for me?"

The waiter gave her a blank stare and blinked. "Well, ma'am. Mr. Hawkins paid out about fifteen minutes ago. He also paid for a cab to take you wherever you need to go."

Vahn felt her mouth open and her face turn scarlet red.

"Can I get you anything else ma'am?"

"No, thank you." She couldn't believe what she had just heard. How could he just leave her there and not say anything. She was so embarrassed. She wanted to close her eyes and dissolve into the floor.

The waiter pulled her chair out for her and escorted her to the front. The valet opened the front door to the restaurant, then helped her into the cab that was already waiting.

Raynor smiled to himself as he and his informant watched Vahn get in the cab and pull off. He prided himself on being prepared for anything.

"She looked pissed."

"That she did. Life is full of disappointments. So you say that he left without confronting her correct?" Asked Raynor.

"Yeah, he bought every word, he was crazy pissed."

"Perfect," said Raynor smiling.

On the ride back to the academy she felt tears stream down her face. How could she be so stupid as to think he was actually going to propose to her? His intentions had simply been to give her a nice goodbye.

"How sweet of him to buy me an expensive dinner to dump me instead of just saying, hey I'll call you!"

She thought. "Damn him!"

She felt all the happiness she had known for the past six-months drain out of her. She should've known better than to let herself be sucked in by some jerk with a nice ass. She wondered how she could've been so blind, and why she had let her guard down.

"I guess that settles it," she thought. "There is absolutely no such thing as love…for me anyway." She vowed to herself right then that she was through with men, and that there was no point in having a heart or being capable of love.

After returning to her room Vahn tried to hide her face from Ricki, not wanting to talk about it right then but Ricki knew something was wrong the minute she walked in the door. Vahn told her what happened, then had to talk Ricki out of storming into Chase's room and tearing him apart.

"I'm so sorry sweetie. I promise I'll never give you advice on men again. Who are we to think that the majority of them are human anyway?"

CHAPTER ELEVEN

Sunday Vahn stayed in her room catching up on some papers that were due. She tried to keep Chase out of her mind but the harder she tried, the more she thought about him. Through the day her emotions went from sad, to being overwhelmingly embarrassed, to sheer anger.

Tomorrow he would be sitting two rows over from her. She didn't know if she could sit there and act like nothing was wrong. She kept wondering how he would act. Would he smile smugly at her, as if to say, "Sorry, but I was through with you." Or would he ignore her completely and act as if she didn't exist.

Vahn became so anxious and nervous thinking about Monday that she had to go to the bathroom twice to throw up.

Ricki came in about 3:00 p.m. and had the cutest little stuffed animal. It was a little brown puppy with a tag that said, "I Love Vahn."

Monday Vahn arrived for class almost fifteen minutes early. She didn't want to have to walk through the room with Chase staring at her. She quickly made her way to her seat and sat down. When people started filing into the room, she tried to keep her head down so she wouldn't make eye contact with anyone but she couldn't help looking up at everyone that came in. Her hands were shaking she was so nervous.

Their instructor stood in front of the class and asked them to pass in the papers they were to have written. Vahn looked over to Chase's seat. It was empty.

"Did he feel guilty about what he had done?" She asked herself. "No, he probably just thinks that if I see him I'll start begging him back. He's so tired of me that he doesn't want to have to deal with me."

After class she watched Adam, Chase's roommate, go up to the instructor. She walked as slow as she could to try to overhear what they were saying.

"Sick huh?" Asked the instructor. "Did he give you his paper?"

"Yeah, it's right here. He's in pretty bad shape though. I don't know if he'll be back the next two days or not."

"Well, his final exam is tomorrow and Wednesday. If he thinks he's contagious he can come down alone after class is over to take it by himself, but I can't let him take it to his room. And if he doesn't take this test, he doesn't pass."

"I'll tell him," said Adam.

Vahn had reached the door and turned the corner when she felt a hand on her shoulder. She turned around to see Adam standing there. When she looked at him, his face froze. He had his mouth open as if he had something to say, but he was only standing there. Vahn tried to ask if something was wrong but she couldn't speak either. Adam then simply gave her a sad smile and walked away.

"What is it with men," she thought getting angry all over again. "Why can't they ever get the balls to say anything?" But on the other hand, maybe she didn't want to hear what he was going to tell her. More confused than before, Vahn returned to her room.

Chase wasn't in class on Tuesday or Wednesday.

She knew it was a childish thing to do, but on Wednesday, thirty minutes after class was out, she walked through the hall to see if he was in the room taking his test. The door was shut, so she assumed he was. Graduation was Saturday night. She knew she wouldn't see him again until then.

Vahn returned to her room, sat down at her desk, and put her head down on her arms. She had just dozed off when she heard a knock at the door. Her heart jumped. She wanted it to be him so badly, but what would she do?

She opened the door. It was one of the women that worked in the office. She handed Vahn a note and walked away.

Vahn opened the note. It was from Darren Torrel. He wanted to see her in his office ASAP. Vahn went into the bathroom and splashed cold water on her face trying to hide the fact that she'd been crying for days now.

Once in his office, she again felt like a small child in his presence.

"Hello, hello," he said. "Come in and have a seat." "Thank you," said Vahn managing a small smile.

"Do you have any idea as to why I've called you down here?" He asked.

"No sir, I don't," she said honestly.

"Well, I'm happy to inform you that you are the top graduate here at the academy. I'm extremely proud of you."

"Thank you," she was so shocked she couldn't think of anything else to say. Top of her class? Wow.

This was actually some good news, amazing.

"I've also heard, just rumors of course, that you have put all the firearm instructors to shame. Is there any truth in that?" He asked smiling.

Vahn felt her face pull itself into a smile without even having to coach it along. "Well, I don't know about that."

"In this little tell tale folder here, it says that you were the top student in firearms. You finished first in all running activities, and you were on the average the top scoring student in all of your class room courses. The only class you lacked the top in was your self-defense courses. But it shows here that you had dramatic improvement from the beginning of the course."

Vahn felt her smile falter. Images of her and Chase endlessly practicing together swam through her mind.

"Miss Carver? Are you okay?"

"Oh, I'm so sorry. Yes, I'm great. I'm just extremely shocked. I had no idea I had done so well."

"Well, we don't have a valedictorian, so to say. Meaning you won't have to give a speech or anything of that nature, but you will receive an honorary award with your Diploma from the academy. You'll be the first in line at the graduation ceremony."

"I really appreciate you telling me," said Vahn.

"It was a pleasure to be the one to inform you of your success. I hope that this will continue over into your duties as a police officer. Also I want to tell you, if you ever need anything, don't hesitate to come to me for help. I must say that I still have a little influence here and there."

"Thank you so much. I really appreciate it." Vahn left his office feeling a little bit better about herself. She decided that the best thing for her would be to completely throw herself into her work. Be the best she could be. That would be the only way to focus her attention away from Chase and men in general.

The next morning Vahn did not want to get up. She didn't have anything she needed to do, and she didn't want to do anything for that matter. There was absolutely no reason for her to get out of bed so she just lay there drifting in and out of sleep.

Finally, she couldn't stand the "morning breath" taste she had in her mouth so she got up to brush her teeth. Ricki had still been asleep the last couple of times she had woken up, but now her bed was made and she was no where insight.

Vahn thought about taking a shower. She looked at the shower, then at her bed. Her bed looked more appealing. She drug her feet across the floor and had just curled up in her covers when the door was practically flung off its hinges.

Ricki was running towards her and screaming at the top of her lungs. Vahn looked up just in time to see Ricki diving into her bed.

"I won, I won! Get up! I did it! Let's go. Get up! I can't believe it! I love you God! I love you! I love you Vahn! Get up, didn't you hear me? Get up!"

Vahn was trying to shield her face while Ricki jumped up and down all over her and the bed. She heard a loud thump as Ricki's feet hit the floor, then felt a loud thump as Ricki pulled her out of bed.

Ricki was now jumping up and down, running in circles, jumping on her own bed, jumping down, and running around. Vahn was wondering if Ricki had gone batty or if she was dreaming. From the pain in her ass from hitting the floor she guessed that Ricki had lost it. Vahn sat up and leaned against the bed just in time to see Ricki sliding on her knees across the floor and ending up with them nose to nose.

"What the hell are you doing?" Asked Vahn.

"I'm celebrating, get this," Ricki's face lit up and Vahn thought her cheeks were going to burst she was smiling so big, "I've just confirmed that I am now, Ricki Kile…Multi-Millionaire. Hah! Do you believe it!" She jumped up again and dove into her own bed screaming into her pillow at the top of her lungs.

"What are you talking about?" Asked Vahn trying to control her laughter. She was thinking that Ricki was going to have to be restrained with a straightjacket.

"Well, last night, the lottery was up to forty million dollars. Can you believe it? Nobody has won in like nine weeks or so. Well, I'm feeling kinda lucky, and stupid, and I just said, what the hell, why not buy fifty tickets." Ricki rolled onto her back laughing hysterically. "I mean, I felt so goofy about spending fifty dollars on lotto tickets. But I thought, hey, if I win, fifty bucks would never again have the same meaning. Fifty bucks would instantly have the value of what…five bucks?

Anyway, I figure even if forty people win, I'll still have a million dollars. Hell, I would've even been thrilled to have won my fifty bucks back. So this morning, I go down and check the paper because I missed the drawing last night. I had a lot of tickets that had two or three numbers and I was really getting discouraged when finally, I came to number fortyseven." Ricki was sitting on her knees holding out her hands, as if the number forty-seven was to be worshipped from then on.

"My forty-seventh quick pick matched all six numbers! Can you believe it? I called to see how many other people had won, and guess what? Guess what?"

"What?" Asked Vahn smiling as big as she ever thought possible.

"I'm the only winner! The only fucking winner!"

The two women both screamed ran to meet each other and started screaming and crying while jumping up and down in a circle.

The first thing Ricki wanted to do was to go buy a ring for Andy so she could propose to him. Vahn went with her to pick it out. The two women argued all day long because Ricki wanted to buy everything in sight for Vahn. Vahn kept telling her not to spend any money on her and to concentrate on Andy's ring. Ricki found the one she felt would be perfect then found her a perfect dress to propose to him in.

Ricki was still going to go to graduation, but instead of being assigned to a precinct, she decided that she would travel the world with Andy as her financial advisor. He had accepted her proposal, then accepted the job offer. They would find the perfect spot, and no matter where it would happen to be, that's where they would build their dream home and become a baby factory.

Vahn was extremely happy for Ricki. She would have made a great cop but she was a free spirit. She needed to get out and live a free life.

CHAPTER TWELVE

Vahn's Uncle Gary and Aunt Roseanne were unable to come to the graduation ceremony and were unable to get in touch with her mother. She wasn't too depressed about it though because she knew that it was a long trip. They did send her a card and a gold chain necklace that had little handcuffs as a pendant.

Vahn and Ricki helped each other get ready for the big event. They waited to put their make-up on until the very last because they didn't want their tears leaving tracks down their faces.

Raynor stared at his reflection in the mirror as he applied shaving cream to his face. For the past six months he had hoped that every time he looked into his bathroom mirror that he would see an image of Vahn. Though each time he found himself staring into his own eyes.

He still wasn't sure exactly how the visions had come about, but somehow he sensed that they had been induced only as a means of introduction, and that there would be no more.

As he ran the blade down his face he thought of how proud he was of Vahn. She was graduating first in her class. He knew that she was special and that she should stand above all others.

Holding the blade under the running water, he twisted the handle back and forth between his thumb and index finger. Being at Vahn's graduation was something he had been looking forward to. Raynor knew that she had no family coming to watch her. No one to cheer and yell and whistle when her name was called. Having no family himself, he knew the feeling well. He hoped that when she walked across the lonely stage, that she would feel his presence, and know that he was with her.

Once they were seated in the auditorium, Vahn could hear nothing over the sound of her heart beating. She was so nervous. She just knew that she was going to trip and fall flat on her face, or that she'd throw up all over the man handing her the diploma.

She hadn't seen Chase when everyone was getting in line, but she hadn't been scoping for him either. She wondered if he was there. She felt the hair on the back of her neck rise as she got the feeling someone was staring at her. She didn't want to look, but she felt her head turning to the right, looking, looking, then, she saw him. Chase was two rows back staring straight at her. She knew her eyes widened and she quickly turned around and faced the front.

She couldn't really tell what expression was on his face. She felt her eyes and throat start to burn as she fought back tears with everything she had.

The man at the stairs had motioned for her row to rise. She was the first to cross the stage so she walked to him and stood beside him.

"Our first graduate was the overall top ranking student here at the academy. She is receiving not only her Diploma, but also an Honorary Achievement Award given only to the top of the class. Miss Jovahna Carver."

Vahn felt the man at her side push her up the stairs. She felt her legs begin to shake. Then she saw Darren sitting in one of the chairs lining the stage. He looked at her and gave her a thumbs up sign. She smiled at him and somehow found the courage to walk across, get her Diploma, her Honorary Award and find her way back to her seat without tripping, or throwing up on anyone.

She watched each cadet walk across the stage in front of her. She began to wonder what each new day would bring to her life. She had actually made it into the academy, and graduated at the top of her class. She could hardly believe it.

Then she heard the words, "Chase Hawkins." She wanted to look at him, but she couldn't. Instead she looked at her feet. She wished she could have all the self-confidence in the world. She wanted to be able to look him in the eye and tell him that he hadn't hurt her and that she didn't need him, but she knew the opposite was true.

When Ricki went across the stage and accepted her diploma, she about took the man's arm off shaking it so hard. She looked at Vahn and winked as she walked across the stage.

Raynor sat four rows back from the floor where the graduates were seated. He sat in a seat that put him just behind Vahn's left shoulder. He wanted to sit more towards the front of the auditorium so that he could see her full face, but he couldn't risk her noticing him just yet. His plan was made, though it still needed a few finishing touches, but it couldn't be altered in any way once it was set into motion.

Vahn had been first across the stage, and her poise and demeanor had been of someone with total grace. Though he knew that she must have been nervous, her face showed only pride. Pride was the only emotion he thought worth feeling. To not take pride in what you do is to not take pride in yourself. And to not take pride in yourself is to be emotionally dead.

Raynor only hoped that in her last minutes she would give him the satisfaction of seeing her wild with terror.

After the ceremony Ricki had insisted that Vahn go out with her and Andy, and some of their family members. She was supposed to meet them at Andy's car, which was parked at the end of the lot. Vahn was walking and staring at the ground wondering what came next. If she was going to like where she would be assigned. If she was going to like her partner. How much action she would really see. And if being a police officer was all she expected it to be.

Vahn looked up to see Chase leaning against the payphones with his arms crossed, staring at her. Instantly, she looked back to the ground. She wanted to turn around and run in the other direction, but she knew she couldn't.

As she drew nearer towards him, she built up the courage to hold her head up. Their eyes met. She walked closer to him and he unfolded his arms and stood as if he had something to say. Vahn stared him straight in his eyes trying to read what he was feeling, or what he wanted to say.

Their eyes stayed locked until she had passed him. He hadn't said anything to her, and she damn sure wasn't going to stop and let her selfesteem be torn to shreds. It felt like she had already taped, stapled and glued it back together. His face had told her nothing.

"Some fucking nerve," thought Vahn. "What the hell does he think he's trying to prove?" Chase had been standing there as if he expected her to walk over to give him some sort of an explanation. She couldn't imagine why he would even expect her to speak to him after doing what he did, much less walk up to him and start a conversation.

It seemed like she had crossed two deserts before reaching Andy's car. Ricki and Andy weren't there yet so she had to wait. Not wanting to make it too obvious that she wanted to see if he was still standing there, she first looked to her left, then slowly swung her view to the front. He was gone. She let out a sigh. She didn't know if she was relieved, pissed off, or depressed.

They all went out to dinner to the best steakhouse in the city. In the middle of the meal, Ricki asked Vahn if she'd go with her to the Ladies' room. Once inside the rest room Ricki said, "I have a gift for you but I wanted it to be just us when I gave it to you," said Ricki smiling and handing Vahn a box. Vahn unwrapped the ribbon and opened the box. In it, was a single piece of paper.

"What is this?" Asked Vahn holding it up.

"It's a deposit slip," Ricki said smiling.

"I know it's a deposit slip. Why does it have my account number on it? And why in the hell does it have a deposit of a million dollars on it?" Vahn didn't know how she was going to accept all that money.

"Oh, give me a break. Don't even try to play the 'no, I can't accept this' game. I love you and I thank you for being such a great friend to me, and hey, it's not even an eighth of my winnings. If I were you I'd be pissed that I'm so cheap."

Vahn just stared at her and smiled. Everything had built up and she didn't know what to think about anything.

"Look, nobody says you have to spend it all. It might take you a while," Ricki said laughing. "I just want to be sure that you have something to fall back on in case of an emergency. I may be in Tahiti or somewhere and you won't be able to get a hold of me. Please just take this and don't think you owe me anything, okay, please."

Vahn closed her eyes and let out a long sigh. "All right, but I have something for you too." Vahn dug threw her purse, then finally pulled out a long narrow box. "It's not quite as astounding as yours is but I hope you like it."

Ricki opened the box to reveal a gold watch. On the back of the face was the inscription, 'Time spent with you always turns to pleasant memories.'

"Just a little something, because you know, you never know what time it is." Vahn smiled through her tears as Ricki let them pour from her own eyes.

PART II

"THE WAIT"

The week after graduation Vahn and over fifty members of Ricki and Andy's family were flown to Jamaica. Vahn had heard that the scenery was gorgeous, unlike any other place on earth. But when she stood on the beach and ran into the water, she decided it was not only gorgeous but utterly breathtaking.

As she stood gazing into the sunset and the crystal blue waters, her mind wandered to thoughts of Chase. Though she had continually tried to push him out of her mind her heart seemed to be holding on to every thought of him.

When Ricki had told Vahn that she planned on getting married in Jamaica, Vahn loved the idea. Ricki hadn't wanted to get married in just any ordinary church. She wanted to do something different. Vahn recalled the conversation well.

"Now you know if I have an ordinary wedding in an ordinary setting then everyone will be convinced that I'm not really in love because when have I ever gone with tradition?

This has to be different and original and something that suits me."

"Really, and since when do you care what anybody thinks?" Vahn had asked smiling.

"All right, so it's not so much them as me. I mean I can count on one hand all the good thinks that have happened in my life, so now that this is all sinking in and it all seems so perfect, I don't know, I guess I just don't want to kid myself. I have bruises up and down my arms where I've been continually pinching myself to make sure this is all real."

"This is definitely real and you definitely deserve it, so that's all that's left is for you to relax and enjoy it. If you continue worrying at this rate your unborn children will have ulcers."

So the discussion about the ceremony began. Ricki went from exchanging vows in hot air balloons, to an undersea diving ceremony, to just about anything wild and imaginable in between. Finally, after several long discussions Andy and Ricki decided to have the wedding on the beach.

As the sun fell below the horizon Vahn found herself wondering if she would ever find the happiness that Ricki had found. Though she had always been independent the thought of spending the rest of her life alone was a bit grim. As darkness surrounded her, Vahn returned to the hotel.

The ceremony was to begin at sunset. There were folding chairs on either side of a sandy runway. All of the family members were seated, Andy's side on the right and Ricki's on the left.

At the end of the runway was a white trellis lined with purple and blue flowers. The preacher, who was also flown in from the church Andy had grown up in, was standing under the center. Andy was standing to the right in a long-tailed white tuxedo with a purple bow tie and cumber bun. Both the men had their pants rolled to mid calf and were barefoot.

A tent had been set up about fifteen feet from the start of the runway. Ricki, Vahn, a professional hairstylist, and a make up artist had all met there early that morning. They had spent all day getting Ricki ready for her big moment.

"I'm so nervous!" Said Ricki shaking like a leaf.

"Everyone's ready when you are," said Vahn. Vahn had been asked to be Ricki's maid of honor and she was proud to accept. Ricki had chosen purple dresses for Vahn and her brides' maids. The bodice of the dresses were satin to the waist, and the bottom were of a light material that let them flow in the breeze. Ricki's dress had a fitted bodice also which came to just above her knees. Her veil had a long flowing train. And of course they were barefoot as well.

Ricki peeked out the curtain to see everyone turned and facing the tent. She looked and saw Andy nervously digging a small hole with his toe. "Oh, he's so adorable, I just love him to death."

"You're right, he's great, now can we get on with this so you can marry him?"

Ricki took a deep breath, then said, "Yeah, okay. I think I'm ready."

Vahn gave Ricki a hug and a reassuring smile, then stepped out of the tent, which cued the pianist that was further up on the shore. Vahn and Andy's brother Todd, who was the best man, were the first to walk down the isle. They were proceeded by three pairs of brides' maids and groomsmen, and a flower girl sprinkling purple petals behind her.

Finally, Ricki appeared looking more beautiful then ever. She walked down the isle gazing at Andy the whole way. Vahn knew that everyone could feel the love they had for each other.

The sunset was an array of pink, purple and blue. The sound of the water and the beauty of the landscape were almost overwhelming. It was hard to believe that a place on our earth could be so perfect.

As the preacher was ending the ceremony the tide began to rise and Vahn could feel the water dancing around her feet. When Andy was told he could kiss the bride, he took Ricki into his arms and kissed her with such passion that many family members started cheering.

Saying good bye to Ricki had been hard because she had been there for Vahn so much. The fact that Vahn knew Ricki was going to be happy and that she knew she would see and talk to Ricki again made things a lot easier to handle.

After returning to Portland, the first thing Vahn wanted to do was buy a vehicle. Having a million dollars in the bank made it possible for her to drive whatever she wanted but she decided against anything that would be flashy and draw attention to her. The last thing she wanted was to attract a pompous asshole, and since she seemed to be a beacon for them she didn't want to make matters worse by advertising she had money.

Unable to decide on a vehicle right off hand, she rented a car and decided to drive through every dealership and test drive anything that looked appealing.

Not being any closer to deciding, she was on her way to get something to eat when she passed the Toyota dealership. She went in, test drove a black Toyota 4-Runner, called Hertz to come pick up their rental, paid the dealer, and left in her brand new black 4x4, 4-Runner.

After picking up some Chinese take out, Vahn returned to her room at the Marriott. She hadn't decided whether she wanted to rent an apartment, or just buy a house. There were pros and cons to each one.

She was also confused about what to do with her life. Being a police officer was what she really wanted to do, but having such a substantial amount of money put things in a different perspective. She searched her mind wondering if there was anything else she might want to do that was not reasonable before but was now possible. Traveling the world as Ricki was doing did sound nice, but being alone the thought of it also sounded depressing.

Unable to repress thoughts of Chase and the times they spent together. She replayed their passing at graduation over and over in her mind on a daily basis. She could see his face but she was unable to tell what he'd been thinking. Was he sad, glad, unaffected, what? Why was he standing there? Was it just coincidence or was he waiting for her, and if he was waiting for her, why didn't he say anything?

She would have liked him to come up to her and tell her that he had no regrets for what he'd done rather than leaving it open to question. There's nothing worse than not having an answer. To have to continually wonder can drive a person mad.

After eating her Chinese food she fell asleep while watching television.

The next morning over breakfast Vahn read through a real estate pamphlet. The pros for a house outweighed those of an apartment. She would have neighbors but at least they wouldn't be able to hear her going to the bathroom. Vahn circled three potential buys and called the agents. She made appointments to see each one for later that day.

Vahn took a shower, got dressed then drove to the first house she was to see. The agent wasn't there yet so Vahn got out and walked around. It was a small brick house, which looked much better in the picture. At the back of the house some of the bricks had fallen away, and the windows were broken out.

When the agent arrived they went through a tour of the inside. It not only looked old but also smelled old. Vahn was polite enough to finish looking at it since the agent had taken the time to come out but told her it wasn't exactly what she'd had in mind.

The second house was white with navy blue shutters. It was a two bedroom, two-story house. The outside was decent enough and the inside was nice also but something about it just didn't sit right with her.

When she pulled up to the third house she thought the day had been wasted. It also looked much "homier" in the pamphlet. The outside of the house was a dark gray with light gray shutters. Very depressing. When the agent arrived Vahn was trying hard to put on a smile.

"Hi, my name is Sarah Parker. How are you today?" She asked extending her hand.

"Just fine thanks. Vahn Carver," she replied shaking her hand.

"Well, I think you'll really like this house. It's just been put on the market and I don't think it will be on for long. Follow me," she said as she bounced up the sidewalk to the front door. After opening the door she stepped aside and let Vahn in as she continued, "This is brand new carpet. A very nice neutral color, so you can do whatever you'd like with it decorating wise..."

The realtor's voice faded out as Vahn looked around the house. She loved it. After entering the house through the front door the living room was directly to the right and a dining room was beyond it, which had, sliding glass doors leading out to a patio in the backyard.

The living room had a fireplace in the front corner of the house. The kitchen was off of the back of the dining room to the left. It had all the appliances, tons of cabinet space, and an island with a pot rack hanging above it.

Down the hall on the right was the main bathroom. The second door on the right was a spacious bedroom with a window that viewed the backyard. It had a walk-in closet with built in shoe shelves.

Across the hall was the master bedroom. It was huge. There were two walk-in closets, both also with built in shelves. On the opposite end of the room were double wood framed doors with frosted glass. Beyond them was the master bathroom. There was a garden tub, which had two steps up to it. A shower stall was on the opposite end with the toilet, and in the middle was a set of double sinks.

Vahn fell completely in love with the house and wrote the woman a check right there. Vahn made her take down the realty sign, then followed her to her office to fill out the necessary paperwork.

Raynor sat half a block away from the house that Vahn, and who he assumed was the realtor, were standing. He watched at they took the realty sign out of the yard and placed it into the back of the station wagon the realtor was driving.

He looked in the rearview mirror and winked at his smiling reflection. This was what he'd been waiting for. In order to set up his plan he had to know where Vahn's place of residence was going to be.

He was glad that she'd picked a house instead of an apartment. He still would've gone through with his plan though it would have made things much more difficult.

As Vahn and the other woman drove off, Raynor slowly pulled up to the house, waiting until they were out of sight before pulling in the driveway. He walked up to the front door and tried the lock. In all the excitement, apparently they had forgotten to lock the door behind them. Raynor pushed the door open and stepped inside. He looked at the back of the door to see what type of locks there were. There was the basic twisting doorknob lock, and above it was a deadbolt which locked or unlocked from the inside by turning its lever.

Walking to the sliding glass doors, he noted that they had only a lock, which slid up or down. He then proceeded to inspect all of the windows in the house. They all had the same set up. Each screen could be easily removed but the windows had very strong steel swing locks, which he knew no simple slim-jim could unlock. They also had two levers, located on the inside of the pane, which could pop out and allow the window to be opened only about two inches.

Though they weren't but an inch long and only a fourth of the lever blocked the window from raising, they proved to be very strong. After pulling out the levers and yanking up on the window Raynor found that there was no way that he could open the window with just his bare hands. And using any type of tool to break them would make plenty of unwanted noise.

After finishing his inspection Raynor went into the master bedroom. He tried to imagine how the room would look with her bed, and her end table, and all the little extras she would add to make it perfect for herself.

He could plainly see her lying in bed, sleeping as soundly as ever. He wanted to lay beside her and stroke her hair, taking in everything about her.

Outside a horn beeped as two children ran into the street after a ball. Raynor blinked and found himself staring at bare carpet. He sighed knowing that it would be possibly two years from now before he would be standing there again, to finally find himself with Vahn. Satisfied with the fact that perfection takes time, he turned from the room and walked to his car. He now had to return to his home and get out the map of the city.

Over the next few weeks, Vahn spent all of her time decorating the house and buying things she needed. She had been assigned to the sixth precinct but she wasn't to start for another two weeks. So to pass the time and keep her mind off things, she went crazy buying pots, pans, furniture, and paint. When it turned warm the first thing she was going to do was to paint the outside of the house an off white color and the shutters were going to be cabernet, or a deep maroon color.

Christmas happened to fall in her two week waiting period. She didn't even bother to get a tree. That made things seem more lonely, though she did set out some holly and burned some green and red candles. She sent presents to her Uncle, Aunt, and Mother. They also sent her gifts which she opened Christmas day after making a fire and drinking some egg nog.

That evening the phone rang. It was Shirley, her mother. Vahn had only given her the address to the house and had told her that she didn't have a phone but apparently she had gotten Vahn's number from her Uncle. Shirley claimed she was only calling to wish her a Merry Christmas, but Vahn knew better.

Shirley tried to talk Vahn out of being a police officer, and went on and on for hours about how valuable life was and how you shouldn't put your own life on the line for people who didn't know or care about you.

After an hour Vahn laid down the phone, finished watching the movie she had rented, and picked the phone back up in time to hear her saying, "Promise me you'll think about it sweetie."

"Okay Mom, I promise," she said hoping her mother's conversation with herself was over.

"All right then, I'll talk to you later. Love you bye."

Vahn sighed, hung up the phone, and went to bed.

CHAPTER TWO

Before she knew it, Vahn found herself standing in the sixth precinct ready to start her first day as a police officer. She was immediately sent to meet up with her partner. He was fifty-eight years old and wasn't exactly what she'd been expecting. He was leaning over the break table rummaging through the box of donuts that was on it and mumbling something about raspberry filled donuts.

"Jack," said her lieutenant getting no response from the man. "Jack, I want you to meet your new partner."

"Huh?" He asked turning around with a scowl on his face. "Oh, my new partner, right. Hi, I'm Jack Randall. Nice to meet you," he smiled and shook Vahn's hand.

"Vahn Carver. Nice to meet you too."

Jack and Vahn went down to their car to start off the day. Vahn watched Jack as they walked to the car. He looked about twenty pounds overweight. Although trying to imagine him any skinnier just didn't seem right. She assumed that he'd been a big boy all his life.

She was shocked at the greeting she had received. In all the movies she had seen and the stories she had heard, the new partner always gets treated like dirt and it takes a while before they accepted each other as partners. Jack on the other hand, seemed happy to have her.

"Well, let me tell ya. When I heard I was getting a woman partner fresh out of the academy I was quite honored. I think we need more women on the force. My wife was a police officer but after we had our first child, Terry, she decided to stay home with him and she just never got back into it. That also could be because we have six kids and she wanted to be home for all of them, but anyway, I'm just glad you're here."

"Thanks I really appreciate you being so supportive."

Jack went on and on about how it was important not to get put with the "wrong kind of cop" right after graduating from the academy.

"We're here to help people you know. Not to see how many people we can take down or beat up, or shoot. You wonder how some of the guys in the department ever got here. It's kind of scary. But don't worry. This may be a depressing job sometimes, but it has its rewards."

"How long have you been a police officer?" Asked Vahn.

"Thirty years next month. My wife thinks I should retire, and so do a lot of other youngins, but I don't feel like I'm ready yet. Yeah I may be a little over weight, but hey, I can still keep up with the best of 'em. I still work out and jog, and keep in shape, I just happen to carry around a little extra luggage."

Vahn never really knew her grandparents because they had died when she was four. But talking with Jack, she thought that he must be not only a great dad but also an excellent grandfather.

Jack pulled up to the drive thru at Dunkin' Donuts and ordered three raspberry filled donuts, and a chocolate milk.

"Would you like anything?" He asked.

"No thanks, I already ate something," Vahn said trying not to laugh.

"What?" He asked looking at her face. "Oh, I get it. You think it's funny because I'm getting donuts right?" He looked at her and smiled. "You're right. It is pretty funny. Just because cops and donuts are like Frick and Frack, they always go together."

"You want to know something even funnier?" He continued, "Before I became a policeman I had never eaten a donut in my life. I never ate breakfast. Then I constantly heard that I should try one because they were great, and because it was inhumane for a cop not to like donuts. Even though we get teased for it and everything, it's become kind of a given tradition. Anyway, I tried a raspberry filled donut one morning because of peer pressure from my fellow officers, and I loved it. So, as you can tell, I'm hooked on them."

The car in front of them was an old rusty Cadillac. It had been sitting there for almost five minutes now. Vahn noticed Jack looking at them suspiciously. She didn't think they'd be stupid enough to hold up the cashier with a police car sitting right behind them.

"Vahn, I think the first thing we'll do today is call in that plate and see what comes of it." He picked up his radio and said, "This is 2116. I need to run a plate check please."

"Go ahead 2116," answered the dispatcher.

"Delta, Juliet, Lima, 6,9,0." Jack put the receiver in his lap and looked around to see if he could see inside the building. They were already pulled up too far and another car was behind them, so they were unable to back up.

About that time two boxes were passed to the car. It pulled forward and went around the corner. Jack pulled up to the window. The woman at the window looked at Jack and smiled nervously.

"Morning officer," she said with a shaky voice.

"Morning ma'am. Everything going okay?" Jack asked picking up on how nervous she was.

"Oh, yes everything's fine," she said handing him a bag with his donuts.

"I just noticed that the car in front of us took an awful long time. Usually this is the fastest drive thru."

"Oh, well, they had a big order."

Jack was handing the lady his money for the donuts when dispatch radioed in. "2116, those tags come back to an 86' Ford Bronco, registered to–"

Jack interrupted while stepping on the gas and pulling away from the window.

"2116, we are in pursuit of a late model Cadillac, tan, with stolen tags. Possible theft at Dunkin' Donuts on Madison and Hawthorne. Request back up."

As they rounded the corner they saw the Cadillac still sitting at the exit. As soon as they came into view the car sped out into traffic. A red Grand Am had to slam on its brakes so it wouldn't be broad sided by the Cadillac.

Jack flicked on the lights and the siren. "Here we go," he said as if they were going on a fishing expedition. They chased the car down about three blocks then turned left.

"2116, we are north bound on 39th, car is not yielding, we are still in pursuit."

Vahn's blood began racing as the sound of sirens and the squeal of tires rang out. They followed the car up to the on ramp of the Interstate. Weaving in and out of traffic the Cadillac looked like a boat out of water. There were a line of cars backed up waiting to get onto the Interstate. The Cadillac jumped the curb and rode along the grass embankment trying to pass the cars.

Jack was right behind them.

Vahn felt a smile pulling at her lips. This was what she had longed to do for so long that it almost seemed unreal. As they pulled onto the freeway a tractor trailer was in the middle lane but had his turn signal on to come over to the right lane to make the next exit. The trailer didn't see the Cadillac come out of no where and continued with the lane change.

Jack slammed on the breaks in time to see the Cadillac being pushed into the guard rail, flipping over it, and rolling down the hill to slide across its top and end up in the intersection below. Jack pulled the car off onto the shoulder, threw it in park and jumped out.

Vahn was right behind him.

As they raced to get down to the car Vahn wondered if the men had survived the wreck. "Do you think they made it?" She asked.

"Oh yeah, I noticed that both of them had their seatbelts on. The only thing hurt is their pride, I'm sure," Jack said smiling.

After reaching the car and pulling out the two men, they cuffed them, and had to be patient as the men stumbled up the hill, still off balance from the wreck. Once they reached the cruiser the ambulance arrived to check the men over. Vahn went back down the hill, crawled into the car and retrieved the two boxes. One box held a dozen assorted donuts, the other held only $165.

Two other men had been picked up after being seen speeding away from the donut shop. After returning to the precinct and questioning all of the men it was established that two men had went into the shop while the other two drove up to the window.

The two men inside had made the women empty the front registers, then walked to the back and told the woman at the drive up to empty her register also and to put all the money in a donut box then pass it through the window to the waiting Cadillac. The men inside had still been holding a gun on the woman when Vahn and Jack had driven up.

The men, not being smart enough to figure out that the shop had just opened fifteen minutes before they robbed it, had only gotten $165 which was about forty dollars a piece.

Vahn went home that night feeling good about herself and things in general. She had loved the way her blood raced when they were chasing that car. Knowing that every day would bring a different challenge made her so anxious she could hardly sleep.

Lounging on the couch and staring at the city map sprawled out on the coffee table, Raynor entertained himself with thoughts of worldwide recognition. His goal was to become the most talked about, and the most feared serial killer.

He had read every piece of literature ever written about every known serial killer to date. He wanted his name to be above all others. Ted Bundy came the closest to being the one he respected the most. He had no respect what so ever for John Wayne Gacy. The clown that abducted and raped all the teenage boys, and would kill them then bury them under his house and in his backyard. Only an incompetent asshole would leave bodies on his property.

Then there was Jeffrey Dahmer. He was one sick bastard. One thing Raynor could never figure out was why he got off on eating some of the people he killed. Now, watching Native American movies, they always would take a bite out of the heart of their kill, which was a ritual and something to be respected. But, keeping body parts in your refrigerator and freezer seemed a little over the edge.

Charles Manson was a man that really pissed him off. Every time his name is mentioned people seem to take in a breath like he's some kind of monster. The man basically had everyone else do his dirty work for him. What bravery he showed. And besides all that he was all about drugs. Which meant that everything he was about, was a delusional vision.

Raynor had never done drugs throughout his entire life. Watching his mother and her friends was enough to deter him from trying them. He had always felt like the most important thing in his life was to always maintain control. To take in excess amounts of any kind of substance that relinquished control was, in essence, to relinquish your life.

Another difference that he wanted for himself would be that he would never get caught. He would never be analyzed by thousands of psychologists. No one would ever have the chance to label him while he sat alone in a cage.

While he either roamed the earth freely, or roamed the after world, because of self-inflicted death, people would be talking and writing about him. They would never be able to ask him any questions or get any answers. They would never be able to break apart his life and try to mold it into the shape of a raving lunatic.

He knew that the deadliest thing about him, was that he was sane. He had no paranoid delusions, no delusion of grandeur, and no schizophrenic traits about him. He had perfectly good, solid explanations behind everything he had done and everything he intended to do, and he planned to do them well.

Earlier that night when he had been slicing green peppers he had realized Vahn's connection to his life, and he felt as if he had experienced a mental orgasm. His body became warm and shook with a feeling he had never known before. Unable to stand, he had sunk down to the floor and rested there, wiping small beads of sweat from his brow.

He laid his head back and stared at the ceiling fan turning slowly above his head. He laughed to himself knowing that what was in his mind was locked there for only him to see. He knew that many stories about him would be fabricated, and he really didn't mind.

But in the end, he wanted Vahn to know the truth.

CHAPTER THREE

Over the next few weeks Vahn found herself growing fonder of her career and of Jack. Though he was old and overweight he was an excellent police officer. He was very intuitive, and he never overreacted to anything. He always kept a cool head about every situation they found themselves in.

The week before, they had been at a cafe eating lunch when outside they saw a boy running with a woman's purse. Vahn reacted as soon as she saw him, but Jack was already in front of her moving with more speed and agility than she thought he was capable of. After catching the boy, he went back to the cafe and put his food in carry out box before taking the boy in.

Jack had invited Vahn over for dinner that evening. After getting off duty, they drove up to his two-story house with green shutters, and a white picket fence. It was perfect. All the stories he'd been telling her started having a picture to go along with them.

Jack opened the front door for her, then closed it behind them. "Norma, we're here!"

Visions of Fred Flinstone slamming the door and screaming 'Wilma, I'm home' flashed through Vahn's mind making her laugh to herself. The inside of the house was as beautiful as the outside. Vahn smelled spaghetti and garlic bread coming from the kitchen.

Norma came out from the kitchen drying her hands on a towel. She was a beautiful woman. She had short brown hair and big brown eyes. She looked about forty though Vahn knew she was fifty-seven, but for Jack's sake she wouldn't tell Norma that she was aware of her age.

"Well, hello there," she said smiling and kissing Jack on the cheek.

"Sweetie, this is my new partner Vahn Carver. She's just as feisty as you used to be," Jack said smiling.

"Vahn, it's so nice to meet you. I'm always happy to meet a fellow policewoman."

"It's very nice to meet you too. I've heard a lot about you. I'm glad I can finally put a face to your name."

"Oh no. You've heard a lot about me huh?" She looked up at Jack and smiled. "I'm not even going to ask what you've heard, but you'll find out that Jack likes to add little sparks to his stories. We call them fibs, he calls them sparks."

"Now Norma, everything I've said has been good and if there were any sparks they only made you look better, if that's possible anyway," he said kissing her.

Vahn followed them into the kitchen where the table was set for four. Norma noticed her looking at the table and smiled.

"I invited our youngest son Jeremy. All my other kids are married and have families but he says he's too busy to try to find a wife, so I have him over for dinner quite often to make sure he doesn't starve."

Jack pulled out a chair for Vahn. "Thank you," she said as she sat down. When she had accepted his dinner invitation she had been worried that she'd feel awkward but they were both so sweet she couldn't help but feel at home.

"Are we going to wait for Jeremy, or are we going to start without him?" Asked Jack sitting down.

"Well, he called and said that they were having trouble with one of the programs and that he'd be a little late." Norma poured Vahn and Jack some iced tea. "Jeremy is a computer programmer. That's about all I can tell you. I don't really understand exactly what he does myself so I know I couldn't explain it. I just know he's always saying something about windows."

Vahn smiled at her. She wondered what it would be like growing up in a home with five siblings, a greathearted Dad, and a Mom who was there for you whenever you needed her.

They heard the front door slam shut and a man's voice yell, "Hey, I'm here. I'll be down after I go to the bathroom."

Vahn heard loud thumps, which sounded like someone bounding up stairs, taking them three at a time.

Jack proceeded to tell Norma everything that had happened to them during the day, while Norma put the pot of spaghetti, the salad, and the bread on the table.

After Norma had sat down they heard footsteps running down the stairs, and then a black haired, blue eyed man stepped around the corner. Visualizing a computer programmer Vahn had expected a scrawny man with horn-rimmed glasses that were so thick you couldn't actually see the true shape of his eyes through them.

Instead, standing in front of her was a very masculine, very good-looking man. He was wearing Levi's and a denim button down shirt. It was obvious that he worked out. His shirt was bulging in all the right places.

Though he looked good, and was single, Vahn told herself not to even think about the possibility. Men were all the same, and she still hurt when she thought about Chase. The worst thing a woman can do is to get over one man with another. You always end up right where you started.

Jeremy obviously wasn't aware that Vahn was going to be joining them. He stopped dead in his tracks when he saw her.

"Jeremy, this is your dad's new partner, Vahn."

"Hi," he said, snapping out of his daze. He walked around his mother to shake Vahn's hand. "Nice to meet you. I hope Dad hasn't tried to push any of those raspberry donuts on ya."

"No, once they're in the car, the donuts don't have much of a chance," Vahn said smiling.

"Very funny Vahn." Jack gave her his 'I heard that' look, and everyone laughed.

All through dinner Vahn caught herself staring at Jeremy. He looked good, he was funny, and he was nice, but there was no way she could even consider going out with anyone anytime soon.

After dinner Norma made a pot of coffee and they all went in the living room to talk.

"Well, Jeremy, have you talked to that Jaime girl anymore?"

"What exactly does that mean Mother?"

"What do you mean, what does it mean?" She asked wrinkling her nose at him.

"Well, because if you mean did I ask her to marry me so that we could give you some more grandkids, then no I haven't talked to her."

"Jeremy, you know your mother doesn't mean anything by it. She's just looking out for you," said Jack.

"That's right. You can't stay single forever. Maybe you should go out more," said Norma giving him a hopeful smile.

"Mother, if you have to know, every time I go out, I end up seeing the woman I mistakenly thought I had a relationship with, walking around with another man. Or, I knock on her door and another man just happens to answer it in his underwear. Then when I get upset, the only explanation I receive is 'well, we're just talking, we never said we couldn't talk to other people'. I'm only twenty six, I'd like to know when being with someone and having a sexual relationship suddenly became 'just talking'."

"You never can be too careful these day Jeremy. Maybe you should try meeting people somewhere besides work and the gym," said Jack.

"Oh, like where Dad, a bar? I think I'll pass." Jeremy put his head back and stared at the ceiling. "Besides that the women who actually want kids already have kids and are married. All the single women are the women that cringe at the thought of motherhood, because they are scared that if they have a child they might just have to grow up and take some responsibilities in life."

"Vahn, honey, do you have any children?" Asked Norma.

"No, I don't," said Vahn, a little shocked at herself for sounding sad.

"Are you ever planning on having any?"

"Mother please! It's bad enough that you pry into my business but you don't need to give our guest twenty questions."

"I don't mind," said Vahn smiling. "I actually haven't really thought about having kids all that much. I'm an only child, and my childhood wasn't exactly peachy, so my first thought when I think about kids is kind of grim. Although when I'm out and I see babies, and kids running around, I have to admit that it makes me feel like I'm missing out."

Norma smiled. "Sweetie, if you imagine the thing that makes you most want to smile, I will guarantee you that after you have a child, it won't even compare. You'll realize that there's nothing in the world more important than that little person who counts on you for everything. And there's nothing more rewarding than raising your children."

As Norma talked Jack shook his head in agreement.

Lying in bed that night Vahn let her mind wander. She wondered if she would ever have a child. It would be nice to have a Daddy to be there for the child too, but at the moment all she was concerned about was the child.

That night she dreamed of swinging in a porch swing. The view from the porch was beautiful. There were rolling hills covered with lush green trees. She could hear birds chirping, and could feel warm air breezing across her face. She looked down, and in her arms was a beautiful baby. It had big blue eyes and strawberry blond hair.

CHAPTER FOUR

Getting home from work Raynor pulled off his coat and hung it on the coat rack just inside the door. The anticipation of the day's end had made this the longest day of his life. He had decided that tonight was a perfect night to set his plan in motion.

Walking into the living room he looked at the clock above the TV. It read 5:45 p.m. Not wanting to eat heavily, he walked to the refrigerator and pulled out a bag of deli-smoked turkey and a block of Colby cheese. He cut himself three pieces of cheese, then placed the block back into the refrigerator, grabbing a can of Sprite before closing the door.

He sat down to eat at the bar in his kitchen. Laying to the left of the counter was his favorite knife magazine. He pulled it towards him to leaf through while he ate.

Knives were something that he cherished. He liked guns too of course, but knives seemed to hold something special. Each blade had a different personality, and left its mark in different ways.

It filled him with pride to know that he was skilled with a knife. Any Jack off the street could pull the trigger to a gun and have a chance of hitting a target. Anyone could also kill with a knife but the thing was, if you were to compare a skilled chef with a restaurant bus boy in the way that they carve meat, the chef would end up with a beautiful work of art, while the bus boy, having no talent with a knife, would end up with a mass of bloody flesh.

Being skilled and precise was extremely important to him. Another aspect of knives that intrigued him was the closeness that comes when using a knife to kill. In order to kill with a gun the victim could be several feet away, but with a knife, the victim has to be close enough that you feel each others breath. Your souls must be able to look and touch one another.

As he swallowed the last bite of turkey, he closed the magazine, threw away the baggie, wiped off the counter, and then proceeded into his bedroom.

In the beginning he had been worried that Vahn was such a hermit that there would be no way to meet women like her. He couldn't go to bars because women like Vahn didn't hang out in places like that. Which he was thankful for because with past experiences, every time he trailed a woman to a bar she usually went home with someone.

It was extremely important to him that the women chosen were as much like Vahn as possible. Each one being a sweet reminder of his final destiny.

One afternoon he had been sitting outside Vahn's house waiting to see if she would go anywhere, when she had emerged in running shoes and sweats. He followed her to a nearby park where she jogged for a complete hour while listening to headphones.

As he had sat with the map spread over the bar he noticed that next to every area he had circled was at least one park if not two. He was pleased in knowing that there were probably several women who ran at the park just as Vahn had. This seemed to be the perfect way to choose his victims.

As he pulled on a pair of sweats, a sweatshirt, and some running shoes he smiled to himself. It seemed so strange that every detail seemed to be falling right into place without much effort on his part.

Raynor drove to Gabriel Park. It was towards the most southern sight on the map that he had chosen, and he figured it the best place to start. Once parked he stepped out of the car and found a grassy area on which to stretch his legs.

He watched the many people passing by. Though it was the middle of January it was a rather nice day. Not too much wind and the sun had melted most traces of the past weeks snow. He had assumed with it being January that he would have few women to choose from but the park was littered with people walking dogs, pushing strollers, and jogging.

After about a half-hour he noticed two women jogging together. One was a blonde, fake as hell, and the other was a brunette with long thick hair. He fell in behind them keeping a safe distance. He watched the way the brunette moved. She looked to be healthy and she had excellent form.

Deciding to change his direction so that he could pass facing her, he turned around. After about five minutes he could see the two women running towards him. He focused on the brunette. As she drew closer, he watched her facial expressions as she talked with the blonde. She seemed to be cheerful, and have good humor.

As he was about five feet from the women they both looked at him and said hello. He nodded back at them, then after passing them, he stopped and stepped over to the side, bending over as if to catch his breath.

The way she smiled had been perfect. Her persona seemed to match with Vahn's. After the women were almost out of his sight he began running again, this time staying behind them at a pace that would let him easily fall back out of sight if they were to stop.

After another twenty minutes had past, the women slowed down to a walk, circling the park two more times, then crossing the street to a car, and getting in together.

Luckily Raynor's car was only four cars ahead of him next to the curb. He quickly ran to his car and pulled out into traffic falling in three cars behind the women. The blonde was driving so he first assumed that she would be dropping the brunette off at her house. Then another thought occurred to him. The women could live together, as roommates or as lovers. That wouldn't work. It also wouldn't work if the brunette lived out of the circle he had designated for this area.

Just as he was about to give up the women pulled into a Protein Shake Bar that was ahead on the left. Raynor made a right turn into a gas station across the street from the restaurant and turned off his ignition.

The women emerged forty-five minutes later. They got in the car then pulled out heading back in the direction of the park. Again Raynor fell in three cars behind them. He followed them to within two blocks of the park where the women made a left hand turn onto Texas St. They pulled up into the driveway of a house on the left side of the block.

He watched as the brunette got out of the car, shut the door, and waved goodbye to her friend as she opened the front door and went inside.

Raynor looked at the house number as he drove past and went home to change while he waited for two a.m. to arrive.

At about fifteen after two Raynor drove past the brunette's house. All the lights were out so the figured it was safe to go in. Though first he wanted to look through her mailbox to be certain that she lived alone. He pulled up to the box and opened the door. Empty. There was no name on the box, only the house number. It made things much easier for him when the mailboxes had last names that were put in plurals.

Such as the Jones', or the Smith Family, etc.

He drove around the block and pulled into the alley, counting the houses back until he came to the brunette's. He pulled down a few more houses and got out of the car.

Everything seemed to be quiet in the neighborhood. There were a few dogs barking a couple blocks over but this alleyway seemed either free of dogs all together or they all were heavy sleepers.

Raynor was dressed all in black and would not be easily spotted if someone were to walk into the alley. He had on a black long sleeve thermal shirt covered by his black leather jacket. He had black fatigue pants on and black combat boots.

Walking back to the woman's house he peered over the fence looking for anything to let him know whether or not she was alone. There were no baby pools or children's toys littering the yard, though with it being January it was a little bit harder to tell. Another problem with the season was that a house with a man could easily be spotted if there were plenty of lawn equipment outside, such as high powered lawn mowers, weed whackers, blowers, trimmers, etc., and with there being only snow or dead grass on the ground these items wouldn't usually be left outside to rust.

Seeing nothing to ward him off, Raynor jumped the fence. He slowly crept along the fence line, covered by the shadows. Once he reached the house he crept slowly to the window to look inside. The woman had mini-blinds covering her windows so he was unable to tell what room it was and what was in it.

Making his way slowly to a set of sliding glass doors, he noticed a set of Venetian blinds covering them that were left open, leaving a perfect view of the kitchen. Raynor reached up and tried the door. It slid open an inch.

Before entering he looked around the kitchen to make sure he saw no sign of work boots, a dog dish, or anything of that sort. Seeing only a dishtowel lying on the counter by the sink, he pulled the door open and stepped into the house.

He stood inside the doorway listening for any noises. Hearing nothing he walked slowly into the living room. On the coat rack near the door, there were three coats, all of them appearing to be for a woman.

Slowly making his way down the hall, Raynor felt his heart begin to pound in his chest. He loved and admired the Bengal Tiger. It was a beautiful, mystic animal that was a ferocious killer. It worked alone on its prey and it showed no mercy. Each time he was stalking a woman, he would think of himself as the fierce animal, walking down the hall without a sound.

It's head down, it's senses all in tune to its prey.

As he came to the first door he slowly peered around the corner. It held a desk with a computer, a filing cabinet and three bookshelves. He moved further down the hallway to the second door on the right. There was a queen size bed, which held a sleeping brunette. She was alone in the room.

Raynor quickly moved to the third door, which was on the left. It was a bathroom. Now knowing that there was no one else in the house he let out the breath that he had been holding and went back to the bedroom.

He stood against the doorframe staring at the woman. She was beautiful. Her hair was laid out almost perfectly on the pillow behind her. She had the covers pulled only to her waist revealing that she wore a shiny satin nightgown that was a deep hunter green.

Raynor pulled the .45 out of the holster under his arm. He checked to make sure the silencer was on tight and he checked the clip. Everything looking as it should, he placed it back in the holster. Not wanting to do anything prematurely he found it necessary to bring a gun along in case of an emergency. If she woke before he planned and saw him, he would have to shoot her.

He could not afford to rush anything and he would not let himself be forced into making her part of his plan until he was ready. He was certain that Michelangelo was never forced to rush a work of art, and he planned on keeping things that way for himself.

While the woman slept he walked through her house trying to find out everything about her that he could. He noticed that she was very orderly. Everything was very clean and seemed to be in its place.

On the wall in the living room he found a picture of the woman with a cap and gown on. There was an elderly couple, which he felt were the woman's parents. Though what was most interesting was a picture of the woman with a man and a child. It looked like a newborn picture of the baby, and judging from the clothes, and the hairstyles of the woman and man, the picture couldn't have been taken more than three or four years ago.

He wondered if they had been killed or if there had been a divorce and the woman was deemed an unfit mother, losing custody of her child.

Going into the office he opened the top drawer to her file cabinet and looked at the files. They were all folders containing bills. There was one labeled car, insurance, mortgage, utilities, and medical. He pulled out one of the envelopes and read her name, Victoria Guiles.

Looking through the medical folder he found hospital bills showing that a Vincent Guiles and a Chelsea Guiles were both hospitalized after a car accident. Chelsea died after two days in the Pediatric Intensive Care Unit, and Vincent died after being on life support for thirteen days. The bill was dated two years and three months ago.

After walking through the rest of the house Raynor came to the conclusion that the woman had no current boyfriend and may still be mourning the death of her family.

After watching her for another twenty minutes Raynor took out his knife. He held it in his hand and smiled at the twisted reflection of himself in the blade. He did not view the knife as an object, but as an extension of his hand. It was exquisite. He had it handmade especially for the occasion. The handle was made of black ivory with vines made of platinum winding their way up the handle to the blade. The blade was almost seven inches long, curved wickedly at the end and was sharp enough to split hair.

Raynor was certain that this woman was perfect for him. He looked at her once more then left his mark. He knew that he was actually doing her a favor, for she would be joining her husband and daughter soon.

Vahn sat straight up in her bed startled from her sleep. She looked at the clock; it read 2:40 a.m. She had an overwhelming feeling that someone had been in her house watching her sleep.

She pushed her back up against her headboard and let her eyes scan the room. Seeing nothing she leaned over slightly and tried to peer into her bathroom.

Getting out of her bed she took her gun out of its holster which had been lying on her nightstand. She searched her entire house finding nothing.

After checking all the doors and windows Vahn returned to her room satisfied that her house was secure. Though the anxiety she was feeling must have come from a dream, she could not shake the feeling that someone had been standing over her, watching her sleep.

Two nights later Raynor returned to Victoria's house. To his delight, she had again left the sliding doors unlocked. He entered quietly, and slowly made his way back to her bedroom. On this night she was wearing a gown of the same style, but it was a wine color. Her hair was braided, which pulled her hair away from her face. She appeared so much younger this way. He liked it, and wondered if she wore it that way often.

Reaching to the inside pocket of his jacket, he pulled out a pad and a pencil. He wanted to write down every thought that came to mind about how to kill her. He wanted each kill within his plan to fit the individual woman's personality. Of course he would always have to leave his trademark, but besides that he wanted each victim to be unique.

After filling two full pages of his notepad, he again pulled out his knife.

As Vahn and Jack drove the streets with not much happening in the city Vahn had to struggle to keep from falling asleep.

"What's wrong Vahn? You not getting much sleep these days?"

Yawning and rubbing her eyes Vahn began to explain to Jack how she had awakened twice to the eerie feeling that someone had been watching her sleep.

"This a nightmare you've been having?" asked Jack.

"I don't know. I can never remember what I've been dreaming about when I wake up. I always wake up with the feeling that someone has been in my house."

"Did you check your house over?"

"Both times," she said nodding her head.

"Vahn honey, maybe you should get a roommate."

Vahn thought about Ricki and smiled. She had sent Vahn a postcard from Maui just three days ago.

"I'm not much for roommates."

"Well a dog then, at least get a dog."

As Jack went on and on about her being alone in her house, she finally promised him she would think about it.

Almost unable to work the next day, Raynor sat at his desk going over the notes he had written the night before. He revised them and wrote them over three times before finally getting them to his satisfaction.

That night as he pulled on his gloves, and slid his knife into the holder on his belt, he felt like a giddish schoolboy. Everything was to begin on this night. The first blood of his vicious quest was to be spilled.

Once again standing outside Victoria's house he tried the sliding glass door. This time, it was locked. Opening his jacket, Raynor pulled a black case from the inside pocket. Over the years he had been able to collect the tools necessary to pick any lock in existence.

Pulling out the two tools needed to slip the lock, he quickly unlocked the door sliding it open an inch, then placed his tools back into the case, and returned the case to his jacket pocket.

Walking slowly into the house, he looked around the kitchen to make sure that Victoria wasn't up for a midnight snack. With an almost overwhelming feeling of power, he made his way back to her bedroom.

The clock on her nightstand read, 2:25 a.m. He was a little late, but not so late that he would have to rush. Victoria was sprawled out on the bed, as if she had been restless through the night. Raynor wondered if it could be possible that she somehow knew that this night would be her last.

Walking back into the living room, he took down the picture of the woman's husband and daughter. Returning to her bedroom, he walked around to the left side of the bed and sat down. Victoria mumbled and groaned slightly but remained asleep. He stared at her for a few moments before deciding to begin.

Tonight her hair was down and lay beside her shining beautifully. Reaching out, he began stroking her hair. Victoria seemed to smile in her sleep and curl her body up into a ball. Raynor smiled then began raking his fingers slowly through her hair.

After a few minutes she seemed to notice that another person was present as she opened her eyes, blinking sleep from them. Rolling over, she peered up at Raynor. At first she lay there frozen, unsure of what to do.

Smiling at her reassuringly, Raynor said, "please, don't be frightened." Though he loved nothing more than the look of terror that began to cross her face.

Victoria quickly sprang up and began kicking away from him trying to make it off the bed and out of the room. Raynor, not expecting this reaction from her, quickly threw down the picture he was holding and leaped across the bed grabbing her ankle as he landed.

Turning around the woman lashed out at his face. He quickly pulled back, not wanting to give her the opportunity to leave his skin under her nails. He grabbed both of her arms and flipped her onto her belly.

"Calm down Victoria. Haven't you ever heard of angels? I've come to grant you something you've surely longed for the past two and a half years."

Pulling her to her feet, Raynor walked her over to the far side of the bed. Keeping her hands in the vice like grip of his right hand, he reached down with his left and picked up the picture he had dropped.

"Your family is waiting for you. I can't believe that you're being so selfish as to want to stay here in this horrid life rather than to go be with them."

Raynor had expected her to plead for her life, but he knew that once he reasoned with her things would be clearer. After listening to his words she said nothing. Her face seemed to cloud over and she gave him no reaction.

This wasn't exactly what he'd had in mind. He wanted her to be passive, not unconscious. He decided to try to get some sort of a rise out of her.

"You know, what do you think old Vincent would do if he were here? Was he a brave kind of guy? Would he put up a grand fight, or would he go quietly?"

Looking at her face, she held only an empty expression. Raynor considered the thought of leaving her conscious to finish his work, but quickly dismissed the idea. Though she seemed to have suddenly fallen into a trance like state, he knew that she would not be able to handle the pain she was to endure and he wanted everything to be perfectly detailed.

The clock now read 2:37 a.m. Unable to waste any more time, he dropped her hands, then quickly reached up and snapped her neck. He then proceeded with his masterpiece.

Driving home that evening Raynor felt more relaxed than he ever thought possible.

Everything had gone perfectly. His only regret was that he wouldn't again choose a victim for at least another two years.

CHAPTER FIVE

Through the next year and a half Jack and Norma continually tried to get Vahn and Jeremy together. Though they liked each other things never progressed beyond friendship. Jeremy was trying to build a long lasting relationship with his girlfriend Jaime and Vahn couldn't seem to get Chase out of her mind.

She knew it was ridiculous to keep thinking of him. And she knew she needed to get over him and get on with her life, but every time she tried going out with another man she would find herself comparing him to Chase. The way he talked, walked, ate, laughed, it didn't matter. No one was Chase, so she would never have more than two dates with a man. Besides that, she made the mistake of thinking Chase was Mr. Right and look what he had done to her.

Vahn loved being partners with Jack and she loved police work, but she couldn't help but want more. Their daily routine usually involved domestic violence calls, small robbery calls, and traffic duty here and there. She did enjoy it, but she longed to be a detective.

Her and Jack sent people away but their busts were usually nothing major and if they were, it was grand theft auto, or aggravated assault, or something along those lines. Those were things that needed to be taken seriously but Vahn never felt as if she really accomplished a lot. They would get a call, show up on the scene, and make the arrest. She wanted to investigate and anticipate the criminal's next move.

Usually, the proper procedure was to have at least five years of working the streets under your belt before you were eligible to be a detective but Vahn was itching to get in. She had talked to her lieutenant and he had told her of a possible opening in Narcotics. She was excited about it at first but the more she thought about it the less interested she became.

If she were to arrest one drug dealer, would that decrease the amount of drugs on the streets? Of course not. Someone else would pick up where the first man left off. The drug dealers usually aren't the ones who actually make the drugs, but if you are lucky to nail one who makes and distributes, then you obviously accomplished something. Though there are plenty more people out there that will still work for him while he's on the inside. Just because one drug dealer is behind bars doesn't mean his business is shut down.

Narcotics detectives were very dedicated and very patient. It takes a certain breed of detective to be able to endure what they go through physically and emotionally. Though she was dedicated and patient, she knew Narcotics was not for her. What Vahn was really interested in was Homicide or Special Crimes. Serial killers held her particular interest. Those cases were usually like a puzzle that needed to be solved. Though all killers are sick, demented people, Vahn was fascinated by the way their minds work. Interestingly enough, most of their problems arise while they are still children. Sexual abuse, mental abuse, and physical abuse usually play a part in their early lives.

She felt that if a serial killer were caught then it would bring great satisfaction. They usually worked alone and if you were able to catch one and put him away, then justice would be done. Unless there were copycat killers, or the murderer escaped from prison the chain of events caused by that person were over.

When Vahn asked there weren't any openings in that department, but her lieutenant told her he'd keep his ears open.

For the fourth night that week Raynor found himself jogging in Woodstock Park. He had staked out two different women he had followed from this park. The first one turned out to have a husband, three dogs, and four kids, and the other lived in an apartment building that fell out of the targeted area. Jogging about twenty feet behind a very slender brunette he hoped that this woman would fit into his plan.

It had been almost two years since he had killed his first victim. The wait was long and tedious, but he knew he had to have self control. He couldn't allow the murders to be connected until he was ready.

Instead of circling the park again the woman stopped at the corner she was nearest to, jogged in place until the street was clear, then jogged across and took off once again on the sidewalk.

Raynor didn't want to risk being noticed by her but his car was on the opposite side of the park and he would take the chance of losing her if he ran to get it. So instead he crossed the street as she did, jogging behind her but keeping a distance of about a block and a half.

After making a right and going down another block, she went left onto S. E. Ellis St. On the third block she jogged up the sidewalk of a house that was centered on the block and went to the front door. As Raynor slowly jogged past he watched her stoop down and pull a key from under the mat and unlock the door.

The woman turned around and made eye contact with him, then waved. Smiling, he looked at the house number, waved back and circled the block back to his car.

The next week Vahn had to pull traffic duty every day by herself. Norma was having her gall bladder removed and Jack had taken the week off to be with her.

The Wednesday after the operation, Vahn took Norma a bouquet of flowers and a card. She looked good and Jack said that he would be taking her home as soon as the doctors released her.

After leaving the woman's house the third night Raynor couldn't wipe the smile off his face. He had been discouraged after learning about the woman's extra curricular activities. She was nothing like Vahn but he decided to use her faults to his advantage. He felt great. There was no doubt in his mind that he was going to be the most feared man on the face of the earth. He was brilliant. A master mind.

His thoughts then turned to Vahn. He had kept close tabs on her as time had past. Watching over her, making sure no one harmed her, and also making sure that no one moved in on her life. There was no room for another man, she was destined only for him.

He trembled at the thought of finally being with her. Each day drew them closer together.

"Carver!" Yelled Vahn's lieutenant waving her into his office.

"What can I do for ya?" Asked Vahn entering his office and shutting the door behind her.

"Well, I just wanted to let you know that there's an opening in Homicide."

Vahn felt her heart jump. This was what she had been waiting to hear.

"Don't get too excited. I called the Captain over there and we had a long conversation. He made plenty of excuses as to why he didn't want you on, but I think all the rumors flying around about him are true."

"Well, what does that mean?" Vahn asked confused.

"That means, he hates women. He believes they're only useful for one thing, especially women only two years out of the academy."

"Well why the hell does he have so much authority if he can't view police officers by their job performance and not their gender? Aren't there any women over there?"

"Look Vahn, I've never known you to be naive so don't start now. The only reason why I told you was so you wouldn't come jumpin' on my back if you heard that the position had been filled. I know you're pissed but until they get someone else in there you can forget it." Looking down and shuffling papers that were on his desk, he waved her out of his office.

"Damn!" She thought. "This is such bullshit!" She knew that she was qualified to do the job whether she was out of the academy two years or five.

She went down to her cruiser and started the engine. While waiting for the car to warm up, she put her head on the steering wheel. Her goal had been to work her way into the Homicide Department and now, just because the Captain was obviously insecure about his masculinity, she was out of luck.

Sitting back and looking out the window at the people passing by she wondered if there was anyway she could get around this little obstacle. She thought about going to talk to the captain herself, but then decided she had better not. More than likely that would only cause trouble for her. She knew her temper well.

Suddenly a thought popped into her mind. Darren Torrel, the academy's director. He had told her if she ever needed anything to come to him. She wanted to go right then but decided against it.

"You will end up looking like a complete whine ass if you go in there complaining to him," she said to herself.

Vahn drove around trying to look for anything inconspicuous but she couldn't keep her mind off of Darren. Finally, at two in the afternoon, she found herself sitting in front of the academy. She wasn't quite sure how she'd gotten there and now she was wondering how she was going to get the nerve to go into his office when there was a tap on her window. It was Darren.

"Well, hello there. Is there a robbery in progress or were you just stopping by to say hi?" He asked with a smile.

After going into his office and trying as hard as she could to explain the situation without sounding pathetic, Vahn finally sighed and leaned back in her chair.

"Well, the rumors are correct. The worst part of the whole thing is that he is proud of it. Strange I know, but overall he is a good cop. I think maybe if I call him and brag on you until he can't stand it anymore he may consider putting you on. Using my psychology background slightly," he said smiling and raising his eyebrow. "Maybe if I make it look like you'll possibly be a better detective than he is, then he'll want you close so that he can keep an eye on you. Hearing good things about you and not having anything to say in retaliation will definitely get under his skin."

Seeing Darren enjoying the thought of getting to the Captain made her suspect that they knew each other more closely then he was leading on.

"And if nothing else," he continued, "he owes me one. We used to work together."

Vahn smiled. Never underestimate women's' intuition.

Feeling a little corny for going to him, but relieved that she did, she hoped that Darren would be able to make something happen.

CHAPTER SIX

"You're pretty quiet today, what are you thinking about?" Asked Vahn. Throughout the day conversation with Jack had been light. Vahn knew something was bothering him.

"Oh, not much. Just life I guess," said Jack smiling at her.

"Life? As in life in general or as in your own personal life?"

"A little bit of both I guess." Jack put his turn signal on and stared out the window.

"Hello. You know you can talk to me. I know that you have this phobia that if you're thinking something bad and you say it then it'll happen, but to let you in on a little secret, that's not true. So go ahead and tell me."

As Jack was making a left-hand turn he sighed.

"Well, I don't know. It's just that when I almost lost Norma, I felt like I would be sucked into this black hole if she died. As if when her life ended then so would mine."

"Well, that's understandable. You've been married longer than I've been alive." Vahn looked at Jack's face hoping she was making the subject a little lighter. Noticing that he was still frowning she asked, "So did you tell Norma how you were feeling?"

"Yes."

"Well, what did she say?"

"She said that is exactly how she feels when I tell her that I don't want to retire."

Vahn didn't know what to say. This was a very tricky subject. Every cop knows that there will always be the possibility that he won't make it to the next day, but that's just something that has to be accepted. She knew that her mother had reservations about her becoming a cop but her mother would also overreact when she went to a late movie at the mall.

Not sharing her life with anyone she never really thought about how it would feel not knowing if the person you loved would walk through the door, or if there would be a knock on the door to say otherwise.

In a shaky voice Jack continued, "I had just always assumed that since she had been a police officer herself that she understood and never worried about me coming home. I asked her when she started feeling this way and she told me that it had always been in her mind." Jack stopped at a red light and looked at Vahn.

She had never seen him so upset.

"Can you imagine that for thirty years she never once told me how she felt? She said that she prayed twice a day. Once in the morning when I left, and once at night, telling the Lord how thankful she was that I had come home."

"Jack, why are you beating yourself up over this? You're fine, Norma is fine. I understand that you're upset but you act as if her worrying is your fault. I love Norma, but you know that you were both police officers when you met. It's not as if you decided to become one against her will during the course of your marriage."

"You're right. I guess what bothers me the most is that she's kept these feelings bottled up inside of her for so long just to avoid making me choose between her or my job. But last night, she told met that the only reason why she decided to say anything now is that all of our kids are grown.

I no longer need to support six children and a wife. It's not like I would have to quit and go find another job. She just thinks that it's time for me to retire. The more I've thought about it today, the more sense it makes. For some reason, I've felt like I was waiting for a reason to retire. Since I'm still able to do my job, I guess I've just thought that I should keep doing it. I actually assumed that to want to quit working would be selfish of me. But now, I see that if I were to keep Norma worrying, that would be the selfish thing. So what do you think? Should I retire?"

"If you decide to retire don't just do it for Norma, do it for yourself. If that's what you want, then that's what you should do."

A small smile played at the corners of Jack's lips. "I think it would be nice, just lying in bed with Norma all day, for as long as we wanted." He looked at Vahn and smiled. "We tried that a couple times, you know. But when you have kids, intimacy becomes something that happens on rare occasions only."

Vahn smiled at Jack then heard dispatch over the radio. "All units, we have reports of a woman screaming. Address is 1509 S. Alabama St. Please respond."

Vahn picked up the radio. "This is 2116. We are three blocks west of the address and en route."

"Copy 2116. The neighbor reports hearing a woman screaming. Number of subjects in the house is unknown."

Jack pulled up to the house. It was a small white house. The paint looked to be chipping away, and the two front windows were broken out, though one of them was boarded from the inside.

As Vahn and Jack approached the house there were no sounds to be heard. Vahn knocked on the door.

"Hello. Police Department, anybody home?"

The front door was open and the screen door, which was torn at the bottom, was gently tapping the doorframe as the wind blew. Jack motioned that he was going to go around the back.

Vahn nodded then said, "This is the police. If you don't come to the door I'm coming in."

After a pause Vahn drew her gun and slowly opened the door. The only furniture in the living room was a single recliner. Two springs could be seen sticking out of the seat and it looked like a board was shoved up under one side to keep it level.

Dishes with food caked on them cluttered the floor. The smell of rotten meat and the sound of flies buzzing were almost overpowering.

Vahn slowly made her way back to the kitchen. The linoleum was ripped up in places and there was pools of what looked like orange juice and curdled milk covering the floor. After checking the pantry in the kitchen, she made her way down the hall. The first door on the left had a dead bolt on it.

Vahn tried the door. It was unlocked. She pushed open the door to reveal boxes of stereo equipment, TV's and some guns. Above the pile the window was boarded up and padlocked. Against the far wall was a desk with bags of crack cocaine scattered across it.

Sitting on the desk was a scale.

It was obvious to Vahn that the profits from this little business were spent to fund other habits and not on materialistic items such as furniture or possibly even a mop.

Vahn continued down the hall. There was a room ahead of her on the right. The door was ajar. As she reached the doorway she quickly scanned the room. At first glance it didn't appear that anyone was in the room, which she now realized was the bathroom, so she stepped inside.

Vahn walked back to the shower. The curtain was drawn. She raised her gun, then leaned to the side to peer around it. Not seeing anyone, she then pulled back the curtain. The tub was full. In it was a woman, face down, floating in the water.

Vahn quickly holstered her gun then pulled the woman out of the tub. She was a light shade of blue. Vahn, having seen drowning victims before and knowing that it was possible to revive some victims, thought for a moment that she could possibly save the woman. She reached up to feel if the woman still had a pulse and was horrified at what she saw.

Looking at the woman's neck, she suddenly saw that someone had broken her neck with such force, that the vertebrae were almost protruding from the skin of her neck. She had bitten her tongue in half. Only a small part was still attached where she had been missing a tooth.

The wild look of terror on her face made Vahn cringe. Not being able to shut the woman's eye lids because her eyes were bulging out of their sockets, Vahn picked a shirt up off the floor and covered her face.

As Vahn was rising to her feet she heard a gunshot come from the backyard of the house.

"Oh God, please not Jack," said Vahn as she ran for the backdoor.

Vahn pressed the radio speaker that was on her shoulder. "This is 2116. We are at 1509 S. Alabama St. One female dead. Shots fired, possible officer down, request back up and EMS."

When Vahn looked through the curtain of the backdoor she saw a wooden shack in the middle of the backyard. The door to it was facing her and on the ground she could see Jack lying on his stomach in the doorway. Not wanting anyone to see her Vahn ran to the front door and went around the left side of the house to the backyard.

Again she drew her gun. Trying to stay low she ran to the shack and put herself against the side of it. She could hear a man's voice and the sound of a child sobbing.

"She was a bitch and you know it. That's all she ever did was bitch and moan. She hated you. She never loved you. She used to tell me that she was gonna give you away. Yeah, and once she said that she wanted to kill you. I did you a favor you little fuck."

"No, that's not true!" Screamed a little boy.

"Mama loved me. She loved me! She loved me."

Vahn knew that the child was on the brink of hysteria. If he had seen his mother, she was surprised that he wasn't already there.

"Do you see that pig over there? Well, you shot him. Do you know what that means? That means that you're gonna go to prison. Do you know what happens to little boys in prison Eric? You will get a beat down every day, and the men in prison will cut you open with steak knives and eat out your insides, and leave you to die. But you know what? If you give me that gun, then we can both run away and I won't let anybody hurt you, okay?"

"No, no, no!" Squealed the boy.

Vahn had first assumed that the man was holding the boy at gunpoint but it appeared to be the other way around. Vahn was trying to think of a way to reach the boy without getting herself killed.

"You think that just because you shot me that I'm not gonna be a problem no more? You stupid little bastard! Give me that gun now!"

Vahn could hear the boy start crying harder. She was going to have to do something. Her only problem was that she didn't know if the man was still mobile or not. If she got the boy to put the gun down, then that would leave the possibility open for the man to grab it.

"You had better give me that gun or shoot me boy. But even if you do shoot me again, I won't die. I told you that I'm invincible! No one can stop me. Your mama didn't believe me and look what happened to her. I can do the same to you, you know. What are you going to do? You gonna kill me? Go ahead, kill me! That still won't get rid of me.

I'll come back and haunt you. My ghost will stick you with knives while you sleep. I'll cut your…"

"Eric?" Vahn interrupted. To your average adult the man's words would be more laughable than a threat, but to a young boy, she knew that he was visualizing, and fully believing, everything the man was saying.

"Who the hell is it?" Yelled the man.

"Eric, are you okay sweetie?" There was no response, but Vahn heard the boy heaving, as if trying to stop crying. In the background was the sound of sirens approaching.

"Don't listen to her Eric. She's a pig too. And you hear that? They're comin' for you. They're comin' to take you to prison. They're gonna think you killed your mom."

"Eric, my name is Vahn, and I just want to talk to you okay." Vahn listened for a reply but heard nothing in return. "Those police officers are coming to take that man away, not you. I'm here to help you. I'm your friend. Can I come stand in the doorway and talk to you?"

"No." Vahn heard a tiny little voice say.

"Okay, you know what? I'll just stay right here then. But if I was to come inside then I could make sure that man won't hurt you. I promise you that I will keep him away from you."

"Don't listen to her Eric, she just wants to kill you.

She knows what you've done."

Vahn creeped around the front of the shack. Police officers were taking position around the perimeter of the yard. Vahn also heard an ambulance approaching.

"Sweetie, nobody thinks you killed your mom. I know that you loved her didn't you?"

"Yeah."

"Your mommy loved you too. You're not going to prison. That man is the one going to prison. I'm just going to come around so that I can see you okay." Vahn edged around the door. Jack was lying on the ground in front of her. His head was facing the opposite direction.

As Vahn looked inside the shack she felt her throat begin to burn. Eric could be no more than five years old. He was sitting on the floor curled up into a ball but had a gun pointing towards the corner. He turned his head to look at Vahn. His face was swollen, his lip was bleeding, and his eye was blackened. Tears were streaming down his face.

Vahn tried to give him the warmest smile she thought possible. "None of this is your fault Eric, okay."

She stepped over Jack and bent down beside him. Her stomach was in knots. Keeping her eyes on Eric she reached back to try to get a pulse from Jack. As she found the vein in his neck she was shocked to feel that he had a strong pulse. She quickly looked down at his face and he winked at her. Courage instantly flowed into Vahn as she looked back toward the boy.

"You know what I'm going to do? I'm going to come in there and hold my gun on that man so that you can give me your gun. Does that sound okay? I bet your arm is getting tired, huh?"

"Shoot her Eric! You better shoot her because she's going to shoot you just like that other pig wanted to. Shoot her now!"

Eric looked from the man to Vahn. His hands started to shake.

"Don't look at him, look at me. You don't have to listen to him anymore. I only want you to listen to yourself and to listen to me okay."

She crawled on her hands and knees into the shack. Looking to the corner she saw a bald man, covered with tattoos, holding his leg. The boy had shot him in the knee. He smiled at Vahn revealing rotten yellow teeth.

"Aren't you a pretty bitch! Just what the hell do you think you're gonna do? Eric, that bitch can't save you. Look at her! She's smaller than your mom and I snapped your mom's neck now didn't I. She couldn't save you could she? And this woman can't save you neither."

Eric looked at Vahn. His eyes were filled with such fear. Vahn sat on her bottom, then scooted towards Eric slowly.

"I'm just going to come sit by you okay. You don't mind do you?"

The closer Vahn got to Eric the more tears flowed from his eyes and the harder his hands shook. Once she got close enough to him, she reached out to stroke his hair.

"You're safe now. You don't ever have to be scared again. Everything's going to be okay," Vahn whispered as she reached up and took the gun from Eric's hand. He leaned against her, crying so hard his body shook.

Vahn looked up to see the man trying to reach for a gardening claw. She held up her gun and pulled back the hammer. Vahn wanted to kill this man almost as much as she wanted to live. Seeing it in her eyes, the man dropped his hand, and leaned back against the wall.

"Not to worry Norma," said Jack laughing. "I think Vahn will make a great mother one of these days."

Vahn, Jack and Norma had just returned to Jack's house from the emergency room. Jack was wheezing slightly when he breathed. He had a huge bruise on his chest. Vahn helped Jack nestle into his favorite chair as Norma brought in some iced tea.

"Well, I'm thankful that she was there to back you up. I can't exactly blame that little boy for not trusting any men."

"I don't think he meant to shoot me. I just kind of scared him and he accidentally pulled the trigger."

"All I know is that when I looked out that door and saw you face down, I just…I just wasn't sure what to do." Vahn looked up in time to see a pillow flying at her face.

Jack laughed as it smacked her. "Yeah well if you'd have left me alone and not made me talk about what I was thinking about all morning then it never would have happened."

"Oh please, will you stop with your superstitions," said Norma. "We should all just be thankful that you're all right."

"This morning I was standing in the shower contemplating our conversation from last night." Jack looked at Norma and smiled. "I just couldn't decide what to do. Finally I prayed and asked to be shown a sign, and you know how I feel about signs. Since I dismiss things so easily I asked that I be able to recognize it. I think maybe I got one."

Norma walked over to him and kissed him. "So what does this mean?"

"This means that after I mosey on in and fill out my paperwork, that I'm going to bring home a bottle of wine and we are going to make love all night and all tomorrow and maybe even the next day. I'm now a retiree at your mercy."

Norma blushed as Jack pulled her onto his lap and kissed her.

After Vahn and Jack had filled out their paperwork, they went to a small diner to have some coffee and to say their goodbyes as partners. Vahn was sad to see him go, but she knew that she would still see him often.

The time with Jack had been good for her. Never knowing a father and never understanding the love between father and daughter, her relationship with Jack had made the picture a little clearer in her mind. For that she was very grateful.

CHAPTER SEVEN

The three days following Jack's retirement were Vahn's days off. She spent them lounging around the house and watching movies. She normally chose action movies to rent, but since she had seen all of the new releases she decided to get a few that touched the heart. She found herself walking up to the counter with A Perfect World; Corrina, Corrina; and When a Man Loves a Woman.

The children in all of these movies were so wonderful. She remembered what Jack had said, "Vahn will make a good mother one of these days."

"Yeah, sure," she thought. "And when will this happen? Since finding the right man is out of the question I guess I'll have to make a few trips to the sperm bank."

She had always felt lonely before but it had never bothered her this bad. Maybe it was because her birthday had been two weeks earlier. She wasn't getting any younger and most couples that get married decide to wait a few years before they have kids.

"Hmm, let's see, at that rate, if I find a man within the next ten years, which includes dating time and engagement time before the actual marriage, then he wants to wait five years before having kids then hey, I'll only be over forty when I have my first kid, no problem."

Vahn threw her head back over the arm of the sofa and stared at the ceiling. "Jack was right," thought Vahn. "I at least need a dog."

The next day she found herself getting dressed and heading out for a K-9 ranch she knew of which was about twenty miles away from the city. This was the place that most of the German Sheppard's used for police K-9 units were purchased from.

She loved dogs and had always wanted to get one but felt guilty since she wasn't home much. So while standing there trying to decide what to do, she looked at two nine month old males. They were so beautiful she couldn't believe it. They were black and tan Sheppard's and their markings were perfect.

The two were biting and pouncing on each other. She couldn't bear to separate them. Finally she decided to get them both. That way they could keep each other company when she wasn't home.

She actually walked out spending only twentyeight hundred dollars. She was shocked at the price at first, but when she was told what it would have been without her police officer's discount, she was quite happy with the amount. The dogs were a thousand each but they were fully obedience and attack trained and all their shots were up to date. She also purchased dog dishes, toys, collars, leashes, food, treats, beds, and a dog door, which she knew she could get Jack to install for her.

Driving home with the dogs, which their trainer had named Zane and Zeke, one was in the front seat with his head out the window and the other was in the back seat, also with his head out the window. Just having them with her made her feel a little more relaxed. She would have someone to talk to even if they couldn't exactly talk back. But since they were males, she considered that a plus anyway.

When they arrived home, she pulled the 4-Runner into the driveway and got out. She opened both of their doors. They jumped down and ran into the yard jumping on each other. Vahn decided that she'd take them into the backyard so that she could unload everything without having to worry about them. She had went over all of their commands at the kennel and they were very impressive but she wondered if they were going to be that easy now that their trainer wasn't around.

"Zane, Zeke, come!"

Both dogs looked up and came running to her. They then sat directly in front of her and stared at her with their ears up and their tongues hanging to the sides. Though they were only nine months old their heads almost came to her waist. As she started walking toward the house they stayed perfectly still waiting for her next command.

"Heal!"

Both dogs came trotting to her left side and stayed directly beside of her. She opened the front door and quickly led them through the house to the backyard so that they could mark their territory outside rather than in. Their trainer had said that they were house trained but she didn't want to take any chances. With the backyard being fenced in by a nine-foot wooden fence that was solid as a rock, she knew that they would be fine and settle in quickly.

After unloading everything she went back out into the yard and practiced a few more commands, then played with them. She threw balls for them to catch. They loved catching Frisbees. She even found herself down on the ground wrestling around with them as they pulled at her feet and licked her face.

The next morning Vahn had just fed the dogs and was ready to climb into the shower when the phone rang.

Vahn picked up the receiver, "Hello."

"Hi Vahn, this is Darren Torrel. I hope you don't mind me calling you so early."

Shocked that it was him and hoping that she was about to hear good news, she replied, "Darren hi, no, no this isn't too early. I've been up for a while now.

What can I do for you?"

"Well, this is still kind of under our breaths, but I just wanted to be the first to inform you that you are going to be moving soon."

"What are you saying?" She asked feeling a smile come across her face.

"Well, I called Captain Reese over in Homicide and I told him that I thought I knew of a certain lady officer that would be a great asset to his department. At first he just laughed but when I told him about your scores out of the academy and the success you've had in the field he was more willing to talk."

"So that's it? You just talked him into it?" She asked feeling her pulse race and trying to hold back the urge to scream.

"Okay, well maybe I might've threatened him just a tad. Not really threatened him but told him a small fib. I may have said that someone from Internal Affairs was asking me about you but that you would rather be on Homicide than Internal Affairs. When I made it clear that he could have the choice of you working for him, or you watching every move he makes because he's basically black-balled you he looked at things from a different perspective. I think it's pretty obvious what choice he's made."

"I can't believe it! This is great. I don't know how to thank you. I appreciate it more than I can tell you."

"Well, don't forget that it's not official until your lieutenant let's you know about the transfer himself."

"No problem. Wow, I'm still shocked. Do you and your wife have plans for this evening?"

"No, not that I know of."

"Okay great, we could meet for dinner somewhere. How about if I treat you both to Portland Place?" asked Vahn.

"Oh, Vahn that's the most expensive place in town. I can think of another place to go," he said.

"Absolutely not. I owe you a lot more than just dinner. I'll make reservations for seven and I'll see you there," she said

"All right, Vahn. That would be nice. We'll see you then."

Vahn hung up the phone and threw herself on the bed. It was still hard to believe. This was what she had wanted and amazingly enough Darren had come through for her. She had surprised herself when she had suggested Portland Place. That was the last place that she and Chase had been together and the restaurant didn't exactly hold pleasant memories, but that was the best place in the city and Darren deserved the best.

Her mind wandered back to that night. She hadn't seen Chase in over two years now, but his face was still so clear, so perfect. She closed her eyes trying to bring back that night. The question of 'why' still remained after all this time. Then she felt a huge pounce and looked up to see Zeke licking her face with Zane right behind him.

Vahn sat up and put her arms around both of them scratching their ears.

"You're right guys. I'm not gonna let thoughts of him ruin this for me. This should be a celebration!"

PART III

"THE REUNION"

CHAPTER ONE

Dinner with Darren and Claire, his wife, went very well. They were both great company and Claire was very light hearted and cheery which made the sting of the atmosphere easier to bear.

When they had first stepped in the door, Vahn expected the Maitre d' to say, "Oh, aren't you the lady who's date left her in the middle of dinner? Ah, but tonight you don't have to worry because you have no date, how lovely. Right this way please."

Instead she didn't seem to be recognized and the table where she and Chase sat was not in view so it turned out to be a pleasant evening.

When Vahn walked into the precinct the next morning her blood was racing. She knew her face looked like a strawberry and she was trying to keep a girlish grin from popping up every second. Walking into the locker room she began changing into her uniform. She could barely button her shirt her hands were shaking so badly.

Leaving the locker room she was walking towards the conference room for briefing before the shift started. Walking past her lieutenant's office she heard him yell.

"Carver I need you in here."

To hide the smile that again stretched across her entire face, Vahn tried holding her top lip in with her bottom. She took three deep breaths before she reached the door, hoping that she could keep from making it completely obvious that she was already aware of what he was going to tell her.

She walked inside and shut the door. Her lieutenant extended his hand, which held a manila folder. She took the folder from him and opened it. Inside were her transfer papers. He then reached down beside of him, picked up a box and threw it at her feet.

"Get your stuff together and report to the sixteenth.

Homicide is on the second floor."

Vahn felt her face burst into a smile. If he looked at her now she knew all he would see would be teeth. She stooped down and picked up the box. As she was walking out the door she heard him say, "Congratulations Detective Carver. Take care of yourself."

Vahn could only nod her head as thanks.

After changing back into her civvies she cleaned out her locker still in disbelief. Packing what few things she had, she tried to imagine what this new change would bring. Would she now feel like she was where she should be? Would this put her life in perspective more so than it was?

On the drive to the sixteenth precinct Vahn became more confident. She knew that she would be a great asset to the department. This was what she had longed to do. Her scores and stats were impressive these last two years but Vahn wanted more. She really wanted to make a difference. She was fed up with traffic tickets and the neighbors being too loud, and one neighbor's dog eating the other's cat, and little nit picky things that are amusing to tell at the dinner table but nothing more.

The only thing bothering her was that she hoped she would be able to handle the face of death. Blood and flesh had never bothered her. Living in Ohio deer hunting was practically a religion followed by everyone. So she had plenty of experience dressing a deer and carving the meat. Though she could never look at its eyes. She had always wondered what it was thinking when it died. Did it look into the hunter's eyes and knowledgably accept death? Or was it simply aware of the presence of danger and had no concept of what would happen if it failed to flee in time.

As Vahn reached the precinct she pulled into the lot and parked. Gathering her reassignment papers together, she headed into the building.

On her way to the second floor she wondered what her Captain would be like. It would be naive of her to assume that he was going to graciously accept her as part of the team but she had dealt with and was forced to tolerate plenty of assholes throughout her life so she figured one more couldn't hurt.

Opening the door that had Homicide displayed on it, she stepped inside and looked around. There were several desks with computers placed around the room in pairs, each facing one another. The wall to the left was a half wall with the upper part being see through glass that showed a smaller room on the other side with large dry erase boards and chairs, which she assumed was the debriefing room.

The door to the room was around the corner out of her sight but she could see maps hanging on the walls and a long table with chairs around it. What appeared to be the Captain's office was in the far right corner of the main room.

A few people were doing deskwork, others talking in a small groups and some were busy on the computers. Looking at the individual people Vahn began to feel slightly intimidated. They all looked to be at least ten years her senior and they they were all men.

Making her way to the Captain's office, Vahn knocked on the door. After hearing a bellow, which sounded somewhat like "come in", she opened the door. Sitting behind the desk was a dark haired, blue eyed, very sleek, masculine looking man. For some reason she had imagined a very obese man with hair growing out of every orifice. This, she was not expecting.

"Please, have a seat." He leaned back as he gestured toward the chair in front of his desk. Vahn walked to the chair and sat opposite of him.

"Vahn Carver I presume," he said interlocking his fingers behind his head.

"Yes sir." Vahn really wasn't sure what to say or do. His voice and whole demeanor had thrown her off guard.

"I'm Captain Reese," he stated not making an effort to shake her hand. "Now I'm really not sure what you have or haven't heard about me. I had a conversation with your old lieutenant concerning you a few weeks ago. I expressed to him my feelings about you transferring to work with us. A week later, I received a call from a Darren Torrel.

Now, he tells me that you were not aware of this call, but I'm going to assume that you were."

As he paused Vahn decided he wasn't asking her a question but stating facts, so she said nothing.

"The outcome of the call is obvious. It's nice to know people isn't it Ms. Carver."

Vahn smirked as she assumed that he definitely seemed to be a prick getting a hard on by trying to intimidate her.

"It helps now and then," said Vahn trying to conjure up her best 'What's your fucking point' look.

"Mmm. Well, this arrangement isn't etched in stone so I suggest you just try your best and we'll see how far that takes you." He sat forward and put his elbows on the desk. "I didn't think you'd be the best fit for the team because you're a rookie and because this is a lifestyle. We live this, it's not something you clock in and out of. Have you thought about what your reaction is going to be dealing with dead women and children?"

"Yes sir I have. I know this won't be easy. I also know that the stats for this division are outstanding. I have no problem working hard and producing results. I'll be fine sir," said Vahn with confidence.

"Know this Carver. The first time you drop a tear, run out of the room, or vomit on my crime scene, you're done. Am I clear?"

"Crystal sir," said Vahn feeling her nostrils flare and her jaws clench together. Grinding her teeth as if to tear apart the words that would surely get her thrown out the door, she raised her eyebrows as if to say 'now what'.

"Now, normally we don't put two rookies together, but your new partner has been here for three months and is a damn fine detective. A new case seems to have surfaced and it looks like it's perfect for the two of you. There have been two murders, both of them look to be connected. Your partner has the files. I'm sure he can fill you in."

As he rose to go to the door Vahn let out a deep breath. She decided she would never again doubt the saying that looks can be deceiving. His voice drove her up a wall. She felt as if her stepfather was sparing her a spanking or some shit like that. She knew that his whole persona was designed to crawl right underneath her skin, and hey, it did just that.

"Hawk, can you come in here please?"

Seeing the wonderful Captain as a role model, she could only imagine what the rest of the men around there were like. That was all she needed. But that was her luck. She got the job she wanted. Never had she been handed a pretty package and there also be something great inside of it. Life is full of 'catches'.

Vahn heard a group of men laughing and footsteps coming from outside the door.

"Hawk, I want you to meet your new partner Vahn Carver."

As the Captain pushed the door open and Vahn rose out of her chair, she found herself face to face with her new partner, Chase Hawkins.

Vahn's mouth fell open, as her knees began to shake. She couldn't believe it. They had lived in the same city, both as police officers for two years now and had never run into each other. Then suddenly the first time she sees him it's as her new partner.

"Carver, nice to meet you," he said extending his hand and giving her a small sly grin.

Thinking that he was now going to act as if they had never even met before, Vahn became enraged. She extended her hand and shook his giving him the best go to hell look she could.

"Hawk, I want you to show Carver to her desk, then fill her in on the case. I want you two to make this case the only thing in life you're living for. I've already had a call from the Mayor today and he wants this wrapped up quickly and very neatly."

"No problem Captain," said Chase nodding at him.

He looked at Vahn and waved for her to follow him.

Walking behind him Vahn shook her head. What kind of a sick joke was this anyway. Vahn looked to the ceiling and said, "I always knew you had a sense of humor but sense of humor but damn!"

Chase stopped at two desks facing each other. One of them looked completely unorganized, the other was empty.

"This is your desk partner," he said pointing to the empty desk. Chase plopped down in his chair and reached into the file beside of him, pulling out a manila folder.

Vahn pulled off her jacket as she muttered words of discontent under her breath. She hung her jacket over the back of her chair and set her paperwork on her desk.

Chase had opened the folder and began spreading photos across his desk. When Vahn looked down, she was not prepared for what she saw.

"We have your classic psycho here. Obviously he thinks he's some sort of vigilante. He seems to be telling a story, or sending a message. Who knows what these sick fucks are thinking."

Looking at the photos, she picked one up and continued to stare at it in disbelief.

"The one you're holding was the first victim. Her name was Victoria Guiles. A woman she worked with found her approximately thirty-six hours after time of death."

Vahn sat down in the chair to her desk, never taking her eyes from the picture she was holding.

"As you can see from the photo her bedroom closet was cleared out, the contents of which were found neatly folded and placed under her bed. The killer then hung a rope from the top of her closet, made a noose, and placed her into it stringing her up off of her feet. The autopsy report showed that her neck was broken before she was placed in the noose, so all this was strictly for show."

Handing her a close up shot of the woman's chest he continued, "The victim's heart was cut out. It was not found at the scene and has never been recovered.

Also her genitals were sown shut with sewing thread."

Vahn felt her body shudder as the words passed over her ears. Instantly she wondered what kind of a monster could possibly do this.

"Do we have any kind of a motive?"

"Well, Detective Carver, no we don't at this time.

That's what you and I have to figure out."

Vahn reached across his desk and fished through the photos. Picking one off the pile she held it up for him to see, wanting him to explain.

"At her feet there was a picture of her late husband and daughter, and beside of that was a page torn out of a journal she had been keeping. It told of how she had felt empty and alone, as if her heart had been torn out. It also said that she had been contemplating suicide, and that she had not had sex since the death of her husband. The passage was dated two weeks before her death. I guess he wanted it to look like a mercy killing."

As Vahn continued to look through the photos, Chase pulled a second folder from his desk. Before he could hand her the second set of pictures, she found something that caught her eye.

"What the hell is this?" She asked hoping that she was mistaken.

"Apparently that is the killers calling card. This murder took place about two years ago. And at the time, we weren't sure what it meant. Until now."

Chase handed her a second picture almost identical to the one she was holding. It was a shot of the back of the second victim's neck. On each woman, were three small marks placed closely together. Each mark was about a quarter of an inch, the first two barely piercing the skin while the third had blood coming from it.

Vahn shook her head needing time to comprehend everything she had just been hit with, when Chase continued with details about the second victim.

"Janis Barker was found approximately twelve hours after time of death. She was strapped to all four bedposts, her anal and vaginal cavities were impacted with condoms, and cause of death was asphyxiation. He apparently stuffed condoms down her throat as well until she continually gagged and vomited, resulting in suffocation."

Vahn looked at the photo of the woman with all fours extended. Her face and throat seemed to be swollen, the veins on her neck and temple were bulging, and she was the strangest shade of blue and purple that Vahn had ever seen.

"The victim had a TV and DVD in her bedroom. There were two videos sitting on top of the DVD, a third was in the player. The killer apparently put it in and set the DVD to repeat so that it would replay after it finished and begin to play again. The neighbor that found the body stated that the DVD had been on when she found Ms. Barker."

"Well, what was on the tape?" Asked Vahn hoping that the man had been stupid enough to videotape the murder.

"They were homemade porno flicks starring the victim and several different unnamed men. In each one there were no condoms used."

"When did this murder take place?"

"This one came across my desk three weeks ago. I had teamed up with Harper, the detective assigned to the first case, and we have been able to come up with nothing. He's been reassigned to a different case so now that you're here, both of these babies are ours."

"And I guess it's safe to assume that we are classifying this as a serial murder investigation?"

"Technically yes. But let's hope we can find this guy before we hit the national news as having a serial killer on the loose. It looks as though we have a killer with a sick sense of humor. He obviously went to extremes to make each murder unique to the victim. He wants to get our attention that's for sure. These murders were two years apart but that doesn't mean he's not ready to speed things up."

Vahn laid the picture down on her desk and placed her head in her hands rubbing her temples. She wasn't sure where to start being dumbfounded.

"It's lunchtime have you eaten?" Asked Chase gathering up the paperwork and putting them back into their proper files.

"No, I haven't."

"Well, let's head out and continue the conversation in the car."

The thought of food didn't sound appealing just then, but she rose to her feet anyway, pulled on her coat, and followed Chase out of the office.

Deciding to eat at a small coffee shop, Vahn found herself staring at Mr. Chase Hawkins over a cup of coffee. Talk in the car had ceased to exist. Though she knew that they should be talking about the case, she couldn't help but wonder what he'd been thinking.

Was he just going to act as if nothing had ever happened between them? He seemed as though he had nothing to say simply because he didn't know her. Leaving her alone in the restaurant that night was one thing, but how could he even consider not acknowledging the situation.

Vahn had ordered a Patty Melt, and Chase a Club sandwich. As the plates were laid in front of them Vahn reached for the salt and salted her fries. Chase reached over and grabbed the ketchup, taking off the lid and holding it over his fries. After a few small shakes the bottle produced nothing.

Vahn put a fry in her mouth and watched as Chase turned the bottle so he could see inside. He muttered something and again held it over his fries beating it on the bottom.

Vahn noticed his face begin to turn red and smiled remembering how the smallest little things used to aggravate the hell out of him. When again nothing came out, he cursed under his breath, made sure to avoid Vahn's face, put the lid back on the bottle, scooted his chair away from the table, turned the bottle upside down and began violently shaking the ketchup to the top of the bottle. After about the third thrust the lid flew off, and ketchup went sailing over the floor, his pant leg, and the two people seated behind him.

Trying as hard as she could, but to no avail, Vahn let out a bolt of laughter. A few of the surrounding tables joined in, excluding the couple that was now covered in ketchup. The waitress walked over with two towels, her face blue from holding her breath.

Chase took a towel from the waitress and glared at Vahn as he slammed the bottle down on the table.

"Is there any left for your fries?" Asked Vahn trying not to go into hysterics.

Getting up from his seat Chase made it perfectly clear that he did not think that her comment was cute, and proceeded to the bathroom.

After helping the waitress clean up and apologizing to the couple and telling them to send her their tab, Vahn moved their food to a small booth in a distant corner of the diner.

As Chase came out of the restroom, one pant leg completely soaked, Vahn stood up and motioned him over to their new table. He sat down across from her and stared at his food. He apparently still had nothing to say. Knowing that he was going to be her partner for who knew how long, she decided it was up to her to get things back on a sociable track.

If he wanted to forget the intimacy between them, then that was fine with her. After all, now that they were partners that was forbidden. The only thing worrying her was that she couldn't think of anything more irresistible.

"Well, I've heard of people doing strange things to break the ice but that was a little extreme don't you think?"

A small smile played at the corners of his lips as he raised his head and gazed into her eyes. Instantly, she knew that the feelings were still there, but she struggled with everything she had to overlook it and focus on their relationship as partners.

He looked back over his shoulder at the couple that looked as though they had just come from a murder scene and smiled.

"Well, it looks like my aim is still a little off huh."

After small talk about what precinct they had been assigned to and how they had liked it, they decided to focus on the matter at hand. Finding the demented man that had killed the two murder victims.

Making their way to the scene of the second crime, Chase began to go over a few details he had previously noted. As he broke the crime scene tape and entered the house, he continued. "There were no signs of forced entry, no fingerprints, no footprints, no nothing.

This place was completely clean."

Vahn followed him back to the bedroom where the bed, dresser, TV and DVD still sat, just as they had in the pictures. Vahn stared at the bed. Besides a small stain near the head of the bed, it looked as though nothing unusual had taken place there. "Was either of the victims raped?"

"No, there was no sign of rape, no semen found at either scene, no skin tissue under the victim's finger nails, no sweat secretions, no blood, other than the victims, and no hair other than the victims. This guy, without a doubt, knows exactly what he's doing. This is not some crazy crack head off the streets. This man put a lot of thought into each murder."

Vahn walked around the room, looking behind curtains, in drawers, under the bed and mattress, behind the headboard, in the closet. She had no idea what she was looking for but she refused to think that there were no traces of the man's presence left behind.

After thirty minutes of finding nothing, and having Chase continually tell her that they had already been over the place repeatedly with a fine toothcomb, she surrendered and they walked to the car.

"Have you ever been to the first murder scene?"

"No, Harper had that case and he said that it was the same as this one, no leads."

"Maybe Harper isn't the best detective on earth and he overlooked something."

"Well, it's going to be a little hard to find now. The murder happened two years ago and there's a new family living there now."

Vahn thought about it for a minute then said, "Let's go anyway."

"Go anyway? Would you be overly cooperative if a couple of detectives showed up at your house and wanted to inspect your bedroom?"

"Sure why not?"

He rolled his eyes at her and headed in the direction of the former home of Victoria Guiles.

As they pulled up to the curb in front of the house, they saw a woman in her late twenties playing with two children in the front yard. She looked toward them and shaded her eyes with her hand. As they got out of the car and walked toward her she smiled and met them at the end of the driveway.

"Hi, what can I do for you?"

"Is this your house ma'am?' Asked Chase showing her his badge and smiling warmly.

"Yes it is." She looked between the two detectives with a beginning nervousness.

"An old case has recently surfaced and we were just wondering if we could have a quick look in your bedroom." Vahn said smiling casually as if this were a daily occurrence in their field of work.

"Is this about the murder that happened here?"

Vahn exchanged looks with Chase, for some reason they had assumed that she wouldn't know about it.

"Yes ma'am."

"Wait just a minute please." She turned and asked her kids to go and play in the backyard. She watched them to make sure that they went through the side gate, then motioned for them to follow her into the house.

"I'll try not to ask too many questions. I don't mind cooperating. My husband told me that we bought this house at an incredible bargain, though he didn't tell me why. I had to find out from the neighbors. It's kind of a shock to receive over casual cake and coffee."

As the woman pushed open the bedroom door and turned on the light, Vahn thanked her and asked if she'd mind waiting for them in another room. She smiled and said that she didn't.

Chase exhaled and turned to look at Vahn. "Well, detective. What exactly do you expect to find?"

Frowning at him, Vahn turned her attention to the closet. She opened the door and scanned it from top to bottom. It was safe to say that this was the single most organized closet she had ever seen in her life, and she was thankful for it.

The top of the closet had a hole in it, which had been sloppily patched with putty.

She knew that this was where the killer had placed the hook from which the rope had been hung.

Looking at the bottom of the closet, which was completely clear of any articles of clothing or shoes, she saw nothing. Only carpet. It looked new, and seemed to have been replaced since the murder. She looked behind her and noticed that there was new carpet throughout the room.

Knowing what she was thinking Chase said,

"You're not going to pull this carpet up, so forget it."

Vahn looked up at him and let out a Humph, then stood up. As before, she began to look under the bed, dresser, and at the window. Chase, not sure of whether to admire, or be annoyed by her, stretched his hands up the frame of the bedroom door and leaned forward.

"Well, Ms. Wizard, is it safe to go now? Have you satisfied your curiosity?"

"No, not exactly."

Pushing his hands farther up the frame, Chase suddenly let out a yell, and drew his hand down to look at his finger.

Vahn ran over to him. "What did you do now?"

His finger had a rather large splinter in it, which he was now trying to excavate by distorting his finger to find which way it had entered.

Looking up at the doorframe, she noticed that there was what appeared to be a small notch taken out of it. Standing on her tiptoes, she was unable to get a good look at it.

Hearing Chase call out the woman came running in from the kitchen. "Are you all right Detective?"

"Yes ma'am thank you. Do you have a needle?"

"No," interrupted Vahn. "Do you have a magnifying glass and a chair I can stand on?"

Smiling, she turned and walked down the hallway after the items.

"What the hell are you doing now?" Scowled Chase.

"Is this your designated day to be accident-prone or what?" She asked laughing.

The woman appeared with a needle for Chase and a stool and small magnifying glass for Vahn. "I crossstitch at night sometimes and my eyes tend to get weak so that little magnifying glass helps a lot. After about five hundred little x's they tend to all run together."

Vahn gave her a complimentary smile, pushed Chase out of the way, and climbed up on the stool. Looking closely at the notch with her naked eye, she noticed that it was three small little nicks in the frame. Putting the glass up to it, she noticed that the third one, or the bottom one, had a dark tint to it.

"Look at this."

After pulling the splinter out of his finger, and giving a sigh of relief, Chase took the glass from her and climbed up onto the stool. After taking a good look, he turned to the woman.

"Have you ever noticed this before?"

"No, I haven't. We've just recently laid new carpet and I've been picking out colors to repaint, but we've left everything as it was."

"There's no way that your husband, or your kids, could have done this?"

"No, I don't think so.'

Vahn looked at Chase knowing that she might have found something.

"Well, ma'am, we appreciate your cooperation and we would appreciate it if you did not touch this. We have to go check in with our Captain, and we should be back within a couple of hours if that's okay." Chase smiled warmly at her hoping to keep her from getting nervous.

"Oh sure that'd be fine. My husband has a late meeting so we'll be right here until about nine this evening."

Walking quickly to the car, they then headed back toward the second murder scene.

"Why do we have to go check in with the Captain?" Asked Vahn.

"We don't but I didn't exactly want to tell her where we are going."

"We should've just cut that part of the frame away from the door. What if she starts messing with it?"

"Would you relax," said Chase. "We need to see if there is anything at the second place to tell us whether or not it's connected. Otherwise we'll have taken part of the woman's doorframe for nothing."

Vahn crossed her arms and stared out the window wanting the cars in front of them to instantly part. She had become too accustomed to the sirens in her patrol car.

Approximately twenty minutes later, they pulled up to the house on S. E. Ellis Street, and Vahn practically sprinted inside. As she quickly walked back to the bedroom, she looked up at the doorframe.

Chase entered the hallway and could see her smile gleaming from the bedroom door. He didn't have to ask her what she saw.

CHAPTER TWO

Raynor glared intently at the punching bag before him. Sweat ran down his face and burned his eyes. With each punch and each kick he felt his adrenaline begin to pump harder. It was everything he could do to remain calm and not rip the bag from the ceiling. He loved this feeling of overwhelming rage. With each blow to the bag he envisioned not taped leather, but faces with blood flying from them, ribs cracking under his foot, knees breaking.

As he felt his climax coming, he closed his eyes and instinctively began performing spin kicks. Every time his foot hit the bag he yelled at the top of his lungs. Each time hitting harder and harder, knowing his body was an unstoppable weapon. He shook with power, his whole body in sync, turning with exact force and preciseness. Finally he slammed his foot into the bag, his body turning perfectly with him and with such force that he fell to the ground and shook as he climaxed.

Lying on his back he looked at the ceiling and steadied his breathing. Above him, was a blown up picture of Vahn, which he had taken one day at the park she frequented. In the picture her hair was pulled back and her lips were slightly puckered in an exhale. Mist danced about her mouth as the cold air had cooled her breath.

He closed his eyes and pictured her face as it must have looked when she stared at the photographs of his work. He suddenly began to laugh uncontrollably at the thought of how perfectly everything was playing out.

He wondered if she could possibly have any idea as to how close she was to the case she was on.

Vahn sat on her couch watching TV and eating spaghetti while on the floor Zane and Zeke laid on top of each other exhausted from playing Frisbee.

As much as she had wanted to, Vahn did not invite Chase over for dinner and he gave her no invitation either. She had asked him if she could bring home the case files to look over the autopsy and forensic reports, along with the case notes written by both Chase and Harper.

She smiled to herself knowing that early in the morning the lab would be busy analyzing two small pieces of two doorframes, which both had three small notches. They had no idea what they signified but it was obvious the killer had left the marks, and that they resembled the marks on the backs of the victims' necks.

After turning off the TV and putting her plate in the kitchen, Vahn walked to her stereo and put in her favorite D'Angelo's CD. She then took the files from the kitchen counter and spread them on the coffee table in front of her. Beside her was a pen and pad to jot down whatever happened to jump out at her.

In his apartment on the seventh floor of his building Chase sat on his weight bench and stared at his feet. Half way through his nightly workout he had drifted off with thoughts about Vahn. Damn that woman! It had taken him almost two years of pushing her out of his mind and he had finally managed to stop thinking about her on a daily basis when she walked right back into his life. And as his partner.

Through a few nonchalant questions he had determined that she did live alone and that if she was seeing anyone it wasn't someone who she spent a lot of time with. But could he trust her again? How could he possibly let himself back into the vulnerable position he had been in before? Never had he fallen for a woman like he had for her.

Closing his eyes he thought of the look of surprise on her face when they had met earlier that day. He had tried like hell to hide his initial shock but he didn't know if he had been successful.

The way she looked, walked, smelled, talked, everything about her drove him crazy. Initially he had tried to put up a guard. Something about as thick as the Berlin wall to protect himself against her. But her sweet little smiles and the little jokes she always made tore the wall to shreds.

So now what? If he were to try to build a relationship with her again it would have to be completely secretive or they would be separated and assigned to different partners. At the moment he could think of nothing more satisfying than being with her every moment of every day. Watching out for her, protecting her.

His thoughts returned to the night at Portland Place. He closed his eyes, and wondered…why?

Raynor walked to his filing cabinets and pulled out the file that he had made for his plan. Walking out of his workout room, where he also kept his vast collection of guns, knives, ammo, and other souvenirs, he locked the door then laid the file on the kitchen counter.

He then proceeded into the bathroom to take a shower. Making the water as hot as he could stand it, he undressed then stepped in bending his head under the showerhead. He let the vibrating water beat down his neck and back.

After washing his hair, and body he pulled the stopper up on the tub and sat down letting it surround him with steamy water. Rolling a towel up and placing it behind his neck, he turned off the water, then leaned back and relaxed.

He smiled to himself thinking of the work he had already done. He knew he was good. The best. He wondered how long it would take them to extinguish the few little leads they could explore. He knew that the only way they could get close to him would be if he allowed it.

As he took a deep breath in, he held it until he could feel his heart pounding loudly against his chest, then exhaled.

Chase Hawkins. Definitely not a problem. Actually an excellent bonus. If he and Vahn were to become lovers again they'd be so busy trying to sneak back and forth that they couldn't possibly have time to track him until he was ready. And of course if Chase became a problem again, he would take care of him again. Though it would have to be a little more permanent than last time, though it could be easily arranged.

Noticing the water beginning to cool down, Raynor stepped out of the tub and dried off. He went into his closet and pulled on a sweatshirt and a pair of shorts. Heading then for the kitchen he got a V-8 out of the fridge then sat down at the bar. He opened the file and laid the map out in front of him. He wanted to keep detectives Carver and Hawkins jumping but he also had to move cautiously so that the case could still be handled by two rookies without several others having to get involved.

He looked at the area he had circled and noted the park that he was to visit next.

As Vahn went down through her list Zeke leaned his head on her knee and nudged her hand up onto his nose so she would pet him. She had made notes and had planned to go over them with Chase the next morning.

As she leaned back and rubbed Zeke behind his ears she thought about all the nights she had sat in that very spot and wondered where Chase was and what he'd been doing. Now it seemed to give her peace to know that she would see him the very next day and several days there after.

When he had finally broken down and started to talk to her that irresistible smile had surfaced. That smile had made her feel so wonderful when they were together at the academy, and so alone without it.

She played through her mind every moment they had spent together. She had often thought about him on lonely nights. His warm body pressed against hers, making her feel things she had never thought possible.

Thinking of him now she longed for him.

How was this going to work? She could see it in his eyes today that he hadn't forgotten their time together. She knew that there was no way to continue to go on as if simply his presence had no affect on her.

As she laid her head back and stared at the ceiling she thought again about that horrid night at Portland Place. She remembered how she had thought that he had taken her there to propose to her when actually he had been giving her a nice formal goodbye. Again, she wondered…why?

CHAPTER THREE

Walking to her desk the next morning, Vahn pulled off her coat and laid it over the back of her chair. Chase hadn't arrived yet so she decided to go over the files one last time before he arrived.

As she opened the folder on the second victim the door to the office opened and a tall, masculine, fierce looking man entered. Vahn tried to look away but couldn't. For some reason her eyes stayed fixed on him. When he passed in front of her, he looked at her and gave her a crooked smile. She quickly looked down and pretended to be overly occupied, when he sat down in Chase's seat.

"How are you this morning? Detective Carver right?"

She looked up to see him smiling and extending his hand. She smiled, nodded, and shook his hand.

"I'm Harper. I see that you're taking over my old case."

Clearing her throat Vahn said, "Yeah, it looks that way."

"Well it's pretty cut and dry. The guy left nothing. He's a ghost. The best I've seen so far. I've never left an open case. He's damn good I'll tell you that."

"It sounds like you admire his work." Vahn held her breath as the words slipped from her mouth. She couldn't believe she had just said that! Where the hell did that come from?

"Admire? Not exactly, but you'll find that if you can't look at this job from different perspectives now and then, you'll crack up eventually. You see dead bodies every other day. If you don't keep an open mind about you, you'll walk around with a heavy mind and heart that will weigh you down before you know it."

He looked at Vahn, cocked his head slightly to the side and continued. "Tell me Carver, would you find it easier to work on a case where a woman was cut into pieces by a loved family member or by someone with no attachments, a random killing. Which one would you rather tell the remaining family?"

"Neither." She said wondering where his sick train of thought was supposed to be leading.

Pushing the chair back and laughing he replied, "then you've chosen the wrong profession sweetheart."

As she watched him walk across the room she searched her mind wondering what kind of an impression he had left. She had no idea what to think about him.

Throwing himself into his chair and making Vahn almost jump out of her skin, Chase smiled at her from across the desk.

"So, did you do your homework last night?"

Quickly gathering her thoughts back together, she looked up and smiled at him.

"Yeah, yeah I did. I just made a list of a few things we need to go over."

Struggling to get his arm out of his jacket he said, "okay, shoot."

Nodding her head, Vahn takes a breath then begins, "It says here that there were two hundred fifty condoms found in the second victim's body.

Have you checked into that?"

"Well, not really because condoms can also be bought at multiple locations. I thought about asking if anyone has noticed someone buying an obscene amount, but he's too smart for that. He would've gone to several different locations."

"I know that there aren't any factories in town, but you can get them in bulk. Did you follow up on that?" she asked.

"No, I hadn't really thought about it. Every time you buy in bulk you have to place an order and I don't think that he would leave a paper trail for us to find."

"I thought about calling the local Health Department and asking where they order from, just to get a general idea," she said looking at him to get his reaction.

Nodding his head, Chase leaned forward to look at her list.

"Let's see, second, have you checked out any of those guys in the videos? Maybe one of them knew both victims. They didn't live that far from each other."

"Yeah, I thought about that myself and that's basically what I've been doing for the past three weeks. But there were twenty-three men in the videos all together and I've only found twelve of them. Though I actually think it's a waste of time."

"Why is that?"

"Knowing that he didn't rape the victim and knowing the way she was killed, I think he was disgusted with her and probably lectured her as he slowly killed her. Making her watch the videos the whole time. Like I said none of the men in the videos wore condoms, so why would one suddenly flip out and do that. Whoever murdered her was sending a message and I'm sure that it wasn't any of those men. This guy is an extremist. He wouldn't not wear one for the camera, then kill the woman in that way. It makes no sense. Why not just stab her and get it over with if it was something personal."

Thinking that he probably had a good point, Vahn forgot about the eleven men that remained unquestioned.

"It says here that the first victim was a loan officer at a local bank and that the second was a secretary in a small local law firm. Have you checked the records of both places to see if they have any matching clients?"

"Sure have. I found nothing," replied Chase.

"Okay, then last on the list your report showed that when you questioned friends and neighbors of the second victim that the only place she frequented was a small bar." Looking back through the file Vahn found the name of the bar, "Delilah's?"

"Yeah, I've been in there several times. How do you think I found the twelve guys?"

Looking back at Harper's notes she said, "Harper didn't have much of anything in here about the first woman. He stated that most of her friends and neighbors said that she was a hermit except for the occasional Tupperware or Mary Kay party."

"And?"

"And what's the connection? Why those two women? One was 5'3, the other 5'7". They both had brunette hair, but other than that they had nothing in common. We need to find out where these women were chosen. I mean, if these murders weren't connected to something the women did themselves then they were probably just stalked and killed by this maniac. We need to know if the guy has a favorite place that he likes to pick his victims from."

"I guess it'd be worth a try to go back and re-question the friends and neighbors of Victoria Guiles. Although I don't think she frequented any bars, but you never know."

"We need to find out where these women shopped and how often they shopped. I want to know what grocery store they went to, where they rented movies from, where they went when they got sick, everything.

There has to be a connection somewhere."

"Well, I guess you did do your homework last night didn't you." Chase smiled at her. "Not bad detective."

Vahn returned the smile and handed him the folders. "Thanks, now why don't you make a list of where we need to go and which ones to hit first so we don't waste a lot of time zigzagging all over the city, while I call the Health Department."

"Yes ma'am." Chase flashed her another smile then took out a pad and pencil and began jotting down addresses.

Vahn picks up her phone and completes a search for the number to the Health Department.

After ten minutes of being transferred back and forth, Vahn was finally connected to the woman who handled the orders received by the clinic.

"This is Harriett Hill, what can I do for you?"

"Good morning Ms. Hill. My name is Detective Carver, I was just wondering if I could possibly have you pull up your files from the last four months on the deliveries you've received?"

"Well, sure honey, but that will take some time. Our computers have been on the blink, so I'm not as organized as I should be. What exactly do you need?"

"I would like a list of the company or companies that you order condoms from. I need to know if you receive your orders directly from that company or if they have a carrier of a different name, such as UPS. I also need to know how many you have ordered for the past four months and a list of what you've received. Specifically, I need to know if you were ever short anything."

"All right honey. Give me until this afternoon then you can come by and pick them up."

"Thank you Ms. Hill." Hanging up the phone Vahn looked at Chase. "You almost ready?"

"Almost." As Chase flipped through a few pages of the file he had open, his phone rang. "Hawkins."

Vahn watched his eyes light up as he looked at her. "We'll be right down." Hanging up he smiled, "Come on, the lab report is in."

Holding one notch of wood with tweezers, under a huge magnifying glass for them to see, Marty the lab tech chomped viciously on his grape Hubba Bubba bubble gum.

"Each mark is a sixteenth of an inch away from the other. Very precise. This blade has to be extremely sharp. Notice how the wood isn't bent in any on the side of the cuts. Meaning that the blade was not forced into the wood at all. It made a clean little incision."

Blowing a large bubble, then making a strange sucking noise as he tried to hurriedly get the popped bubble back into his mouth, he continued. "The third incision definitely has blood in it. The darker one. This guy must have wanted it to be noticed. It wasn't just a chance that a little blood happened to be on the blade. This type of wood would have soaked up a little bit of blood fairly quickly. He must've gotten a good amount on there and kind of caked it full. He was real meticulous though."

Vahn took in a deep breath trying to concentrate on what he was saying. She wanted to hit him in the back of the head to make his gum fly out of his mouth.

"Well, what do you mean by that?" Asked Chase.

"Well, under the microscope it shows traces of blood underneath the mark. You can't see them just by looking at it. So that means that apparently he was wiping away the excess so that it only stayed in the mark. Which backs up my theory that he was placing the blood in the mark. If there were blood all over the knife then it most likely would have also gotten into the small cut above it. But he was extremely careful not to get any in anything but the last, see what I mean?"

Crossing his arms, narrowing his eyes and chomping his gum, he said, "Yep, I definitely think it means something." Nodding his head and smiling as if extremely impressed with himself. "Most definitely has to be a sign of some sort. Third times the charm type thing."

Looking at the wood one last time Chase shook hands with Marty and thanked him.

Watching the rainfall as they drove to the Health Department, Vahn thought of the maniac they were after. What kind of a man could he be? What did he look like? She pictured him looking like a mad man with eyes sunk deep into his skull, with wild hair, and gaunt features.

How did he live? Was his apartment or house, or shack, a total disaster? A place of chaos where only he could make sense of things. She thought of the woman's heart that was cut out. What had he done with it? She felt her stomach churn at the thought of him roaming the city for his next victim.

"So what do you think?"

"Huh?" Vahn broke away from her train of thought to look at Chase.

"I said what do you think? About those notches?"

"I don't know."

"Well, I think Marty was right. He put it there as a sign, but for what?"

Vahn sat silent watching the rain hit the windshield.

"The only thing I've been able to come up with is that maybe it means that he plans on having three victims altogether. But that doesn't explain why he would put blood only on the last notch. It's not as if it symbolizes that blood will only be spilled on the last victim. And as far as gruesomeness goes, I hope that he isn't saying that his last victim will be the bloodiest."

Looking at Vahn and noticing her pale face, Chase tried to coax her out of her trance. He reached over and patted her on the shoulder.

"Hey, are you all right? I know this is hard but you can't let this guy get to you. This is what he gets off on. I have no doubt that he sits at home and laughs his ass off at the thought of us throwing up our lunch in the victim's backyard. He's playing games Vahn. And the only way to get him is to play along with him and try to beat him to his next victim."

Feeling his hand rubbing her shoulder and listening to his voice she began to feel a little more at ease. She tried to focus her mind on visioning the killer in a cage being torn to shreds by his cellmates. That helped, a little.

As they pulled up in front of the Health Department Vahn looked at Chase and gave him a smile to let him know that she had her mind where it needed to be.

Making their way through the halls, they came to the office of Harriett Hill. The door was open and she sat behind her desk with her reading glasses resting on the end of her nose. Her plump rosy cheeks and warm smile were the most inviting thing Vahn had seen all day.

"Detective Carver right?" She asked shuffling through the piles of papers on her desk.

"Yes, and this is my partner Detective Hawkins.

We really appreciate your time Ms. Hill."

"Oh, don't be silly. It was really no trouble. I'd do just about anything to help catch the bad guys. I've been trying to imagine why a couple of detectives are so interested in our records but I know you can't tell me so I won't ask. Maybe when your case is finished you can drop by and satisfy my curiosity."

Smiling and taking the files, Chase said that they would be sure to.

After getting half way down the hall, they heard the woman yell for them. Vahn returned to her office to find her shuffling through the piles on her desk once more.

"Well, honey, after I talked to ya I got to thinkin' that you were probably looking to see if anything was stolen from us and used in some sort of crime, so then I thought that maybe I should also give you all of the inventory files for the last four months because, ya know, employee theft and all. We've been trying to control it. We've put a camera in the stockroom, but it's not exactly hooked up because we don't have the money but I think it's a little intimidating just being there none the less. Ahh, here it is."

Handing Vahn the paperwork she smiled and added, "I hope you find what you're lookin' for sweetie."

Raynor stepped inside the grocery store and shook off, wiping his feet on the rug.

He hated rain. Rain was depressing. Pulling a cart free from the others it was lined up with, he pushed it through the isles, crossing off things from his list as he placed them into his basket.

He had planned on going to the park to run but the rain had changed his plans for him. It was possible that there would still be people out jogging but they would be the die-hard joggers who would be more likely to notice a new face on a day like this and remember it if asked.

Raynor remembered quite well gawking through his old apartment window at the idiots running in the rain. He wondered what kind of a force could drive a person into the freezing rain to run. Why not buy a treadmill?

As he rounded the corner and stepped into isle three he noticed a woman bending over to tie her shoe. Her breasts were almost falling out of her shirt due to the fact that she wasn't wearing a bra.

Not impressed, he pushed his cart past her and stopped at the coffee. Both Maxwell House and Folgers were running a sale so he was comparing the unit prices when the woman brushed up beside him and reached to the top shelf for a jar of Taster's Choice.

"Excuse me," she purred giving him a sly look.

Raynor said nothing and hoped that she would get the hint as he put a five-pound can of Maxwell House into his cart.

"Haven't I seen you in here before?" She asked stumbling over her own feet as she tried to keep up with him.

"No." He never shopped in the same place twice for that particular reason. He had seen on countless numbers of talk shows that the best place for single people to meet was the grocery store. After hearing that, he made it a point to go to a different place every week. The only problem he ran into was that nothing was ever in the same place.

After eating dinner Raynor stretched out on the couch and found a basketball game to watch. His mind wandered back to the woman from the grocery store. Just the thought of being with the woman made bile crawl up the back of his throat. He would much rather beat her to death than give her any type of pleasure. He tried to erase the images of her from his mind by concentrating on the game.

During half time he closed his eyes, only for a moment, then drifted off to sleep. His mind flew through a series of tunnels. He went back in time, he searched endlessly and each time he reached for something reassuring, he was ripped away from it and tumbled through a cold, vast place, until he was there.

His eyes searched frantically for a way out while he screamed into the darkness. "I have to get out, have to get out. I hear them. I can hear them, all of them. They're laughing. They're moaning and laughing.

They're coming for me. I have to get out."

He crawled across the floor, he was cold, he was so cold. He found the wall, he stood trying, trying, trying to find the doorknob. "Where is it? I have to find it, I have to find it, I have to get out, I can hear them, they're coming. Found it, I found it, I found it. It won't turn, it won't turn, it won't turn, it's locked, it's locked! Oh no! They're coming for me. I can hear them, I can smell them, I can."

The door creaked open. Everything was in slow motion. He closed his mouth as tightly as he could but his mind was still screaming out. "Why, why, I have to run, I have to run. There she is. There she is. There they all are. Staring. Laughing. Staring. Laughing. My mother, her rotten teeth, sharp, rotten, laughing.

The rubber cord, still around her arm, purple arm, always purple, sometimes black, she's naked, they're all naked. They smell, they're laughing."

He stood shaking with fear. He knew what was next. He didn't want them to touch him. "Don't want them to touch me, don't touch me, don't touch me. I'll try to run." He felt his frail legs move, still in slow motion. He could see the door. "Have to get out, have to run." Then he felt himself being dragged backwards.

"No, no, no! He caught me, a big man, he has me. I want my clothes, I need to get out. My mother is lying with another man, but she's looking at me, she's looking at me, she's laughing. The big man is behind me, everyone is looking at me, they're all looking at me, what is he going to do? NO, NO, no don't do it, don't do it, don't do it, don't do it, don't do it, don't do it..."

Raynor bolted up off of his couch knocking over his coffee table, putting his back against the wall, he shuddered and he was shaking furiously. He looked around confused as to where he was. His mind raced.

"Are they here? No, no. It's okay."

He worked his way down the wall until he came to the corner. He shoved the small table with plants on it out into the middle of the floor and curled up into the corner.

He held his breath. Listening. He heard nothing. He wanted to close his eyes, they were burning, and unfocused, but he knew he couldn't. He knew he couldn't close his eyes.

He looked at the clock, and he watched, and he waited, and he listened. After two hours he was finally back in his house, he was alone, and he was safe. He slowly rose to his feet, and gradually made his way to the bathroom.

Raynor stood in the shower letting the scalding hot water run over his body. He scrubbed furiously, to the point that his skin was cracking, ready to bleed. After using up all the soap he stood with his face down.

An hour had passed before he realized that ice cold water was pouring over him. He wondered when he had even gotten in the shower. Quickly turning off the water he stepped out of the shower and dried off.

Putting on a pair of sweats and a T-shirt he went into the living room to watch TV and noticed that his coffee table and his plant stand which he kept in the corner had been knocked over. He instantly ran to get his gun and searched the house wondering if someone had gotten in past his security system.

CHAPTER FOUR

"Did you want fried rice or steamed rice?" Vahn asked as she placed the different cartons of Chinese food on her table. They had decided to grab a bite to eat and take it back to Vahn's house before going over the paperwork they had taken from the Health Department.

Having Chase in her house made Vahn feel like a high school kid inviting her boyfriend over for the first time. She had tried to stay focused and keep her mind off their past, but for the two years that she was on the streets as an officer she had sat in that house wishing that he was there and wondering where he was, what he was doing, and why their relationship had failed.

Looking on her living room floor, Chase was hardly noticeable due to the fact that two black and tan bundles of fur were pouncing all over him. Putting the Sweet and Sour Chicken down on the table she couldn't help but stare at the three of them with a smile on her face.

"Okay, okay, I surrender, you got me!" Chase laughed trying to get to his feet.

"Does this mean you're ready to join me?" Vahn asked.

"After I wash dog slobber off my face and hands I'll be more than ready."

"The bathroom is down the hall. It's the room with the toilet and shower."

"You're too helpful," said Chase narrowing his eyes at her then disappearing down the hall.

Zane and Zeke ran over to Vahn excitedly wagging their tails. She bent over and rubbed noses with both of them.

"What do you think guys? Think we should have him over more often?" She whispered. Zane licked her earlobe and Zeke let out a muffled bark.

Chase came back from the bathroom with a slightly depressed look on his face like something was bothering him. Vahn opened her mouth to ask him what was wrong but decided otherwise wondering if he too could simply be thinking about the past and what could have been.

"Did you want a plate or do you just want to eat it out of the box?"

"This will work. I'm starving," he said keeping his eyes fixed on the food.

"Tell me again, what do you think the notches are supposed to mean?" Asked Vahn.

"I'm not sure what to think," he said taking a bite of his chicken.

"I don't think it means there's only going to be three victims. I think it has something to do with each individual victim," she said taking a drink of her Sprite.

"What do you mean by that?"

"Well, three notches in both doorframes. The last notch has blood in it. The first victim had her heart cut out, which obviously spilled blood. With the second victim there was minimal blood. Obviously the first two marks can't represent the first two victims since there was blood involved with both murders. Maybe the blood in it symbolized that on his third encounter with the victim he spilled their blood."

"Not bad Carver. A little far fetched maybe but not bad."

Vahn winked and nodded having a mouthful of food.

"But what do you mean by third encounter?" He asked.

"I don't know. It was just a thought. Did either of the two women report being stalked or threatened before their murder?"

"No, neither one. That's the first think I looked into."

"Well maybe he knew them and the third time they got together he made his move."

"That's a possibility. Both of the murders were based on things that only people close to them would know. But for some reason I don't think the women knew their killer."

"Why is that?" Asked Vahn. "There was no forced entry, for either victim. It would make sense that the women could have known the killer and let them in."

"True. I just have a feeling that they didn't know him that's all."

"So he is either telepathic or he was slick enough to find out intimate things in the house to tell him about the women without them catching him," said Vahn.

"He could have broken in their homes while they were at work. That would minimize his risk of getting caught," said Chase.

"Like the lab tech said, third times the charm. The notches were the only evidence left in the house and the fact is they were intentionally, not accidentally, left behind. He wanted us to find them and he wanted us to know his methods," said Vahn as she got up from the table to get another can of Sprite out of the refrigerator.

"Do you need more to drink?" She asked.

"No. Actually, I need to ask you a question."

Vahn closed the refrigerator door and looked at Chase. He had the same look on his face that he had when he returned from the restroom earlier.

"What is it?" Asked Vahn growing very curious.

"Is your divorce final yet?" He asked staring at her with such intensity that it made her nervous.

Letting out a little laugh and not quite sure if she heard him correctly, Vahn could only say, "Excuse me?"

"You heard me Vahn."

"I heard you, but I don't know what you're talking about."

Standing up and pushing back his chair he raised his voice. "Cut the shit Vahn. We're not together anymore you can lose the charade. All I want is the truth. I think I at least deserve that much."

Vahn was stunned. His words were swimming around in her head and she could not for the life of her understand what he was trying to say.

"Chase I don't know what you're talking about. I can't be divorced when I've never been married."

Becoming enraged Chase stepped around the table and was face to face with her.

"I already know the truth. I met your husband that night in Portland Place."

Feeling her mouth fall open, Vahn could not believe her ears. Hearing him speak about that night made her feel like someone had punched her in the stomach. She couldn't catch her breath.

Zane and Zeke came running into the room, ears back and growling hearing Chase's raised voice. Vahn signaled them to sit. They obeyed yet remained on the defense at the edge of the kitchen.

"Do you have any idea why I asked you to dinner that night?"

Vahn could only stand there in disbelief.

"I was going to ask you to be my wife. My wife!" He yelled.

At this point the dogs stood up and Vahn had to signal them to leave the room.

"Lucky for me I got a little nervous and went to the men's room, where I was fortunate enough to meet your husband. I believe he said his name was Neil.

Ring any bells Vahn?"

She could only shake her head 'no'. She felt her face flush and a nauseous feeling come over her as she replayed that night in her mind. He had went to the bathroom and never returned. Leaving her sitting there feeling embarrassed, abandoned, and confused.

"What the hell is wrong with you? Can't you respect me enough to be honest with me now? Don't stand here and act like you don't know what I'm talking about. Don't deny it Vahn. He said that the two of you were separated because you wanted to run off and 'play cops and robbers'. He told me that he was at the restaurant for a business meeting and that he didn't appreciate me being there with his wife."

Opening her mouth to talk and feeling her tongue thick and her throat dry, she cleared her throat and said, "Chase I'm sorry, I don't know what to say."

"That's apparent Vahn. I'm sure you don't. This is obviously something you didn't want me to know otherwise I would have heard it from you instead of getting caught with my pants down in the middle of my marriage proposal to you. Can you imagine how ridiculous I felt holding the ring I was about to place on your finger while that prick was cussing me out for being with his wife?"

Chase turned around and leaned on the table. His hands were balled into fists and she could see from where she was standing how white his knuckles were.

"Chase look, I can tell by the way you're acting that you're serious, but I have no idea who this man was or what you saw, but I'm telling you I have never been married. I don't know anyone named Neil and I have no idea why anyone would tell you otherwise."

Turning to look at her with tears in his eyes Chase whispered, "You just never stop do you?" He then turned and walked out slamming the front door behind him.

Sitting on her couch, head cupped between her hands, Vahn could not believe what had just taken place. For two years she had hated Chase Hawkins for leaving her that night in the restaurant, when all along he had planned to ask her to marry him. She couldn't believe it. But what the hell had happened in the restroom?

Apparently some sick bastard had decided to play a prank for whatever reason and had said that he was her husband. That was insane.

Johnny would be the only one she knew who would want to ruin a relationship she was in, but Johnny did not have the brains to fabricate a lie that elaborate. "Damn it!" She yelled, making the dogs raise their heads and stare at her. Knowing there was only one solution, she sighed and got up. She would simply have to prove him wrong.

Vahn went into her bedroom and changed into a pair of sweats and a heavy sweatshirt. "Come on guys, let's go for a run," she said returning to the living room and grabbing her running shoes from beside of the front door and pulled them on. She knew she would have to blow off some steam before she'd be able to go over the paperwork from the case with a clear mind.

Chase blinked as the overhead light slowly came into focus. He let out a sigh as Brett, his trainer, leaned over top of him.

"Haven't I told you not to step in the ring if you're not going to concentrate on the fight?"

"Yeah, yeah."

Chase grunted as Brett pulled him up. He tapped gloves with Jason, the man he had been sparring with, and who had just knocked him on his back. Stepping out of the ring Chase took his headgear off.

"It's a woman isn't it?" Asked Brett.

Chase simply gave him a disgruntled look and began unwrapping his wrists.

"I thought you weren't serious about any woman."

"So did I," said Chase as he walked off towards the locker room.

Standing in the garage of the blond woman's home Raynor had followed earlier that night, he was in awe. She was an artist. Not your usual boring flower and trees oil painting artist but a strictly deep soul searching artist. Placed on different easels scattered through her garage were chalk sketches using only black and white chalk.

Each canvas portrayed different scenes in magnificent shades of gray. One canvas had a view of a night on the ocean. Another was a full moon viewed by a pack of wolves standing over their prey in a thick forest. Yet another was of a woman kneeling in the middle of a brick street crying in the rain.

When he had first entered the house he had almost left. The woman was sleeping on the couch surrounded by boxes. She had apparently just moved in. All of her belongings were still packed making it very difficult to distinguish whether or not she lived alone, and also making it difficult to find out intimate details of her personal life.

One would surely notice tape being removed from a box and aside from making too much noise, rummaging through unorganized boxes would do nothing more than annoy him. Yet something had beckoned him in none the less and now he knew why.

Pulling out his knife, he stepped not to her bedroom doorframe, but to the entrance to the garage and ever so cautiously left his mark. He then returned to the living room, gently kissed the woman on her forehead, watched her stir slightly, and left for the evening.

CHAPTER FIVE

Not being able to sleep, Vahn showed up for work early, only to find Chase sitting at his desk buried under paperwork with huge black circles under his eyes. As she walked toward their desks he stood up and held out his hand as if to stop her from saying anything.

"I apologize for the way I acted yesterday. Obviously I misread you and I realize I need to get over it and get on with things. I did it once, I'm sure I can do it again. My personal life is left at home and at work, I work. It's that simple."

"Let's go," stated Vahn as she turned and walked toward the door.

"Vahn what the hell are you doing?"

"I said let's go," she yelled over her shoulder as she walked out the door.

Pissed off by her tone of voice, yet curious, Chase grabbed his coat and followed her. Neither of them said a word in the car. Vahn simply drove to the courthouse, parked, got out of the car and looked at him as if to demand that he follow her.

Reluctantly Chase stepped out of the car and followed Vahn to the fifth floor where on the door was printed Marriage Licenses. Vahn walked up to the counter showed her badge and requested the woman search the computer for a Vahn Carver having filed for a marriage license over the past ten years.

Vahn had brought her birth certificate to show Chase that her maiden name was Carver to prove that she wasn't going by another name, and that the license would have been applied for in that name.

Chase sat down in one of the wooden chairs lining the wall while Vahn continued to stand at the counter. Fifteen minutes later, the woman reappeared stating that she found no record of a Vahn Carver ever applying for, or receiving a marriage license.

Walking out to the car Vahn stopped Chase and looked at him. "Since we've now established that I never had a marriage license, hence, was never married, I would hope that you'll believe me now. We can do this same thing for every county in Oregon, and every county in Ohio but I can promise you the result will be the same."

Chase began to say something and Vahn put her fingers on his lips. "I don't know what the hell happened that night, and I honestly have no idea who would go so far to fabricate a lie to keep us apart. Now, if you stop saying I'm lying about being married, I won't say that you're lying about the incident in the restroom. Agreed?"

Looking forlorn, Chase nodded in agreement, then pulled her close to him and hugged her.

Back in the precinct, both of them feeling a little lighter in their backsides, they shut the door to their Captain's office and went to their desks. They had just given him a progress report. It consisted of having only the good news of the notches in the doorframes, of which they had no solid evidence as to what they meant, and that there seemed to be no connection between either women whatsoever.

Back at their desks Vahn suggested they go back to the Health Department.

"And why is that?" Asked Chase.

"If I tell you, you'll think I'm ridiculous."

"I already think that, so what do you have to lose?" He asked smiling.

Rolling her eyes at him and moving around to his side of the desk she put the inventory sheet in front of him.

"Right here, next to the box of condoms, box meaning two hundred and fifty count, there is a two."

"And?"

"First of all, look at the date. This is dated less than a week before the murder took place. Each box contains exactly two hundred and fifty condoms, and besides that everything else on the list has a check."

"So maybe only one of everything else was checked out at a time."

"Exactly. Now look at that," she said pointing to a little dot to the upper right corner of the two.

"That would be a dot."

"That would be a dot or that would be the remains of a check that was whited out and replaced with a two."

"So you're suggesting we drive all the way down to the Health Department to interrogate the staff about a dot."

"No, I'm suggesting we interrogate A.S., the person whose initials are beside of the two and the dot."

Giving Vahn an odd look, Chase shook his head. "Well, hell, we don't have anything else to do, and after getting our asses chewed it's more intelligent that just sitting here."

"Great, let's go."

Harriett Hill looked up from her desk and a huge smile spread across her face.

"Well, hello Detectives. Nice to see you again."

"Good morning Ms. Hill. How are you today?" Asked Chase.

"Well I'm fine of course. What can I help you with today?"

"Well," said Vahn laying the paper in front of Ms. Hill. "I was wondering if I could see the original sheet for this date and also if I could find out who initialed this, A.S., and if I could speak with him or her."

"Well honey that's easy enough." She grunted slightly as she got up and made her way to the filing cabinets.

"A.S. is Allison Shepard. She's one of our nurses here. Today we're actually short handed and she's one of the two nurses seeing patients right now. I'll run and let her know that you need to talk with her as soon as she gets a moment."

Almost losing her head in one of the drawers of the filing cabinet, she clicked her tongue and said, "well, all righty now, here it is." She smiled shutting the drawer and handed the paper to Vahn.

"Hah! I knew it!" Cried Vahn as she spotted the whiteout on the paper with the two written over top of it.

Chase just laughed, as Ms. Hill looked puzzled.

"Knew what darlin'?"

Vahn blushed slightly. "Well, I had suspected that one box of condoms was originally checked out and then it was whited out and replaced with a two."

"Hmm, that is odd. We usually use less than one box of condoms a day. The numbers pick up slightly when the seasons change, hormones and all, but still two boxes seems a bit much for a days supply."

"Would you mind letting Ms. Shepard know we're here and we'd like to speak with her?" Asked Chase.

"Oh, no problem hon." She waved as she waddled out of the office and descended down the hall.

"Don't even give me that look."

"What look?" Asked Vahn batting her eyelids.

"I now know exactly what you must have looked like when you had your hand stuck in the cookie jar as a kid."

"How's that?"

"Because every time you discover something, you get that sneaky look on your face."

"And is that a bad thing?" She asked gazing up into his eyes.

Licking his lips and leaning towards her he said, "no, that is definitely not a bad thing."

"Detectives!" Yelled Ms. Hill, snapping them out of their trance. They turned around to see her waving them towards her.

"Allison will be with you in just a few minutes. In the mean time, you can wait in her office."

Having just sat down in their seats, Ms. Allison Shepard came bounding through the door, shoes squeaking, white uniform very starched, and perfectly pressed. Her hair was in a bun so tight Vahn expected her hair to be pulled out by the roots at any second.

"Well hello there," she stated shaking their hands vigorously. She appeared to be in her early forties and seemed eager to be of help. "What can I do for you today? Harriett has told me that you have some kind of secret investigation going on. I must say that's a lot more exciting that taking pap cultures and giving penicillin shots all day long. I just love James Bond movies and anything that has suspense and mystery is my thing. I'm glad you need my help, I'll do my best to help you crack this case!"

Vahn and Chase looked at each other trying desperately not to laugh. They knew it would break this woman's heart to laugh at what she had just said.

Clearing her throat, Vahn stated, "could you possibly tell me why you changed your mind about how many boxes of condoms you needed on this date." Vahn handed her the inventory sheets, both the original and the copy.

Putting on her reading glasses, which were on a chain around her neck, she let out a "Humph." She then walked behind her desk and sat down. "Well, this is odd," she stated.

"How so?" Asked Chase.

"Well, I've worked here for more than twelve years and I've never taken more than one box of condoms in a day. And these check sheets are logged each day."

"Who else has access to these sheets?" Asked Vahn.

"Well, anyone that walks into the stockroom. It hangs on a clipboard that hangs on a nail on the wall."

"Who usually frequents the stockroom?" Asked Chase.

"Well, that would be the nurses, Ms. Hill, Mr. Grady, and the stock boy." "Who is Mr. Grady?" Asked Chase.

"He runs the place. He's the Director of Operations."

"Let me ask you this Ms. Shepard, why would someone change the sheet rather than just take something and not log it?" Vahn asked.

"Well, that one I can answer. We were having items disappear all too often around here and we barely have enough money to run on as it is. Well, Mr. Grady made some changes. He put a camera in the stockroom. It isn't hooked up, but not everyone knows that. Also he began doing inventory himself. He checks the order log to the shipment when it comes in and he then checks these sheets and does inventory every month. He has already told us if anything comes up missing, we will live in his office until someone confesses and then they will be handed a pink slip."

"Why wouldn't he ask you about this if it has never varied over the past twelve years?" Asked Chase.

"Because he only started doing that a few months ago. He's not really that familiar with the usual amount of supplies used."

"Do you always order the same type of condom?" Asked Vahn.

"Yes ma'am always do."

"Could we possibly get a few of those?" Asked Chase.

"Well sure," said Ms. Shepard rising from her desk. "I would imagine you would like to see the stockroom as well."

"You're one step ahead of us," smiled Vahn.

As they walked down the hall, Chase squeezed Vahn's shoulder as a small vote of confidence. They entered the stockroom with Ms. Shepard pointing out everything. "Our boxes of condoms are kept here and the clipboard is kept over there…"

Her words drown out as Chase noticed a dark haired man in his late twenties crouched over some boxes in the corner. As the man stood he had a box in his arms and turned to face the door. Instantly Chase recognized him as the man from the restroom in Portland Place. In the same instant the man's eyes widened as he looked from Chase to Vahn.

Chase felt his face flush as he stepped toward the man. He was met by a box being thrown in his face. The man bolted out of the stockroom shoving the nurse and Vahn out of the way.

Vahn sprinted off after him. She could hear Chase's feet hitting the floor behind her. The man ran out into the hallway tipping over a mop bucket and throwing the mop at them. Slipping and falling to her knees, Vahn watched as Chase leapt over the bucket and tackled the man by his legs.

As she ran up to them, Chase already had him in handcuffs. He looked at her and exhaled, shaking his head.

CHAPTER SIX

s Chase escorted the man back to Harriett Hill's office, Vahn went to make sure that Allison Shepard was okay. She had a few scrapes on her forearm from where she had fallen into the shelves but other than that she was fine and a little too excited over what had taken place.

"Detective can you tell me what's going on? I mean Kyle has been a great worker. He is always here when we need him here, he works hard. Did he steal a box of condoms or something? Is that what this is about? I didn't know that a person could be drug down and handcuffed for stealing a box of condoms especially since we didn't even know they were stolen, and we would have to report them stolen for him to be charged with them, isn't that correct? Or wait, did he do something else? I guess a couple of detectives wouldn't be coming all this way and asking all these questions if condoms were the only thing of concern. I-"

"Ms. Shepard," Vahn interrupted, "I understand your concern and interest. To be perfectly honest with you, I'm not quite sure what is going on myself, okay. So could you please just calm down and wait in your office. We are going to have plenty of questions for you later and I promise you, you'll be brought up to speed just as soon as I know where we're at okay?" Smiling reassuringly Vahn led her back into her office and exited as quickly as she could.

Back in Harriett Hill's office, Chase had the man's forehead leaned against the wall and was patting him down.

"Do you want to fill me in now or later?" Asked Vahn.

"Actually, I was hoping that this joker could fill us both in but he seems to have amnesia. He can't remember his name, why he ran from us, and most importantly, whether or not he was in Portland Place posing as your husband."

Vahn stared at the man in disbelief. She had never seen him before. This being the man whose cruel joke, or whatever the hell it was, turned her life upside down. She wanted to bounce his head off the wall a few times herself. She took a deep breath and exhaled slowly knowing they would eventually get it out of him once they got him back to the precinct.

"I want you to see if this place can function without both Ms. Hill and Ms. Shepard. I want them to come with us and tell us everything he's not. I'm sure they'd be willing to help. And this asshole is not getting out of my sight again."

Amazingly enough, both women punched out and said that they would ride together to follow the two detectives downtown to answer any questions asked of them. Though they both repeatedly stated they thought this whole situation must be a misunderstanding due to the fact that Kyle was surely a model citizen.

Looking in the rearview mirror, Chase stared intently at the man in the backseat. Who was he? How in the hell was he connected to all of this, and why would a possible murder suspect know who he and Vahn were? Know things about their personal life, and why would he fabricate a bullshit story like he did. Nothing made sense.

"So what's up man?" Chase asked, hoping he would be ready to start talking. Chase was too impatient to wait until they could get him into an interrogation room.

The man stared out the window, face flushed, biting on his lip.

"You don't have anything to say or what?" Asked Chase.

The man said nothing.

"You look a little nervous, anything you want to tell me?"

Vahn stared at Chase. She knew his emotions were running high. She just hoped that they could make it to the station without Chase pulling over to see exactly what he could beat out of this guy. She was sure that the only thing stopping him was that both of the women from the Health Department were following closely behind them.

"Why did you run from us?" Asked Vahn. She had no idea where to start questioning this guy or what to question him about, so she decided to start with the basics.

The man continued to stare out the window and bite on his lip so hard she could see that it was on the verge of bleeding.

"So do you know the drill or what? Should I give you the bullshit speech about how it'll be easier on you if you talk to us, or have you already been through all that and you have your lawyer's number memorized? Or maybe, it's your parole officer you're thinking about?" Vahn asked.

The man's facial features never changed. It was as if he heard nothing that either of them was saying. Whatever he was thinking about, it was obvious that he was scared to death of it.

As they entered into the precinct, they had to wait for both Harriett and Allison so that they could register the man as being detained. He had been carrying no wallet or forms of identification, so they needed the women to tell them what his full name was.

He was entered in as Kyle Weathers, date of birth - unknown, address - unknown. The two women stated that they would be more than happy to look that information up in the personnel files just as soon as they returned to the office.

Chase took Kyle Weathers to the interrogation room that was the most secluded. There were cameras in each room, which they were supposed to turn on as soon as a suspect entered, but in this particular room, the camera was broken. Until someone caught on and made him move the suspect, Chase planned on keeping him there and getting the answers he wanted, no matter what it took to get them.

Pulling back the chair at the table Chase shoved Kyle into it. Kyle had to steady himself with his feet to keep from falling out of it onto the floor. His hands were still handcuffed behind his back.

"All right Kyle, I don't know if you know why you're sitting in this room. I don't know if you know why we were even at the Health Department today, and I don't know why you think I don't recognize your scandalous ass from the restaurant, but I'll tell you right now, I do. Don't think you're gonna play me for some fucking fool who is going to believe some bullshit story you try to through my way.

I remember your smooth talkin' arrogant ass in that fucking pin striped suit so don't sit there and try to play like you're the stupid little stocker. I don't know what you're up to but we're not leaving this room until I'm satisfied that all my questions have been answered."

Kyle sat in the chair staring at the tabletop, not saying a word. He had not spoken a single word since Chase had tackled him in the hallway.

"Who are you hiding from?" Asked Chase stepping around the table.

Vahn walked in and shut the door behind her. She had just finished getting the two women the soft drink of their choice and answering about a thousand questions. After telling them she'd be back to ask them some detailed questions about Kyle, she knew she had better get into the interrogation room with Chase. She noticed he had chosen the one in which the camera was broken. Kyle did not shift his gaze at all as she entered the room.

"I got your number you slick bastard. I'm telling you that I know damn well that you're not as stupid as you look. You're hiding out from somebody and you're also working for someone, am I right?" Chase grew more and more furious as Kyle continually sat there staring at the same spot on the table, biting his lip and not saying a word.

"Okay, I told you what I do know," said Chase as he began pacing the room. "Now let me ask you what I don't know. How do you know who she is?" He asked slamming one fist on the table and pointing to Vahn with the other.

Still, Kyle refused to look up. Chase grabbed a fist full of his hair and his chin and made him look at Vahn.

"Did you comprehend my fucking question? How in the fuck do you know who she is?" When he refused to talk Chase slammed his head into the table making Vahn jump.

"Why did you pose as her husband that night?"

Vahn could see a purple knot appearing on the man's forehead. He had blood coming from his lip where he had bit it when Chase slammed his head down. Now he sat motionless staring at the table with his jaws clenched.

Chase paced back and forth behind him like a wolf stalking its prey. Vahn had never seen him this angry before and she knew he would do whatever it took to get the truth.

Vahn walked over to the table and placed her hands down, trying to look Kyle in the face. He would not meet her eyes but seemed to loosen his posture slightly, possibly taking comfort in the fact that Chase was less likely to nail him again with her standing there.

"Kyle, right now we are investigating a murder. And guess what, we have no leads. Imagine that. We went into that Health Department today basically so that we wouldn't be sitting on our asses in front of our boss, and we wind up having you throw a box at us and run down the hall. That basically winds up our day. Can you tell me what kind of sense that makes?" Asked Vahn.

Pulling out the chair that was across from him, Vahn sat down and continued. "One of our victims was killed by asphyxiation. Exactly two hundred and fifty condoms were shoved into her body. It just so happens that you are the only place in the city, that I've located so far anyway, that orders condoms in bulk and receives them in, guess what quantity? Can you guess? Oh, that's right, you don't have to guess. You know. Because you're the stocker right. So if you stock the condoms, then you've probably noticed that they come in boxes of two hundred and fifty count.

Apparently a box came up missing from your stockroom not more than a week before she was killed. That's a bit of a coincidence don't you think? Now here's the really funny part. You are the stocker in the stockroom where the missing condoms, possibly the murder weapon, oddly enough, came from which would naturally make you a suspect does it not? And to make matters just a little bit worse for you, you ran from us and you had to be tackled and handcuffed just so that we could talk to you. You are aware that now, thanks to you, we have our lead. We have our number one suspect, and he's in custody.

As a matter of fact, I believe that just this morning I left my Captain's office with half an ass because he had just gotten off the phone with the Mayor, who said that he wanted results. Something he could give the press so that the good citizens of Portland could rest easy tonight. I know that this may be a little hard for you to follow, but basically what

I'm saying is that it doesn't matter if your lawyer is the best of the best. There is no way in hell that you're going anywhere, so you might as well talk."

Vahn looked from Kyle to Chase. Neither of them had heard a word she'd been saying. She had been talking to the table. Kyle continued to stare blankly, not saying a word.

Vahn knew that the main thing on Chase's mind was not the murder investigation but why this guy had posed as her husband. Pushing her chair back Vahn motioned to Chase to leave the room with her. As they were leaving Chase turned around and looked at Kyle.

"I'll give you about fifteen minutes to get yourself together so that I can tear your ass apart as soon as I step back in here if you're not ready to talk."

Vahn walked with Chase down the hall towards the room where the two women were eagerly waiting for them.

"Chase are you okay?"

"Hell no I'm not okay. I have about a hundred things going through my mind at once. I don't even know where to start with this guy. I swear if you hadn't walked in that room when you did I would have fucked him up. His little silent charade is about to send me over the fucking edge."

"All right, well do you want me to go back in there while you talk with the ladies?"

The look he gave her answered her question.

"Okay, how about we get a cup of coffee and then question the women together. By the time they're done talking our ears off maybe he'll be ready to give a little."

"Fine. You get the coffee, I'll be in after I go outside for a minute."

Vahn walked toward the vending machines as she watched Chase walk toward the front.

Looking through the window of the interrogation room Raynor could only stand there with a smug smile on his face. At first he was irritated at the fact that Kyle was sitting in that room. He never expected Vahn and Chase to track him through the condoms.

Though this was a little premature for his taste, it did makes things interesting. He wished that he didn't have to dispose of Kyle. Kyle had come in handy, doing his legwork for him when necessary, but he couldn't risk having him talk.

Watching Kyle sit there motionless through that entire episode with the two detectives made Raynor proud. Proud of the fact that although he had to be scared and intimidated by Chase, the thought of Raynor and what he could do was far worse.

Holding a cup of water in his right hand, Raynor reached into his left pocket. He pulled out a baggie containing four pill capsules, which he always kept with him, just to be prepared for an unexpected situation, such as this.

As Raynor opened the door to the interrogation room and stepped inside, Kyle continued to look at the tabletop.

"Nice to see you Kyle," he said as he closed the door behind him.

Kyle looked up from the table with a terrified look on his face. "I didn't tell them anything man, I swear to you, I didn't."

"I believe you. I know this is a bit awkward, and I apologize for the inconvenience. I seem to have underestimated the detectives on this case. I honestly thought that there would be no chance that they would follow up on the condoms since condoms are sold in every drug store in the city and also since the Health Department is not the only place in town that orders condoms in bulk. I guess they just got lucky. What do you think?"

"I don't know. All I know is that we're still cool. They have no idea what's going on and since they don't know anything about you then there's no way for them to find out right?"

Raynor sat in his chair and leaned forward twisting the baggie between his fingers.

"I never asked you why you wanted those condoms, and hey man, if what they say is true then so be it. I mean I didn't murder anyone. I don't know what night it happened on, but I'm sure I have an alibi, so we're straight right? They'll have to let me go when they can't pin me with the murder. Like I said before, I'm not talking no matter what that asshole thinks he's going to do to me so there's nothing to worry about, am I right?"

"Of course you're right Kyle," said Raynor smiling. "That knot on your head looks nasty. That's gotta hurt. Chase has a bit of a temper I guess. He's usually so calm and collected. Hmm, anyway, I brought you some Tylenol to get rid of the pain a little. I know you're only supposed to take two but you've been known to exceed the prescribed limit a time or two haven't you?" He asked smiling.

Kyle's hands were still handcuffed so Raynor leaned over the table holding the baggie up to Kyle's mouth. As he opened his mouth Raynor shook the bag letting all four capsules fall in. He then put the cup of water to Kyle's lips and washed the pills down his throat. After having Kyle open his mouth, and making sure that all the pills were swallowed, Raynor pushed his chair back and headed for the door.

"It was real nice doing business with you Kyle," he said as he winked at him. He then chuckled to himself as a look of complete helplessness and desperation washed over Kyle's face as he realized what Raynor had meant. Hearing a faint trickle, Raynor smiled smugly at Kyle, as he looked under the table noticing that Kyle had lost control of himself he was so terrified.

Shutting the door behind him, Raynor walked down the hall whistling a tune he had heard on the radio that morning which he couldn't quite seem to get out of his mind.

"So you're telling me that you've worked with this guy for nearly three years and that all you know about him is his name and that he's single?" Asked Chase pacing back and forth in front of the two women. Vahn sat in one of the chairs across from them smiling to reassure them that everything was okay.

"Well like I said, he's such a sweet boy, and so quiet. I mean maybe he's just quiet because he doesn't have much in common with us, but I cannot remember a day that he has ever missed work," stated Allison.

"As a matter of fact, he is so reliable that when the supplies came up missing, he is the first person we ruled out. We always assumed that it was the new nurses coming in and out. We have quite a high turnover for some reason. Actually Allison is the only nurse we've ever had that has lasted more than a couple of years. Most nurses last about four months on the average," said Harriett.

"Did he have a locker there at the department?" Asked Vahn.

"No we don't have lockers. We have always wanted them, but they aren't in the budget."

"There was no place in the building that he could have put his personal belongings?" Asked Chase.

"None that I can think of," said Allison shaking her head no.

"Did he drive or take the bus or what?" Chase asked becoming more irritated with each question.

"He drove. He drives a little black Ford Escort if I do remember right. It's a little beat up, but I think he's driven that car since he started working with us," answered Harriett.

"Did he drive it to work today?" Asked Vahn.

"Yes, I believe he parked about three cars down from where I was parked," replied Allison.

"Hopefully his driver's license or something we can use is in that car," stated Vahn.

"If he's not being cooperative, maybe you should let us talk to him. I do know that he doesn't have any family. I believe that he said they were all killed in a plane crash or car crash or something while on the way to see him. Tragic isn't it," said Harriett shaking her head. "Anyway, I think he thinks of us as his adopted mothers, I mean, we don't know much about him, but we would always make casseroles and such for him because he said that he wasn't much of a cook."

"That's very considerate of you Harriett, but I don't think it's a good idea that you speak with him right now. You ladies have been very helpful and we appreciate you coming down here to talk with us during your workday with no notice," said Vahn.

"Oh, we're happy to help. We know that Kyle has to be innocent of whatever it is you think he's done, Detective Carver," said Allison looking at Harriett, both of them shaking their heads.

"Ladies, we will be sure and call you if we need anything else and we will be down either later today or tomorrow to pick up his personnel file okay?" Vahn stood and began walking toward the door trying to wrap things up.

"We'll be sure and have all that ready for you when you come in." Both ladies talked over top of each other, saying the same thing.

As they pointed the women in the right direction, Vahn took a deep breath and looked at Chase.

"Are you ready?" She asked.

"I've been ready," he said bounding off toward the interrogation room.

Reaching the door to the room, Vahn put her hand on Chase's back. "Could you please let me see where I can get with him before you start pounding his head in?"

"You saw him Vahn, he's not going to give unless I make him give."

"Look, we have all night. All I'm asking is that you give me fifteen minutes with him, then you can come in and take over. I promise I won't say another word after that."

Sighing and looking down at her, he said, "fifteen minutes."

Vahn smiled at him and pushed the door open. She held her finger out as if to say wait here while she shut the door, watching him as it closed.

"Okay Kyle." she said as she turned around. She stopped dead in her sentence.

Kyle was lying on the floor with his chair toppled over. She ran around the side of the table and noticed his eyes were rolled up into the back of his head and the veins in his neck and temples were bulging out. A thick foam was coming from his mouth and his nose. As she bent down to check his pulse, she yelled for Chase. He opened the door and ran over to her.

"Get a medic in here. He doesn't have a pulse." She quickly uncuffed him and began giving him compressions, knowing that it was going to do no good. He was gone.

As Vahn watched the paramedics take Kyle's vitals and pronounce him dead on the scene, she felt as if she was in a dream. Not even an hour ago they had a lead, a suspect. Actually, in all honesty they weren't quite sure exactly what they had, but the outlook was more promising an hour ago than it was then.

Who was Kyle? Was he the killer? She wasn't sure whether or not to be happy about the fact that he was keeled over dead on the interrogation room floor. If he was the killer, then she supposed that the case would be closed and they could be thankful for that. But the only way to know would be to find some hard evidence in his car or apartment; otherwise, it would go back to being a waiting game.

The first two murders were years apart. She didn't think she could handle not knowing for a fact who exactly Kyle was and what his role was in the case. It was also still a mystery how he knew who she was and why he had posed as her husband to keep her and Chase apart. She had never seen Kyle that night but Chase seemed certain of the fact that it had been him.

As Kyle laid on the floor, eyes rolled back in his head, entire face and body looking to be distorted in agony, she tried desperately to remember if she had ever seen him before then. Could he have been one of the junkies that used to buy drugs from her ex-fiance Johnny?

If what Chase had said about him was true, that he had been in a pin striped suit and he pulled off being a very suave businessman to Chase, then she doubted he was one of Johnny's friends.

Vahn looked at Chase who was standing to her right, arms folded, teeth clenched, face red. She wanted to say something but not knowing what to say she decided she would watch and wait.

"Excuse me sir," said one of the paramedics as they wheeled in a stretcher. Chase moved out of his way, nodding his head.

"Do you have any idea what killed him?" Chase asked the coroner.

"I have no clue. I'll be taking him down to the medical examiners office from here. I'm sure you'll want an immediate autopsy done to determine cause of death."

Chase walked to the table and wrote down his cell phone number on a piece of paper and handed it to him. "Be sure he calls me first."

"No problem."

As they zipped up the body bag and placed Kyle's body on the stretcher, Vahn walked out of the room. Detective Harper was standing at the end of the hall leaning against the wall and drinking a Coke.

Vahn looked at him wondering why he looked so smug. He was obviously going to be an asshole once they solved the case, simply due to the fact that he was pulled off of it.

Chase stepped out into the hallway with her so that they could wheel Kyle's body out of the room.

"I want this room sealed off until we find out what he died from," said Chase through clenched teeth. "Maybe that's why he wasn't saying anything," said Vahn. "For him to die that quickly he must have been having some sort of symptoms."

Following the medics down the hall, Chase and Vahn came up to Harper who was still leaning against the wall.

"So was that your big break?" Harper asked nodding his head back towards the passing stretcher.

Chase glared at him. Vahn could see his jaw bone moving he was clenching his teeth so hard.

"Carver, did they say what he died from?" He asked.

"They don't know. The medical examiner is supposed to call us first thing."

"Sure would be nice to roll back the video and see exactly what was going on in there when he keeled over on ya wouldn't it? I guess that pretty much sucks that you decided to use the room with no eye in the sky huh?" He said smugly.

"Fuck you Harper!" Yelled Chase taking a step toward him.

"Hey man, I was just wondering if you helped the man on his way or what? It's usually smart to get the goods out of him before you completely bash his head in ya know."

As Chase took off for Harper, Vahn stepped in between them and began leading Chase down the hall.

"Give your mouth a rest for once huh Harper," said Vahn still trying to get Chase to walk down the hall. Turning the corner in front of them was Captain Reese.

"Well detectives. I see we've been busy today. At this point I don't know whether that is a good thing or a bad thing. I will tell you this, if that autopsy report comes back showing that your perp died from anything other than natural causes, Internal Affairs is going to have a fucking field day with this. I'm sure they'll be curious to know why he was taken to the third interrogation room, the one without the camera, while the other two remained empty. I would normally have you in my office asking you the same thing right now, but I think I already know the answer.

I believe you know that my point is that the two of you had better be walking on eggshells for the remainder of this case. Was that perp the killer detectives? Please tell me that you at least have the case wrapped up except for the paperwork."

"We're not a hundred percent on that, yet, sir," stuttered Vahn.

Captain Reese inhaled deeply and pursed his lips together then said, "Well, I assume then that you were on your way out to try to gather some more information, am I correct?"

"Yes sir," she stated trying not to look intimidated.

"Great. Hawk, I want an incident report on my desk ASAP just as soon as you get that autopsy report, am I understood?"

"Yes sir, that's not a problem," said Chase as dryly as he could.

"Fine," he said as he walked down the hall to the interrogation room.

Harper was still standing against the wall, loving every minute of the conversation he was overhearing.

"Harper, since you can't find anything to do besides hold the wall up, get your ass on the phone and get the repair man in here to fix this camera. Also tape off the door. We may have a damn crime scene in our own house. How fucking pathetic is that," he mumbled as he walked into the room where you could view the interrogation room through the glass.

Closing the car door, Vahn looked at Chase.

"This is some bullshit isn't it?" He said looking at her. "I can't fucking believe that the first lead we get is gone in a matter of minutes."

"Where to now?" Asked Vahn.

"Back to the Health Department. I'm going to tear the hell out of that car of his."

Pulling up to the black Ford Escort, Chase called in the plate number to dispatch and was able to attain Kyle's full name and address. While he was writing down the information Vahn stepped up to the driver's side door and found it to be unlocked. She sat down in the driver's seat and flipped down the visor. The keys to the car fell out in her lap. Picking them up and looking at them, what appeared to be the key to his apartment was on the ring as well. Looking up she smiled and whispered, "Thank you."

Reaching over and pulling open the glove compartment she went through the contents; a pack of gum, a tire gauge, a comb, a pen, the operator's manual to the car, a folder which held insurance information and registration, and a wallet.

"Bingo," she said pulling out the wallet. She opened it up and pulled out the driver's license. The license had been issued the previous year and she believed that the address listed was the same address she heard the dispatcher relay to Chase.

Also in the wallet she found a Red Cross card showing that Kyle Weathers was CPR and First Aid certified. Behind both of those was a picture of himself, a woman and a small child, which appeared to be around twelve months old. The picture was creased and the edges worn. In the picture Kyle was wearing a very nice suit, the woman a dress, and the infant was in a velvet dress. The wedding ring on the woman's finger looked more like a rock than a ring. Vahn held it up and stared closely. It looked to be at least a three-carat diamond.

"Whatcha got?" Asked Chase leaning his forearm on the car and bending over to look in.

"Looks like Mr. Weathers was married once.

There is nothing written on the back, so it's hard to say when this was taken. But look at this," she said jingling the keys.

"At least something is going our way today," he said. "Now let's just hope we find something in that apartment that tells us that Kyle is our man."

Vahn and Chase went through the rest of his car with a fine tooth comb and found nothing else of any importance.

The address they had for him was only about ten minutes from the Health Department. As they pulled up to the building it looked to be about eight stories high. It was red brick with parts of the brick around the base of the building chipping away. Getting out of the car Vahn noticed that there was one main entrance door, and that to get to the desired apartment, you had to take either the stairs or an elevator to the designated floor.

Opening the door to the vestibule, the building smelled about as old as it looked. On the driver's license, it said apartment 582. Assuming that the apartment had to be on the fifth floor, Vahn pushed the button for the elevator.

"I wouldn't think that a person could have much privacy in a place like this. What do you think?" Asked Chase.

"Well, I guess that depends on the people around you. I mean, if the guy brought home a human heart in a baggie and just decided to carry it up to his apartment, yeah I guess there's a good chance that he would run into someone. Hopefully they would think that it was a little awkward, but you never know."

As the elevator doors opened, an elderly woman with a cigarette hanging out the side of her mouth, and holding a cat in her arms, came waddling out. She was coughing, and sounding like she was ready to cough up a lung, yet managed to keep the cigarette in her mouth.

Stepping onto the elevator and pushing the fifth floor, Chase looked at Vahn and raised his eyebrows as if to say maybe a guy could carry a human heart to his apartment without anyone questioning him.

As they reached the floor and stepped out of the elevator Vahn got the keys out of her pocket. They walked down the hall and found a door that had a five, a blank space, and then a two. The apartment across the hall was 583, so they assumed that they were at the right place.

Picking out a gold key on the ring that was the only key that didn't have either Ford or U.S. Postal on it, she tried the bolt on the door. It unlocked without any problems. The same key also worked on the lock for the door handle.

Stepping inside, the apartment looked to be neat and tidy to their surprise. There were two closets with sliding doors that lined the wall on the left. In the middle of the room were two plush couches, both a rust color, which were positioned to be facing each other. They appeared to be pretty run down but looked comfortable none the less.

Vahn walked towards the kitchen, which was to the right of the living area. There was a small table on the far side of the kitchen by the window with two small chairs. The sink and cabinets lined the wall on the right. There were a few dishes in the dish drainer, and a glass, a bowl, and a spoon were sitting in the sink. A box of Corn Flakes was sitting on the counter.

A door led off of the kitchen, which was across from the table. Vahn walked toward it, continuing to look around as she heard Chase opening one of the sliding doors to the closet.

As she pushed open the door it revealed a small bathroom with a sink, toilet and an old bathtub which stood on four legs. There was no shower curtain because the tub was for baths only. Opening the medicine cabinet above the sink revealed two toothbrushes, one blue and one purple, a tube of toothpaste, a bottle of Tylenol, some dental floss, a pair of tweezers, a blue razor and a pink razor. No body parts, no blood.

Nothing of importance being in the bathroom, Vahn returned to the living area. The apartment didn't have a bedroom, which would explain why the couches would have to be so comfortable.

"Didn't the ladies at the Health Department say that he was single?" Asked Vahn.

"Yeah but there's some women's clothing in one of these closets," said Chase.

"There's a purple toothbrush and a pink razor in the bathroom," said Vahn. "I wonder if it's the woman from the picture?"

Looking around the room, Vahn could find no pictures framed for display. There was a small TV on a stand by the door with only a plant on it. She also couldn't see anything that showed signs of a child in the place.

"You got anything interesting?" Asked Vahn joining Chase at the closet doors.

"There's some duffle bags that have some gym equipment in them, like some gloves and a back brace for lifting. Here, look through this box for me," he said handing her a shoebox that felt ready to fall apart.

Vahn took the box to the couch and sat down. The box contained several snapshots. Looking through them, she noticed that they were mostly of Kyle and the woman in the picture from his wallet. They looked like they went back several years from the way they were dressed. The pictures that were taken indoors looked like they were in a house from Lifestyles of the Rich and Famous.

One picture showed the woman on an oversized bed with a velvet comforter in a long satin nightgown. She was smiling and holding up her hand as if to show off her ring. Another showed Kyle sitting on a leather couch laughing, trying to hold his hand up. Apparently he was a little camera shy. Behind him there was a painting that looked like a Van Gogh.

In the bottom of the box there was a satin pouch which closed with a drawstring. Vahn held her breath as she opened it. She shook the contents of the bag out into her hand and felt her throat tighten. She was holding the three carat diamond ring from the woman's hand in the picture, a man's wedding ring, which probably had around a carat's worth of diamonds in it, and a baby's ring and necklace. A Rolex watch for a man and a small slender Rolex watch for a woman.

Also in the bag was a piece of paper that was rolled up tightly and bound with a rubber band. Unrolling it, Vahn stared at what appeared to be an obituary, and a Memorial that had 'In Loving Memory' printed on the outside. Reading the obituary it stated that both Samantha Mochova and Lyndsey Mochova would be buried on a Saturday morning dated four years ago. It also stated that their living family existed of their loving husband and father Ricky Mochova, and continued to list the grandparents and other relatives. The cause of death was not stated in the obituary, nor was it in the Memorial, which was apparently handed out at the funeral.

"You need to come look at this," said Vahn.

Chase was holding a hanger with a vinyl cover protecting what was inside.

Unzipping it revealed a black pin striped suit. "Hah, just thought I wouldn't remember, stupid bastard. I knew that was him. This is the suit that fucker was wearing at Portland Place," said Chase showing Vahn the suit. Looking at what Vahn was holding he asked, "what have you got over there?

"I'm not so sure that Kyle Weathers is Kyle Weathers."

"What's that supposed to mean?" Asked Chase hanging the suit back in the closet and joining Vahn on the couch.

"It looks like Kyle Weathers is actually Ricky Mochova," she said handing Chase the obituary. She put the jewelry back in the satin bag and pulled the drawstring then placed it back in the box.

"Damn, this guy is going to be more of a pain in the ass dead than he was alive," said Chase shaking his head and reading the obituary.

"Did you find anything else in the closets?" Asked Vahn.

"Not a damn thing," he mumbled as he looked through the pictures in the shoebox.

"We need to find out who this woman is that's living here with him," said Vahn as she returned to the kitchen and began going through all of the kitchen drawers.

"Can I help you with something?"

Vahn turned around to see a slender blond standing in the doorway with a waitress apron in her hand looking shocked to see two people in her living room.

She was definitely not the woman in the pictures.

Chase stood up and showed her his badge. "Hello ma'am, I'm Detective Hawkins and this is Detective Carver. Do you live here?"

"Yes I do, what's wrong? What's the problem?
Who let you in?"

"Could I ask your name please?" Asked Vahn joining Chase in the living room.

"It's Rebecca Morris, exactly what the hell is going on?"

"Ms. Morris, could you please sit down on the couch so we can ask you a few questions?" Asked Chase motioning for her to come in and sit down.

The woman walked over to the couch and reluctantly sat down. Her eyes shifted between both Vahn and Chase and she began wringing her hands in her lap.

"What is your relation to Kyle Weathers?" Asked Chase as he took out his pocket notepad.

"He's my boyfriend of about a year," she said.

"How well would you say that you know Mr. Weathers?" Asked Vahn.

"What do you mean how well do I know him? We live together. I can tell you what kind of underwear he likes and that his favorite thing to eat is fried chicken and mashed potatoes and gravy," scowled the woman.

"What do you want to know?"

Holding up a picture of Samantha Mochova from the box, Vahn asked her if she knew who the woman was.

"Yeah that's Kyle's ex-wife. Her and his baby died in a car crash about four years ago."

"Do you know her name?" Asked Vahn.

"No, I never asked her name. Kyle was real sensitive about the subject. This is the first time I've ever even seen that picture. I've only seen the one he keeps in his wallet. Where did you get that?"

"It was in the closet," said Chase looking at Vahn. "How is it that you live here and you've never seen it, and we're here for ten minutes and we're standing here with it in our hands?"

"I've never went through Kyle's things. He is a very private person and he's very big on respect. I can't remember how many times I've been told not to disrespect him or his things."

"So what would happen if you did disrespect his things?" Asked Vahn. "Would it be safe to say that Kyle was a violent person?"

"I've never even heard Kyle raise his voice. I just said that he has said not to disrespect his things. He never said it in a threatening tone. It was more like a sad tone, which made me think that what I would find is exactly what you're holding. Memories of his wife and kid. Something I don't much want to look at anyway."

"Does Kyle go out much Ms. Morris?" Asked Chase.

"Never," she said shaking her head. "He doesn't go to bars, clubs, strip joints, nothin'. If he isn't at work, he's here. He drinks beer, but he will always go get a twelve pack after work and then come straight back here to drink it. Where is Kyle? Is he in trouble for something?"

Knowing that this conversation was going nowhere, Vahn decided to ask the only question she could think of that could possibly give them a hint as to whether or not Kyle was the killer.

"Ms. Morris," she said sitting on the couch across from her. "There have been several things happen today, all of which we'll be more than happy to tell you about in time. I have a question for you and I know that it is a bit personal to be coming from strangers, but it's very important."

"Well, what is it?" She asked looking at Vahn as if she was annoyed at the idea of the question.

"Did the two of you use birth control at all during intercourse?"

Wrinkling her face at Vahn, yet answering the question she stated, "no, I'm not able to have kids so we never worried about it why?"

"So he never wore a condom when the two of you were together?"

"Huh, no. He hates the things. I tried to get him to wear one when we first got together, just because of AIDS and all. He told me that he'd go down and get tested before he'd put a rubber on. Now will you tell me what is going on?"

As Chase began to inform the woman that Kyle had been taken into custody for questioning and that a medical complication had occurred, Vahn could hear the woman's voice begin to crack as she asked several questions.

Vahn got up from the couch and walked to the window. As she stared out at the city listening to the woman's sobs in the background and Chase telling her that she would have to come down and identify the body, all Vahn could think about was the fact that she was sure that Kyle was not the killer.

At first she thought that maybe he had snapped after the death of his wife and child, but everything about his profile so far said otherwise. Vahn heard Chase asking the woman if Kyle had any kind of medical problems that they should be aware of. If he had ever had a seizure or suffered from convulsions of any kind.

Hearing the woman answer no to all of his questions, Vahn stood there feeling numb. They had no suspect, and the one lead that they did have was a complete mystery.

Now what were they supposed to do? This guy was only close to one person, the woman sitting on the couch, and she didn't know a damn thing about him except for the fact that he went to work, came home, drank beer, and ate chicken.

"Vahn, you ready?" Asked Chase.

"Yeah," she said turning from the window.

Ms. Morris stated that she would be down to identify the body just as soon as she could pull herself together and change her clothes.

As they were taking the elevator down Chase's cell phone rang. "Hawkins," he said after flipping down the mouthpiece.

As the elevator dinged and Vahn walked off the elevator towards the door, she stopped to wait for Chase who had come to a dead halt in the middle of the lobby.

"You've got to be fucking kidding me," he said in disgust. "Don't give them a damn thing until I get there," he yelled shutting his phone.

"What's going on?"

"That was the medical examiner. Seems as though they've determined the cause of death, but the Fed's are there to confiscate the body and the autopsy report."

Running out to the car, they drove to the medical examiner's office as fast as they could.

"What do you mean it's on a need to know basis only? He died in my interrogation room, he's the prime suspect in a serial murder investigation, and he's the only lead I have. I want to know what he died from and how he died and I want to know now!"

Chase and a FBI agent by the name of Caldwell, were nose to nose in the middle of the hallway. Caldwell was holding the file on Kyle while his partner, Pillers, was calling in transport to take Kyle's body back to Florida.

"Look Detective, if you have no leads on your case that's not my problem. From what I understand you're a rookie who's obviously in over his head."

"Kiss my ass Caldwell," yelled Chase.

"Excuse me," yelled Vahn walking up to the two of them. "Caldwell, would you mind stepping outside with me for a moment please?"

Giving her a look of disgust, yet walking toward her Caldwell followed her outside. Walking out a few feet from the entrance, Vahn stopped and crossed her arms.

"I know you think that giving us the information in that file is on a need to know basis only, but you know as well as I do that once you two suits leave, all we have to do is walk in there and sweet talk the medical examiner to get what we need anyway."

Looking at her slyly and shrugging his shoulders he said, "and your point is?"

"I'm more interested in knowing about Ricky Mochova than I am about why Ricky Mochova died in our interrogation room today."

"How the hell did you get that Detective?"

"Well, that would also be a need to know, wouldn't it Caldwell."

"A bit of a smart-ass I see," said Caldwell giving her a small grin. "Why don't you tell me what you know and I'll decide whether or not I want to fill in the blanks for you."

"Fair enough," said Vahn. "Ricky Mochova had a wife and a child. So far speculation is that they died in a car crash, but I would imagine that's not the case. Ricky Mochova's wife's three-carat diamond ring is in Kyle Weathers apartment, and there's a picture of Kyle, or Ricky, and Samantha and Lyndsey Mochova in Kyle's wallet.

It also seems that Kyle is somewhat of a hermit. He suddenly dies and the Feds show up to extradite his body back to Florida. Which leads me to believe that Kyle Weathers is in fact Ricky Mochova. Why he changed his name or why you changed his name is the question that I need answered."

"Not bad Detective," he said smiling at her as he took a cigarette out and lit it. "It seems that you're a little more in tune with things than your partner is in there."

"Testosterone always seems to cause men to overreact. Thankfully I don't have to worry about that. My partner is concerned with his cause of death because his ass is on the line. Hawk was a little rough with him while he was still alive. We left the room so he could cool off and when we came back in, he was lying on the floor dead."

"Hmm," said Caldwell taking a long drag off his cigarette then slowly exhaling. "Well, the cause of death was not from any sort of inflictions from your partner. The cause of death was suicide."

Vahn laughed and said, "You expect me to believe that a man who was handcuffed in a police interrogation room committed suicide?"

"Yes ma'am."

"And just how the hell did he do that?" "Red Phosphorus."

"Red Phosphorus? That's it?"

"Yeah, that's it."

Not sure what that meant, Vahn threw up her hands saying, "okay, could you be any less vague?"

"Okay Detective, you win. Let's have a seat, this will take a few minutes," he said leading her toward a bench that was about five feet away.

He then proceeded to tell her that Ricky Mochova worked for one of the biggest drug cartels in the Florida Keys. Ricky was about three men from the top. This was because everything went by seniority and where you were in the family. Ricky was a cousin to the man in charge.

Ricky was in control of imports. Heroin was their biggest moneymaker. One particular evening, all of Ricky's men and his shipment were confiscated by the DEA as soon as it docked in the Keys. The men in custody were too scared to roll and give up the goods on Ricky and the Mochovas but the big boss was steamed none the less. The Mochovas lost around eight million dollars worth of Heroin in the bust.

To teach Ricky that he shouldn't leave loose ends and that he shouldn't make any future mistakes, the Mochovas killed his wife and his baby girl. They drown them both in the pool at their house.

Instead of scaring Ricky into silence and getting him on the right track, he turned himself in and offered to give up everything if he would be placed in the witness protection program as far away from the cartel as possible.

"The two of you picked him up thinking that he was a suspect in a murder. I can tell you right now that Kyle was not your man. You'll find that out on your own I'm sure, but he's not the man, trust me. That was one thing that held him back with the Mochovas. He didn't have the killer instinct he needed to off people when necessary. He took care of his men instead of threatening them. The Mochovas thought he was soft.

Ricky ingested enough Red Phosphorus to kill two men. It was probably taken in pill form, but we can't determine that since the caplets were dissolved.

More than likely, Ricky knew that unwanted attention was about to come his way. If any reporter were to snap his picture for the paper, or any jailhouse snitch catch wind of who he really was, his life would be over.

I'm sure he probably carried the pills with him. That stuff eats you from the inside out, but you're dead in a matter of minutes. I'm sure he chose this as opposed to the torture that would have been inflicted on him if the cartel were to ever get a hold of him."

"My partner patted him down though," said Vahn wondering where he could've had the pills.

"He probably had them down in his sock or something. I've seen it a thousand times. He had them somewhere that he could reach and probably threw the pills on the floor, then crawled over to them picking them up with his mouth. Trust me Detective, it's not a hard thing for a determined man to do, handcuffed or not."

"One more question," said Vahn leaning forward on the bench. "Do you have any idea if Ricky knew who Chase or I was around two years ago?"

"What do you mean Detective?"

"Well, it seems that Ricky had posed as my husband, for reasons unknown, in a restaurant here around two years ago. I just wondered if you would have any clue as to why he would do something like that?"

Standing up and laughing Caldwell said, "You've got me there Detective. I think it's very unlikely that he would want to be involved with anyone in or around law enforcement. I can't see Ricky wanting to be in the middle of anything like that."

Shaking hands with the agent and thanking him for his help, Vahn walked back in the medical examiner's office and had Chase follow her out to the car where she filled him in on everything she had just been told.

They sat together in silence, both wondering how Ricky fit into the picture, and both knowing that the answer to that question may never be answered.

CHAPTER EIGHT

As Raynor watched Melinda Davis sleep soundly on her couch for the second night, he could not remember a time when he had ever felt so at peace with himself. It had taken him a lifetime to feel this way but he now had a purpose, a goal, a plan which he had already set into action and which would soon be accomplished.

Walking back through the kitchen and into the garage, Raynor took out his tape measure and measured the dimensions of the open area of the garage floor. He was glad that he had Kyle purchase an excess amount of supplies that he would need to finish his work before Kyle's little run in with Vahn and Chase had happened. Now all he had to do was to determine the exact dimensions that he needed and go from there.

He had enjoyed all the murders he had performed in the past and was quite proud of himself for their originality, yet he knew that this one would be the most fun for him. Being the art buff that he was, he had always wanted to watch an artist at work. He knew that with his and Melinda's talents combined, that this would not only be in the papers but would also be in every art magazine frequenting the tables of the most eccentric art galleries in the nation.

He made a mental note to himself to remind Melinda while she was begging for her life, that he was in fact, doing her a favor. She was obviously a starving artist at this point, and of course it was common knowledge that every artist becomes overly famous only after a dramatic death.

Returning to the living area, Raynor sat on the floor in front of Melinda. He watched her mouth, slightly open, pucker as she exhaled softly. Her eyes were moving rapidly showing that she was in the REM stage of sleep. He wondered what she was dreaming about. She seemed at peace. Could her dreams be as solemn as her art?

Reaching up and stroking her hair that laid across her pillow, Raynor thought to himself that out of the three women he had chosen so far, that he had the most respect for this one. The first victim had been suicidal after losing her husband and child. Though he could understand how a loss like that could affect a person, he couldn't understand why she couldn't be strong enough to accept the fact that she obviously wasn't meant to live the life that she had chosen and that she was given an opportunity to change it. Instead, she had sat in her room every night sobbing over her loss and writing in her journal.

The second woman, well, what could he say about her. What a piece of trash. It's bad enough that women make pornographic films as a way of living, but that bitch had a decent job and chose to make that filth for fun and personal entertainment.

This woman, however, expressed her pain in the form of art. He had found no sappy journals, no physical means of release, such as drugs, no pornographic materials, etc. She merely smeared her pain on a canvas for the whole world to see. He liked that. He too was an artist, who would no doubt be remembered by many.

Thinking about how he watched each individual woman as they ran with poise and vigor just as Vahn had, made him wonder. Why were they running? None of them looked like they needed the exercise. They had all had such serious looks on their faces, such motivation, exactly the way Vahn looks when she runs.

Apparently none of the women were completely satisfied with their lives. Were they running to try to get away from the lives they were leading? Were they running to try to cleanse their minds of the demons that haunted them when they sat and thought about their purpose in life? What was their motivation?

For his three victims, he wasn't sure that he had an answer, yet he knew Vahn's motivation. Vahn was not only running to get away from the demon seeds from which she was born, she was trying to fill an empty void that she felt, yet could not possibly understand.

She was running with everything she had, trying to catch up to something she lost. Trying to find the one thing that would fill her every need. The one thing that would make her whole again. She was trying to find something she was bonded with, the thing that would make her soul complete. She was trying to find what had been ripped away from her at birth. She was trying to find him.

He closed his eyes as he continued stroking Melinda's hair and he could almost feel the soft baby fine hair Vahn had as a baby. Her big blue eyes staring at him as if she knew that he was her only savior. The only one who would live his life as her protector and do anything for her. They were one.

He opened his eyes and chuckled to himself as a small stream of drool stretched from Melinda's mouth to her pillow. He rose from the floor, and taking out his knife he proceeded to the doorway of the garage to leave his mark for the second time.

Life was funny, he thought to himself. Funny in the sense that even though life can be rough and throw you a few curve balls now and again, it always seemed to work out in the end. Like a finely scripted play.

He had always thought of himself as a savior, in different ways, of course. So far, he felt as though he had served his purpose well. With his first victim he had helped her end her life when she didn't have the courage to do it herself. His second victim, he had probably saved several lives by putting her out of her misery. The woman had probably contracted and passed on so many diseases that she had become an abomination. His third victim, of course, would become the famous artist she longed to be. And his sweet Vahn. She would finally know what it felt like to be whole again, as would he.

Vahn moaned as she awoke to the phone ringing. She looked at the clock, which read three a.m. and reached for the phone.

"Hello," she said trying to clear her throat.

"Vahn honey. This is your Uncle. How are you this morning honey?" He asked with a nervousness in his voice.

"Well, it's not exactly morning here. It's only three o'clock."

"Did you hear that Shirley? I told you there was a four-hour time difference. Let's say we just let the girl sleep, huh?"

"Give me the damn phone Gary."

Vahn rolled her eyes hearing her mother's voice in the background. What in the world could possibly be so important that they would wake her up at this hour? Knowing them, they were simply having breakfast at seven in the morning there and began arguing and needed her to settle it. Compassion was something that was lacking in the family.

"Vahn, are you awake honey?" Asked her mother with genuine concern in her voice.

"I am now Mom. What's the problem?"

"Well sweetie, I had a mild heart attack a couple of days ago–"

"And you're just now calling me? Are you okay?" Interrupted Vahn.

"Yes baby, I'm fine. The problem is that it got me to thinking. Hold on." She covered the phone as she asked Gary to hand her a cigarette. He refused which ignited her fuse and they began arguing again. After exchanging pleasantries, Vahn heard the flick of a lighter and her mother inhale. Raising her eyebrows not surprised in the least, Vahn continued to listen as her mother began again.

"What I'm about to tell you is very hard for me. I didn't want to do this over the phone, but I know that you can't come home at the drop of a hat either. I honestly am very tongue tied right now and I don't even know where to start. I don't even know if I should tell you the whole story or part of it, or what."

"Mom," said Vahn sitting up in bed, now curious as to what the news could be, "I'm a grown woman, I think I can handle whatever it is you think you need to tell me. Just spit it out, how bad could it be?"

"Honey, are you sitting down?"

"Yes mother, I'm actually laying down if it makes you feel any better. You're not pregnant are you?" That's all Vahn needed was for her mother to tell her that she was pregnant yet unable to raise the child, and that she was just calling to see if the responsible older daughter she had could take on her new sibling.

"Vahn, this is serious. When I had my heart attack, I got to thinking that if something were to happen to me, I wouldn't want you to find out by going through all of my paperwork. That just wouldn't be right. I want to start by saying that I'm sorry. I should have told you a long time ago. Every year I've thought about telling you, I've waited for the perfect time, but it just never seemed to come. Unfortunately, not by my choice, this seems to be the right time."

Vahn sat in her bed in a daze as she listened to her mother tell her that she had been adopted. Her mother and her husband at the time had been on the waiting list for an infant for several years when they received a call from the adoption agency telling them that they had a baby girl who was up for adoption who was seven months old.

Apparently the biological mother had sold the baby a month after birth for three thousand dollars. The police were tipped off and arrested the mother, and the purchasing parents. The biological mother also had a son. The son was placed into a home for boys. Being twelve years old there weren't many people who would want to adopt a boy that age coming from the environment he was raised in. So she had been separated from her brother and put up for adoption.

"Vahn sweetheart, I know that this is a lot to take in at once. The main thing that I want you to remember is that I love you. I know that I haven't given you the best life, but I hope it was at least a life filled with love. I know that what I told you about your biological mother comes as a shock. I wouldn't have told you that part except for the fact that I know you're a detective and all and I was sure that you'd be curious and want to know who your biological parents were and why they gave you away, as most adopted kids do. Vahn, I wish that I could give you a sugarcoated story about how your mother's parents made her give you up or something like that.

I'm so sorry that things happened the way they did, but you have to remember that it had nothing to do with you. That woman was a complete psycho to want to sell a baby for money."

Still not wanting to believe Shirley's words her mind flashed to her holding her birth certificate in her hands to show Chase not but a few days ago. It had Shirley's name and who she had thought was her father's name listed on it.

"But what about my birth certificate? Are you sure? I don't understand." Vahn put her head in her hands trying to contemplate everything.

"Oh honey. My best friend was a nurse on the maternity ward. Those certificates are kept blank in a file in the office. She took one for me and I just typed in the information I wanted. At the time, you were just a baby and I honestly didn't ever want you to know the truth. It was just easier that way."

Trying to find her voice, Vahn cleared her throat and asked, "and where is she now? Is she still in prison?"

"No, she died of a drug overdose when she was out on bail before the trial. Heroin I believe. I'm really not sure of the details sweetie."

"And the father?"

"I don't think she knew. I'm sorry. One other thing," said Shirley taking in a deep breath. "Remember how I absolutely did not want you to move to the West Coast?"

"Yes," said Vahn remembering Shirley going into hysterics when she told her she was moving to Oregon.

"Well, that's partly why. All of this happened in Oregon sweetheart. I've always been afraid you would find out somehow. And it seemed a bit strange that out of the fifty states you two kids could have run off to, it just had to be Oregon."

Vahn said nothing. She couldn't believe what she was hearing. Shirley's words sent chills over her body. Vahn pulled her knees up to her chin and rested her head as she listened to Shirley apologize repeatedly.

After hanging up the phone Vahn stared at the ceiling. On top of everything else going on in her life, why did she have to hear about this now? How could it possibly be true? Growing up she never once thought that there was a possibility that she could be adopted. Everyone that ever crossed her and Shirley's path always said that they thought they looked so much alike.

As a kid she had hated the fact that she was like Shirley. She had driven her crazy all her life. But that was also the thing Vahn loved about her. Now to think that she wasn't even her mother, how was she supposed to handle something like that? How was she supposed to handle the fact that she had been born the daughter of some smack fiend that had sold her at birth?

Vahn held her head in her hands. She couldn't believe this was happening. And didn't Shirley say that she had a brother? Who was he? What could he possibly be like, and did he live in Oregon now?

For a moment, she thought about searching for him. Yet something inside told her that finding him was one of the last things she should do.

CHAPTER NINE

Their Captain had wanted Vahn and Chase in the office every waking hour of every day to try and get somewhere on their case. Today, however, was a Saturday, and the Captain had actually decided to let them have the weekend off. Vahn assumed that this was because he was still hoping that Kyle, or Ricky, was the killer.

After going out and jogging for an hour and a half, Vahn returned home and took a shower. She then loaded the dogs up in her 4-Runner and took them for a drive. They stopped at a roadside rest area that had two fields of grass for animals to exercise in. The three of them played Frisbee for about an hour then loaded back up and went home.

Back at the house Vahn sat outside with the dogs. She lounged in her lawn chair as they chased, tackled, and drooled all over one another. She had turned the ringer off and was screening her calls with her answering machine. Shirley had called three times to make sure that the news she had given her that morning had not sent her 'over the edge' and that she was okay.

Vahn knew that she should answer the phone and let Shirley know that she was fine, but for some childish reason she felt betrayed by her. She knew it was petty to feel that way. It was just that she never really had much family, and the family that she did have drove her nuts. But, that's what made them her family. Now for some reason she felt lost, as if everything she had felt and known growing up had been a complete lie.

She knew that was a ridiculous way to think. Her life seemed pretty great next to what it could have been, so she did at least have that to be thankful for. Maybe if she were a mother herself, it would be easier to understand why Shirley hadn't told her before now.

The news was a little hard to digest at a time when her career was going down the tubes because there was a maniac killer on the loose and there was a dead mobster who liked pretending that he was her husband.

Nothing made sense anymore.

Watching the sun on the horizon Vahn felt her stomach grumble. She hadn't eaten anything all day. The dogs were lying on top of each other on their favorite blanket, which they had dragged out into the yard again. Which meant she would have to wash it, again, before they drug it back inside along with all of the grass and dirt that they had smeared on it.

She pulled her sunglasses up and rested them on top of her head as she looked at her grill. A steak and baked potato with tons of butter and sour cream sounded great. Now if only she could find the energy to get out of the chair and start the grill.

About that time she heard her doorbell chime. She felt her stomach flutter hoping that it would be Chase standing at the door when she opened it. As she walked through her house to the door she looked down at herself. She had on cut-off shorts, a sweatshirt, and her legs and hands had dirt and paw prints on them.

Cute. Very cute.

Opening the door revealed Chase standing on her porch with a little grin on his face. He was wearing jeans, a T-shirt, and a Nike pullover and he was holding a six pack of beer. She couldn't remember a time when he looked more irresistible.

"Hey, I was just driving by and thought maybe you could use some company. I'm also kind of hungry and didn't want to go eat by myself. You want to go grab a bite or something?"

Vahn smiled and motioned for him to come inside. "I was just about to throw some steaks on the grill, so you're just in time. You've now been designated Chef Hawkins, so if you'll head outside and get the grill started I'll bring you the steaks." She smiled as he looked at her and shook his head. "Oh," she said taking the beer out of his hand and opening one, "I'll take these." She smiled again as she strutted off past him toward the kitchen.

"Thanks, I think," he said walking toward the back patio.

As the sun went down they threw the Frisbee back and forth while they waited for the steaks to achieve 'perfection' by Chase's standards. At one time the dogs had distracted Vahn long enough for her to look away from the Frisbee that Chase had just thrown. When she looked up it nailed her right between the eyes.

As she fell to her knees with her eyes watering, Chase fell to the ground with tears in his eyes as well. He was laughing so hard he was crying. Though he did feel sorry enough to try to crawl over to her and console her.

After they had eaten they sat outside and looked at the moon. Luckily it was still too cold out for mosquitoes, so they relaxed and enjoyed the cool night. Once they finished their beer they decided to go out for an ice cream at a local drive up that stayed open until one in the morning.

On their way to the ice cream parlor Vahn found herself blurting out everything that Shirley had told her earlier that morning. They had been having such a great time that she hated to add a depressing note to the mood of things but Chase was so easy to talk to and she felt better after she had confided in him.

He pulled over to the side of the road and held her while she cried. When she was through he looked into her eyes, and knowing that there was nothing he could say to make her feel any less betrayed, he simply wiped her tears away and kissed her cheeks.

Wiping the steam from the bathroom mirror, Raynor smiled at his reflection. He felt ecstatic. The time was around midnight. He had planned on leaving his house around two-thirty in order to be at Melinda Davis's house by three a.m. He had already loaded what he needed into the back of his car.

His shower had left him invigorated. He felt fresh and ready to go. The manner in which he was to kill this evening would be a new experience. He knew he would be magnificent. He was simply a genius. There was just no other word fitting enough for him.

Walking into his bedroom he pulled on a pair of shorts and a tank. He had plenty of time to relax and have a small snack before he set out for the evening.

—∞◦◦❧◦◦∞—

Returning to Vahn's house, they had decided to pick up another six pack and play two-handed spades for a while, though it was late. They didn't have to work Sunday so they figured they could act like teenagers and stay up until dawn if it suited them.

As they finished their second game to two hundred and fifty points, Vahn had won, again, and by over a hundred points each game. Chase being the graceful loser that he was had decided that he had enough cards for one evening and they made their way into the living room. Vahn put her Christion CD in the player and sat down on the couch, resting her feet in Chase's lap.

"Okay, so not only am I forced to cook, forced to clean, forced to be your chauffeur, forced to buy you ice cream, forced to listen to you talk shit as you beat me in cards, now you expect me to rub your feet?"

"Well, you did lose. Twice," she said smiling and wiggling her toes.

"And you will remember this next time when I win, correct?"

"Next time you win what? A card game?" She asked laughing.

"Yes, a card game."

"Yeah sure, I'll remember. But I'm not worried about that happening anytime soon."

Squeezing her foot and making her yell he pointed at her to behave herself.

"I know we agreed not to talk about the case today," said Chase as he rubbed her feet. "But I'm stunned I guess. I don't know if I'm just missing something somewhere, if this does actually make sense and we're just not putting everything together right, or if I'm losing my mind."

"I think it's safe to say that nothing makes sense and that we have both lost our minds."

"Maybe. I guess my main question is this. If Kyle wasn't the killer, then where does he come in? Do you think it was just a fluke that we ran into him? I mean, we never really established the fact that it was him that took the box of condoms. And how do we know that the missing box is the box that was used by the killer?"

"Come on Chase, I think that's throwing a little too much to chance don't you?"

"Like I said I don't know. Do you think that he was the killer?"

"You know I don't."

"Well what then? Did he work for the killer? And if he did then why?"

"Monday I think we should start questioning everyone that lives in his apartment building to see if we can find anyone that knows anything more about him."

"Are you sure that you didn't know him from somewhere?" Asked Chase.

"I'm positive. I'm terrible with names but I never forget a face."

"So if you didn't know him, then why would he pose as your husband like that?"

"And you're sure that it was him that night? I mean that was two years ago."

"How the hell can you ask me a question like that? That man's face was clear as day. There's no way that I would forget some shit like that. Besides that, he obviously recognized us at the Health Department. We hadn't said anything to him when he took off running. He didn't even know why we were there. And don't forget the suit I found in his closet. I'm telling you, that was the suit he had on that night."

"The only thing I can think of would be that maybe he bought some weed off of Johnny or something, and knew him that way and did Johnny a favor. But like I said before, his clientele was limited to slums, believe me.

Since you told me that, I've went over it a thousand times. The night we were at the restaurant, it was almost graduation. We had been in the academy for six months. I had been away from Johnny for about seven months. I know for a fact that Kyle had no relations with Johnny before I left him. And considering who Kyle really was, there's no way he would go to extremes and possibly expose himself for a piece of shit drug dealer that he had know for less than a year. It just doesn't make any sense."

"Exactly."

Making his second round on Melinda's block to make sure that everyone was asleep, Raynor decided to pull up into her driveway. What the hell. He was feeling overly brave on this beautiful night. Besides all that, he had a lot of things to carry and he didn't feel like hauling them in from the alley.

After getting out of his car and walking around to the back of her house, he took his tools out of his pocket and proceeded to let himself in her back door. She still hadn't had time to put up a curtain across her sliding glass doors and he could see her sound asleep in her usual spot on the couch.

After letting himself in, he took some chloroform from his pocket and dabbed his handkerchief with it. He had to bring in several things from his car and he didn't want her waking up prematurely.

He knelt down on the floor beside her and began stroking her hair. As she stirred in her sleep he smiled to himself. He let his fingers go from her hair to her face where he made circles around her eyes, then let his fingers slide down her nose to her lips. He watched as her eyelids fluttered and she opened them, revealing a set of beautiful hazel eyes.

As her pupils dilated and her eyes realized what they were seeing, fear flashed across her face as he pressed his finger down hard on her lips.

"Shh, it's not time to wake up yet," he said as he moved his finger and cupped the handkerchief around her mouth.

Her eyes steadily rolled back into her head, and again, she was asleep. He stood up and put the handkerchief back in his pocket and walked toward the front door. He had a lot of work to do.

"I know this much. If we don't come up with a solid lead soon, the Captain is going to have both our asses," said Chase as he leaned his head back and stared at the ceiling.

"I wonder how long it will take this sick bastard to kill again?" Asked Vahn.

"With years between the first two, there's no telling."

"Why do you think the Captain gave this case to us? Why not let Harper and another veteran detective handle it?"

"I don't know. Harper had pretty much buried the first murder and when the second one rolled around he seemed reluctant to want to do much with it. He insists that the killer is a ghost. I'm beginning to think he's right."

"I wonder about him sometimes. Don't you get the feeling that he's a little odd? A little off his rocker maybe?"

"He's just an asshole as far as I can tell," said Chase.

"There's something creepy about him."

"Creepy?"

"For lack of a better word right now at this hour in the morning, yeah, creepy."

"Well, he's been in Homicide a lot longer than we have. I'm sure after a while, after you've seen a lot of 'creepy' things, it tends to get under your skin and affect you somehow."

"I guess maybe that's all it is."

Vahn watched Chase as he sat there staring intently at her feet. They had finished a twelve pack now between the two of them and she was feeling pretty mellow. She wasn't sure if it was the beer, the way he looked, or the way he was rubbing on her feet, but she knew if he was to start traveling north with that massage, she would be in trouble.

Raynor stood in Melinda's garage and dusted his gloves off on his pants. That little task hadn't taken him as long as he thought it would. He had removed everything from the garage floor and had placed several canvases together on the floor. There was a total of ten canvases placed together. Two rows of five canvases.

He had placed a tray that had large pieces of black and white chalk, a piece of charcoal, and several different sizes of sponges on it to the left-hand side of the canvases.

He then took off his heavy black leather gloves and replaced them with a new pair that he had bought just for this occasion. They had cost him about three hundred dollars, yet they were worth it. They were the thinnest pair of leather gloves you could buy. This left ones fingers covered with leather, protected against fingerprints and such, yet the leather was so thin that it felt like he was wearing latex gloves. He wanted to be able to participate in the making of the artwork, yet he didn't want to leave any evidence behind or have his heavy gloves hinder him from feeling the energy coming from Melinda and their masterpiece.

Raynor returned to the living room and sat down beside Melinda on the couch. He began calling her name and slowly shaking her to wake her up. She stirred slightly, but not enough. He was excited. He didn't want to wait for her to come out of her trance. He was ready to get started. He pulled a smelling salt out of his pocket and held it under her nose. She moaned slightly shaking her head from side to side then bolted upright, eyes wide.

"Hello beautiful," he said smiling at her.

She looked quickly around the room to see if he was the only one posing any threat to her.

"We're alone," he said, reading her every thought. He pulled out his knife and put his finger to his lips as if to tell her not to scream.

"I'm here to help you Melinda. But, if you scream or don't cooperate in any way, I'm afraid I'll have to cut your tongue out. It will be swift, I promise, though it's very painful. It's quite messy too. You'd be surprised how much blood comes from one's tongue."

She clenched her jaws together and stared at him, eyes wide, not saying a word.

"I want to tell you from the start how much I admire your work. I'm a bit of an art fanatic myself. Come," he said standing up and holding out his hand.

The woman crouched back away from him scared to move.

"Come, we have work to do. It'll be great I promise. I made sure that I brought everything we'd need. You already had some supplies, but I wanted to be sure that we wouldn't run out. Everything is going to be in your style."

Looking at her confused face he knew that she couldn't possibly understand yet. He grabbed her arm and pulled her off the couch, walking her back toward the garage. As they neared its entrance he pulled her in front of him and stood her in the doorway letting her see what he'd done.

"You see, we're going to create a work of art. Live art if you will. It will be perfect. I think we will call it 'Desperation'. If you can think of a better title, feel free to share it. We can brainstorm together if you'd like. After all, this will be your last piece. This is going to make you famous."

Pushing her forward and making her walk down the stairs, Raynor led her to a stool that was sitting to the side. He sat her down then proceeded to tell her about the piece.

"First, we'll use the chalk to draw or create the floor of a dark room. The far end here closest to the garage door will be a doorway of some kind. There will be light coming in from the doorway so we'll have to be sure and use white chalk to make the light spread out into the dark room toward the center of the canvas. The farther back on the canvas we go, the darker it has to be. You will have to be naked. You're going to be here in the center. We will use the charcoal to paint your body so that you will blend in with the backdrop. It's going to look like a dark room with the door open and light coming in, and there's a woman lying on the floor reaching for the light. You're the woman of course. I was thinking that we could leave your right hand from the elbow down clean because you'll be reaching into the light with that hand. Make sense so far?"

Looking at Melinda, she had tears streaked down her face and she was trembling so badly that she looked as if she was going to fall off of the stool. "You'll be happy to know that I was originally going to make several lacerations all over your body, yet after thinking it through I decided that all that blood would interfere with the chalk and it just wouldn't look right. So, I'm simply going to slit your throat at the end. Perfect don't you think?"

Vahn flushed the commode, washed her hands, and looked at herself in the bathroom mirror. She sighed to herself. She loved having Chase around. Everything seemed so perfect. She didn't want him to go home but it was almost three-thirty in the morning and he had already said he needed to leave twice.

Walking out into the hallway she glanced in her room at Zane and Zeke who were both sprawled across her bed leaving her no room whatsoever.

"Figures," she muttered.

In the living room Chase was sitting on the couch with his head in his hands. When she sat down he looked up at her with the same look he used to give her before he would make love to her. She felt her breath catch in her chest.

Raynor had already taken off all of the woman's clothes and shaded her body with the piece of charcoal he had brought with him. Her face was smeared with tears. She had attempted to plead for her life only twice. She was quickly reminded that they had work to do and that talk would not be tolerated.

He sat on the stool and watched as she held the chalk on its side and created the perfect bleak floor of the room that he had described. The front of the canvases, towards the garage door was a light shade of gray, with the open doorway and the light shining in toward the center of the canvases. Farther back, she had made the created room seem dark and cold. It truly showed that there was pure evil in the darkness. Evil from which she was trying to crawl away from, going toward the light.

As the woman took the sponge and blended in the strokes, tears fell on the canvas, actually creating a nice wet look. He was thankful for the fact that only tears fell and that she made no weeping or balling noises.

Chase stood up and walked to the sliding glass doors. He leaned his head against the glass and stared into the darkness. Vahn walked up behind him and placed her hand on his lower back.

"Chase, are you okay?"

He slowly turned toward her and cupped her face in his hands. "No, I'm not okay." He looked at her with such intensity she felt weak. "Vahn, if that asshole wouldn't have come into the restaurant, for whatever reason. If I had asked you to marry me that night, what would you have said?"

Looking deep into his eyes and feeling her words catch in her throat, she whispered, "I would have said yes."

Chase leaned down and kissed her. Burying his hands in her hair, making fists as he pulled her close against him. His tongue was so soft and wet. She ran her hands up his back and pressed her body against his. He let his lips travel down the side of her face to her neck where his tongue caressed her, then slid to her collarbone.

She moaned as she felt him grow hard against her. She put her hands underneath his shirt and felt his chest, then slid her hands down his stomach to the button on his jeans. She quickly unfastened them, then slowly slipped the zipper down.

Chase took his hands from her hair and pulled her sweatshirt off. Throwing her hair back she slid her hands inside of his jeans. He groaned and bit softly on her shoulder as he slid down the straps of her bra.

He knelt down cupping both of her breasts in his hands, running his tongue over them and nibbling them softly as her bra fell to the floor. He let his tongue slide down her belly as he slid his hands up the backs of her legs and under the back of her shorts. He unbuttoned her shorts with his teeth and quickly pulled off both her shorts and her panties.

Vahn felt her knees begin to shake as he kissed the insides of her thighs. In one swift motion, he picked her up and laid her on the table. She held her breath as he knelt back down and pulled her towards him. She felt his tongue hot against her. She couldn't stop from moaning as she felt his tongue slide in and out of her as his fingers explored how wet he had made her.

As he stood up and pulled his jeans off Vahn looked at their reflection in the glass doors. She was naked on the table, her hair a wild mess. Her face was flushed, her breasts were moving up and down as she breathed and her legs were spread open waiting for him. His entire body was flawless. Every inch of it was muscle. He stepped closer to the table pulling her hips toward him. As he entered inside of her she threw her head back and held her breath.

As she arched her back he ran his arms underneath of her. She felt the muscles in his arms flex as he quickly lifted her towards him. She wrapped her legs around his back as he stepped away from the table and held her as he slid himself in and out of her. He put one of his arms underneath her as he held her back and neck with the other.

She wrapped her hands around his neck and wetly kissed his mouth between gasps. As she looked up she felt herself getting more wet simply from looking at their reflection in the glass.

Chase then turned toward the living room and walked with her to the couch. He turned around and sat down leaving her to sit on top of him. Vahn grabbed the back of the couch and began sliding herself up and down. Feeling him hard inside of her, she was trying to take in every inch of him. As she moaned with delight she felt her face get hot and her mind begin to swim wildly.

Raynor stood over top of the woman who was now lying in perfect position on the canvas. She stared up at him with her hazel eyes full of fear. She knew that this was it. This was her time. She was so beautiful. He pulled his knife out and watched as tears streamed down her face and her lip quivered as she watched the cold steel come toward her.

He would simply make one perfect swift slash to her throat then lay her head down and let her bleed out onto the canvas. As he held the knife to her neck, Raynor felt his breath catch in the back of his throat. His face was suddenly hot and the woman's face faded away and was replaced with an image of Chase.

Chase's face was sweaty and he had a wild look in his eyes. Raynor blinked trying to get the image to come into focus. He fell to one knee as he felt himself sliding up and down, on top of Chase. No, NO! This couldn't be happening.

He felt ill. He felt like he wanted to vomit. His mind was in agony though his body felt hot and wet. He watched as brown hair fell over Chase's face and it was then quickly whisked away by Vahn's fingers, which returned to Chase's face. She put two of her fingers in his mouth as he sucked on them and bit them. Damn it, damn it, NO!

Raynor shook his head trying to get the image out of his mind. The woman's confused face and Chase's distorted face mixed together, swirling in and out of focus. Raynor gripped the knife tighter in his hands then began slashing at the image. Feeling his body responding to Vahn sliding up and down on top of Chase enraged him.

As he slashed at the image before him he felt the knife delve in and out of the woman's skull. He felt blood on his face and felt relief yet the image still would not fade. As Chase's grinning face looked in his eyes he screamed and closed his own eyes slamming his knife into Chase's image as hard as he could.

Vahn tightened her knees around Chase as she felt her body on the verge of climaxing. Chase ran his fingers up her back and again buried his fists in her hair. He tightened his grip pulling her head back slightly, making her arch her back.

She could feel him growing slightly inside of her. Knowing that he was on the verge of climax, she tightened herself around him, which made her moan with satisfaction, as she felt hot fluid slide down him from her. Feeling her climax Chase arched his back and held her to him as he released himself inside of her. Trembling, both of them being out of breath, they leaned over on the couch and lay beside one another, entwined together.

CHAPTER TEN

"What's up Zeke?" Vahn heard Chase say as she opened her eyes.

Zeke and Zane's noses were resting on the edge of the bed looking at them, possibly a little irritated at her that she had let Chase take their usual spot on the bed. She felt Chase kiss her on the neck and she turned over to face him.

"Good morning," he said smiling.

"Mmm, morning," she said snuggling up to him.

"I think the natives are restless," said Chase still petting the dogs.

"Well, that's exactly why I had that dog door put it. Because on mornings like this I'm afraid my comfort would win out over their bladders."

"Are you hungry?"

"It's too early to eat," said Vahn feeling famished yet not wanting to get out of bed to cook anything.

"It's twelve-thirty."

"What? You're kidding me?" She asked a she rolled over and looked at the clock. "Great, I guess that means that I have to get out of bed now."

"You don't have to. I think I remember seeing some bacon and eggs in your refrigerator. You want me to make you some breakfast? I haven't forgotten how lazy you are in the mornings, and your stomach was growling so I know you're hungry."

Vahn laughed and kissed his chin. "Okay detective. You have me figured out. Feel free to knock yourself out in the kitchen."

"My only request is that I take a quick shower if that's okay."

"No problem. Towels are in the pantry in there, just save me some hot water."

Kissing her on the forehead then crawling out of bed, Chase walked toward the bathroom. Vahn couldn't contain her smile as she watched him walking out of the room naked.

"Damn that man has a nice ass," she said laughing.

As she heard the water turn on, the phone began to ring. Thinking it was Shirley calling and rolling her eyes Vahn picked up the receiver, "Yes mother?"

"Detective Carver?" Asked a male voice on the other end.

"Yes."

"Ma'am, this is Sgt. Byers. I was told that you are one of the two detectives I need to speak with."

"What's the problem Sergeant?"

"We have a crime scene over here on Neklickitat Street. A young woman has been murdered."

"Okay Sergeant. What's the address?" Vahn cursed under her breath as she wrote down the address.

Pulling up to the scene together, Chase in the clothes he had been wearing the previous evening, and Vahn looking thrown together as well, she looked around for the sergeant who had called her.

Once she located him, he explained to both Vahn and Chase that one of the children who lived next door to the victim had been playing tag when she ran across the driveway and slipped and fell in blood.

Due to the gruesomeness of the murder, the scene was taped off making the barriers past the adjoining yards of the neighbor's houses. This was to keep on lookers back far enough to keep them from seeing the gory scene.

The garage door was now raised, revealing the most atrocious sight that Vahn had ever seen. Blood seemed to have flowed into the driveway about a foot and a half under the door. The blood was smeared where the small girl had slipped and fallen in it.

Stepping into the garage Vahn clenched her teeth together and held her breath as much as she could. Though the smell wasn't that bad, she had never seen anything like this before. Apparently the murder had taken place the night before. Most of the blood still looked fresh and moist.

The garage appeared to be some sort of art studio for the victim. She had several canvases set up around the garage, all of the pictures in different shades of gray. Lying on the floor was what appeared to be a life size drawing. There were canvases laid out on the ground, with a woman's torso in the middle. She appeared to have been covered with chalk or soot in order to blend in with the art. Though what remained on the canvas was strictly a heap of flesh.

Looking at the corner of the canvas on the right side closest to them, Vahn felt her face flush. There were three small marks matching those that psychotic bastard had placed on the other victim's. He was obviously unable to put it in its usual position, which was at the base of the victim's neck. He had apparently severed her head from her body. Vahn saw nothing that resembled a neck at all.

What was left of the woman's upper body was slashed so badly that bone and flesh were exposed. What appeared to be the woman's head was approximately two feet from the body. It laid on the cement, distinguishable as her head only due to the fact that hair remained attached to it. Her facial features were obsolete, and her skull seemed to have almost been split in two.

Tracks of blood marked the walls, ceiling, and floor showing how violently he must have been swinging his arm as he stabbed her. Plastic had been laid in small areas on the floor. Though this would disturb the crime scene, there simply was no place to stand that was not covered in blood.

There were several places marked with numbers. These areas seemed to be the areas that the killer had stepped, yet there was not one clear footprint. Apparently he had tried to cover his tracks by smearing each footprint with a towel or cloth of some sort as he backtracked his way through the house.

They followed his trail through the house to the backyard where he had used her water hose to wash off. Pressed grass from the wet prints then led from the back of her house around the front to the driveway. He had been cautious enough as he pulled out not to leave any tire marks on the driveway.

"None of the neighbors remember seeing any car here last night?" Chase asked the sergeant.

"No, none of them did. The neighbor across the street said that he had stayed up until around twelve thirty and he had looked out his window when he turned his porch light off and there wasn't a car here. The victim's car was put in the shop yesterday and the neighbor said that he had seen her get dropped off by a cab around seven o'clock, which was her normal time to get home. Neither he or any of the other neighbors saw anyone at the house at all."

After making sure that everything had been documented and that all the pictures they needed had been taken, Vahn watched as they began to gather the woman's body together for transportation.

Returning to the doorframe of the garage, Vahn looked at the three marks in the wood and felt herself become enraged. This time the killer had been less methodical. He had let his emotions surge out of control and he had made mistakes. Leaving a mess behind that should have left them with something to go on. And yet again, they had nothing.

Sitting in the waiting room of the morgue, which smelled of embalming fluid and dirty mop water, Vahn drank a cup of coffee and watched Chase beat on the soda vending machine which had taken his money. After putting in another fifty cents and receiving the Coke that he had bought, Chase sat down beside Vahn and sighed.

"I think he's losing it," he said as he opened his Coke.

"I think he lost it a long time ago."

"You know what I mean. This was way too messy for his style. He likes things to be neat and tidy. Perfect. This was anything but."

"Maybe she said something to set him off," said Vahn.

"Something sure as hell set him off. It looked as if he planned on having everything staged like he did with his other victims. The death fitting their life, that kind of thing, but he flipped out and lost it for some reason. I just wish his ass would have slipped up and left us something."

Four hours after the medical examiner had begun the autopsy he joined them in the waiting room. Almost everything was inconclusive. The only fact that he could be sure about was that the murder weapon had to have been of at least six inches in length and at least two inches in width in the center of the blade.

Number of times stabbed was unknown. If the woman's body would have been dumped somewhere identification would have been close to impossible. Her skull was so badly damaged that there would have been no way to identify her by her dental records and her fingers were severely cut from defensive wounds, trying to shield herself for the few seconds that she was alive when the attack started.

Chase had called the lab and confirmed that there was only one blood type found at the scene, which was the victims. Leaving there with no more answers than they had started with, they drove back to Vahn's house.

As Raynor sat on his couch eating a banana he stared at the picture he was holding. This picture was one of the few things that he had taken from his mother. It was a picture of him holding a baby. The baby was Vahn. Her face looked so sweet and innocent then, just as it still did today.

He sighed to himself as he regretted losing control of the situation the night before. He could not contain his rage at the time, therefore he knew that he should stop dwelling on the fact that things didn't go exactly as they had been planned. One of the things that he prided himself on was the ability to keep his cool, and always strictly staying with what he had planned. That was one of the main reasons that he spent three evenings with the victims. To plan things out perfectly so that there would be no margin for error.

Unfortunately he had not anticipated having another vision through Vahn's eyes. It had been several years since he had one and it came as quite a shock. He was very displeased with what he had seen in the vision yet he knew that Vahn could not be blamed. She was unable to control her womanly urges, as most women were. He had been furious with her at first, but after leaving Melinda's house and taking a nice hot shower, he had time to refocus and to calm down.

Sitting on his couch now, looking at her innocent face, he knew what he must do. He had originally planned for there to be six murders. When a killer is determined to be a serial killer and he begins to acquire several victims, there is always a map that is set up in the homicide detectives' office, which is used to mark the different locations of the murders. He had planned on making a pattern, which would have eventually made a happy face, in essence, his mark on the city.

The first two locations were near the south side of the city and were both to make up parts of the mouth. The third location was the right eye to the person looking at the map. There was to be another eye of course and then one more location for the mouth. All of these locations would appear to make a circle around the city, but Vahn's house was located in the center, which would have been the nose.

Only after killing Vahn would they have noticed the altered face on the map with its eyes slanted and it's crooked smile. After what had happened with the third victim, he decided that he should make a change in plans.

Though he had left no evidence behind, he had become careless. It took him almost more time to try to cover up his footprints than it did to arrange the garage and have Melinda make the canvas look perfect. He could not risk making any more mistakes. He would have to make his peace with Vahn. She would be his next and last victim.

He smiled to himself as he kissed her picture then picked up a pad and pen to write down the details of their reunion.

CHAPTER ELEVEN

Monday Vahn and Chase returned to Melinda Davis's house. They had already been to her place of employment, which was a shoe store in the mall. Her co-workers stated that she had recently moved there from Los Angeles and that she was not sociable with anyone other than the people that she worked with. Knowing that none of them fit the killer's profile, they returned to the victim's house to look for anything of importance.

Going through her closet, Vahn noticed that the woman owned several different pairs of running shoes. In the garage there had been a set of clothes that were folded and set to the side on top of a pair of Adidas running shoes. The woman had apparently been wearing jogging pants and a T-shirt when the killer had undressed her.

On a hunch Vahn walked to the neighbors' house that had seemed to know the victim the best. She asked the couple if they knew whether or not the victim was an avid jogger. They stated that yes she was. The victim had gone jogging for at least an hour every evening. She would leave her house and jog to Joseph Wood Hill Park, the closest park to her house, and would jog home after completing her workout.

Returning to the house Vahn asked Chase if the other two victims had been joggers.

"I know that the second victim was. I'm not sure about the first. It was Harper that did all the questioning for that case. I don't remember seeing anything about it in his notes but that doesn't mean much."

"I'd be willing to bet that she was. What other connection could there be? None of the women knew each other. There's no other connection between people they know. The bastard has to be following them home from the parks where they jog."

Getting in the car Vahn and Chase drove to Joseph Wood Hill Park and parked the car. They watched as several people jogged around the park. After watching the joggers for about fifteen minutes, and not seeing anyone that looked out of place, Chase stopped one of the joggers and questioned him as to whether or not he knew the victim. He stated that he did not. When asked if he had noticed anyone out of the ordinary hanging around the park within the last week he stated that he hadn't. When asked if it was usually the same crowd of people who frequented the park, he stated that when he ran he had tunnel vision and had no idea which people were regulars and which weren't.

Frustrated Chase returned to the car.

"This is going to be next to impossible," said Chase.

"Well, this looks encouraging," Vahn said as she held up the city map, which had been in their glove box. She had circled all of the parks that were located near residential areas. The map was covered with red circles.

Back at the precinct they brought out the board with the map on it. They marked the three parks that were near each victim's house. They then stared helplessly at the map wondering which park the killer would target next.

Vahn chewed on her pen cap and thought about the park that she jogged in. She had hated to admit to Chase that she was the same as the jogger he had questioned earlier. When she was running she was completely lost in the moment. Her mind was clear and she focused on nothing but the sound of her feet hitting the pavement and her breathing pattern. She felt a little embarrassed about the fact that she was a detective, supposed to have an eye for detail, supposed to be more aware of her surroundings, yet she could not think of one face that she saw every time she went jogging.

She felt a chill go up her spine as she thought about the possibility of the killer watching her run in the park. She imagined a psychotic freak in a trench coat and dark hat pulled over his eyes. Always keeping his face in the shadows. Hands always buried deep in his pockets, them being stained with the blood of his victims.

"Vahn what do you think?" Asked Chase.

"Think about what?" She asked snapping out of her trance.

"All of these women have worked. It may be safe to assume that the killer works as well. All three women pretty much had banker's hours. They all probably jogged between six and nine in the evening. I think it's safe to say that we're going to find him between those times during the week. The weekends are wide open though."

"So what, we're supposed to go to every park and look for some guy wearing a sign saying that he's our man?"

"Don't be a smart-ass Vahn. You know as well as I do that we don't have a choice but to try to find him like this. It's going to take some time and a lot of patience but there's no other way."

"You don't think that we should go back to Kyle's apartment and start questioning the tenants?"

"I think we'd have a better shot finding him in the park. Someone who is not in their right mind would be more noticeable in the park than he would in that building," said Chase.

Nodding her head in agreement, Vahn looked at her watch. It was getting close to five o'clock. "Well, I guess let's go through a drive thru and grab some food then start casing out all of the parks to see what we can see."

Chase pushed his chair back and followed Vahn to the door.

Around eight thirty Vahn and Chase pulled up to the third park they had been to that evening. There were several people walking, running, playing with their kids, playing with their dogs, etc.

"I'm beginning to wonder if we're ever going to get anywhere," said Vahn.

"What do you mean? You think this is a lost cause?"

"I'm just saying that if we knew specifically what park to look at, or even if there were more of us to spread around at all of the parks then this could work, but right now I think we're fishing. There are just too many strikes against us."

"Why do you say that?"

"Well for one thing, we're sitting here in an unmarked car watching joggers as they go by. I don't think this guy is stupid. Psychotic maybe, but stupid no."

"All right then, I hope you're ready to whip yourself into shape. Starting tomorrow night we're going to come in our running gear and we can drive either your car or mine, and we'll just run our asses off until we see something suspicious."

"Don't worry about whipping me into shape. I think I can handle myself okay," said Vahn.

"We'll see."

After waiting until ten o'clock when the park had pretty much cleared out for the evening, Vahn and Chase returned to the precinct and made plans for the next day.

As Vahn drove toward her house she felt an uneasy feeling that she couldn't explain. Her mother had always spoken of anxiety attacks and how they affected her. Vahn had never had one that she was aware of, but for some reason she felt like she was short of breath, her muscles were tense, and she continually checked the rear view mirror.

She tried to ignore the feeling, knowing that she had simply spooked herself by imagining the killer carefully selecting a victim as they ran in the park. She felt like a little kid who had watched a scary movie and was too terrified to sleep alone. She had thought about asking Chase to come over but she didn't want to rush things and with this last murder laying heavy on her mind she didn't think that she would be the best company.

Turning onto her street she noticed a car put its signal on and was turning down the street behind her. She knew that she was probably just being paranoid, yet she felt as if the car was following her.

As she neared her house she contemplated driving past it so that the person behind her would not know where she lived. Being about two houses away from her, the car pulled into the driveway of a house on the left-hand side of her street. She felt relieved as she let the air out that she had been holding in her lungs. Though the car had stopped and the occupants had exited the car and were heading toward the front door of the house, she still felt an uneasiness that she couldn't explain.

Pulling up into her driveway Vahn laughed at herself. She was letting this case get the best of her. When she had decided that she wanted to be a homicide detective, she had told herself that this was exactly the way she would not be. She felt ridiculous and angry with herself for being so paranoid.

Shutting the door to the 4-Runner and walking toward her front door she stopped dead in her tracks at what she saw. She whirled around to see if anyone was watching her. Her eyes frantically searched the area. The neighbors' sixteen-year-old son across the street was sitting in his car in their driveway listening to his CD's with one of his friends. Other than that the street was empty.

Vahn slowly turned back around to her door and cautiously walked toward it. On the front door there was a white piece of paper that was folded in half with three small marks resembling the killer's marks, stuck to her door. Watching her hand reach up for the note, it was trembling so bad she had a hard time taking the note off of the door. Vahn held her breath as she opened the paper. She felt a chill go up her spine and she was terrified to move. On the paper was a computer image of an old photograph. It was of a young boy sitting on a couch holding a baby. Under the picture were the words, "I've missed you. I am coming for you. Your life will no longer be empty. We will be together again soon. You have until tomorrow night Detective."

Vahn felt her chest and throat begin to burn. She felt her skin crawl as she felt like she was vulnerable to the world. She clenched her teeth, pulled her gun out of its holster and gripped her gun so tight her knuckles began to turn white.

"You mother fucker," mumbled Vahn under her breath as she became more pissed off that she could not steady her nerves.

Vahn took out her cell phone and called Chase. She knew her mouth was moving but she wasn't even aware of what she was saying. The only thing on her mind was making sure the bastard was not still at her house. As she hung up the phone she examined her front door and saw no sign of forced entry. She began making a sweep of the exterior of her house. No matter how hard she tried she could not shake her fear.

She seemed to be moving in slow motion.

After determining that the only way he was in her house would be with a key, Vahn unlocked her front door and began working her way through the interior of her house. Both Zane and Zeke initially ran up to her to say hello but they stopped in their tracks picking up on her fear. They themselves instinctively began sweeping each room as she did, without her having to say a word.

Once she had cleared the house, Vahn pulled a chair from the kitchen table and put it up against the wall of the kitchen so that her back was to the wall and she would be able to see if either entrance to her house was penetrated. As she sat there still gripping her gun, both dogs sitting at her side waiting to be given a command, she looked again at the note that was still in her left hand. It was now wrinkled from her gripping the hell out of it. What the fuck was it? As she stared at the picture, though she had never seen it before, it stared back at her with an eerie familiarity. The paper seemed to be hot, not from the death grip she had on it, but hot as in the fact that the note actually seemed to be radiating some type of energy from it.

Raynor sat in his living room smiling. In his hand he held his .44 Magnum. He wanted his and Vahn's reunion to be special. He had planned everything out perfectly. And this time, there would be no mistakes. He sat the gun down and picked up the six bullets he had laid on the table. He wondered which bullet would get to do the honor of sealing their reunion ceremony.

It would be perfect. He would sit on the floor and hold Vahn in his lap. He would make her straddle him and he would rock her and let her know that she would be okay. He would tell her about their time together as children. He would tell her about the ritual that brought them together as one. And after she understood, he knew that she would lift her head off of his shoulder, he would wipe away her tears, she would place her forehead against his, then he would put the gun to the back of her head and pull the trigger.

He knew that his gun was powerful enough to go through both of them and it was extremely important to him that they go at exactly the same moment. He did not want to be separated from her again.

As he began putting the bullets into the gun his phone rang. He smiled to himself and answered it saying, "hello."

After listening to the panicked voice of the man on the other end, Raynor bit his lip and tried not to sound excited. "Try to calm her down and I'll be right there Chase."

Hanging up the phone Raynor threw his head back and let a deep evil laugh pour from his mouth. He then stood up, grabbed his coat and headed for the door.

CHAPTER TWELVE

As they drove back to the precinct, Vahn stared out the window. She watched the pavement race underneath of them. She could not remember ever feeling the way she felt at that moment. She felt numb to the world. As if everything was a dream. Reality did not exist, could not exist. What was happening was beyond anything comprehensible.

Her mind had raced a mile a minute as she had sat in her kitchen waiting on Chase. Chase had searched her house and found nothing. It didn't appear that the killer had entered into the house, and the dogs were not acting strangely. Upon questioning the neighbors, as was expected, no one had seen anything.

Vahn felt violated. The bastard that they had been tracking had been at her home. His filthy blood soakedhands on her house. The only place she felt safe now felt as if it were a lion's den. No longer a sanctuary but somewhere that she would be devoured if she entered into it.

Pulling up into the precinct's parking lot, Chase parked and turned Vahn's chin so that she would be looking into his eyes.

"Vahn look at me."

She looked blankly into his eyes and said nothing.

"I don't know what you're feeling right now. I know you're confused and I know you're scared, but I also know you. I'm not going to try to sweet talk you. I know that this is intense but you need to be the hard ass that I know you to be. Don't let this guy get in your head and fuck you up. I'm here for you. I will do everything I can to protect you and you know that, but you need to pull yourself together. You have control over you. Don't let this bastard in Vahn. Don't let him control you, this is exactly what he wants. This is exactly what he gets off on. If you focus and be everything I know you are you'll nail this guy's ass to the wall, but you can't do it just sitting here feeling sorry for yourself. Now either you snap out of it or I'm going to knock the shit out of you before we walk up into that office, now what's it gonna be?"

Vahn blinked and felt a rush of adrenaline go through her body. She knew he wasn't going to hit her and simply said that to piss her off and get her going. She sat up straight and looked at him knowing that everything he had said was true. How dare that sick bastard think that he was going to send her crying by leaving a fucking letter on her doorstep. If the psycho thought that she was going to be a helpless victim, he had another thing coming.

"You're not going to knock the shit out of anybody. Let's go," she said as she opened the door and stepped out.

"That's my girl," he said following behind her.

Chase stood in front of their detective squad and pointed at the blackboard in front of the room. He had made a crude drawing of Vahn's street. He pointed to the board as he detailed their plan of attack on the killer.

Harper and three other detectives were to inform all of the surrounding neighbors that the entire block was to be evacuated. They were going to be set up in hotel rooms for the night and well compensated for their trouble by the mayor himself. Only on the condition that they told no one what was going on.

There would be a sharpshooter on the roof of the house directly across from Vahn's house. Her bedroom window was in the front so she was to leave her blinds partially open to give him a clear shot. The captain and another detective would be in position, hidden in the alley behind Vahn's house to alert them if he entered through the rear. Chase and Harper would be watching from the living room picture window across the street. Two detectives would be in position at the house to the right of Vahn's, and two more would be across the street from them, ready to respond when needed.

They didn't want to risk placing anyone on the street. They knew that their man was good. He had managed to be at four different locations, three of which he had committed murders at, and a fourth being Vahn's front door, and there were never any eyewitnesses.

They decided that Vahn should put her dogs in a kennel. This would protect the dogs from harm and would allow the killer to feel right at home as he entered into her house. They knew that the only way to get him was to use Vahn as bait. She was to be positioned in her bedroom with a night light on. This would make the killer think that she was asleep with there being only a small light on, yet would provide enough visibility for the sharpshooter across the street.

Vahn's 9mm was to be in her hand at all times under the covers. She was to shoot him on sight, no questions asked. As everyone took a coffee break Chase walked over to Vahn's desk.

"You holding up okay?"

"Yeah, I think we have it covered."

"You up to this?"

"I'm up to this," she said nodding her head.

Chase called down to the lab and asked if they had any prints off of the note that was left on her door. The lab technician stated that it was cleaner than a hospital bed, which didn't surprise them in the least.

Closing the door to his office, their Captain stepped up to the blackboard. "All right people listen up," he said motioning for everyone to gather around him. "I think we have this thing pretty well mapped out. Is everyone clear on their duties and assigned places?"

Everyone stated that they were and he continued, "I don't have to remind you that the mayor is breathing down my neck and expects us to wrap this thing up tomorrow night. If this guy gets away and he kills again, we're all going to be looking for employment elsewhere. So, let's be thorough, let's be alert and let's get this finished. I also don't think I need to bring to everyone's attention that this guy thinks he's good enough to try to take one of our own. We need to show him just how mistaken he is."

He pursed his lips together and looked everyone in their eyes before continuing. "Right now it's two a.m. I want everyone to go home and sleep for three hours. That will be your one and only power nap between now and show time. We will meet back here at five and I want those neighbors notified so that there's no confusion, no room for error. Am I understood?" "Yes Captain," they stated.

"See you in a few hours." He waived them all toward the door. "Vahn, Chase, hold on a minute I need to talk with you in my office."

As they walked in his office they sat down and watched as he paced the room. He seemed to be searching for the words to say what was on his mind. After a moment he walked behind his desk and settled down in his chair.

"I want the two of you to know that I'm aware I've been hard on you but it's been for good reason. I won't have a serial killer make himself famous by using citizens of our city and making a mockery of our department. I know that this guy is practically flawless. I also know that the two of you can handle him. I caught a lot of heat for having two rookies on a case like this but I had confidence in you and I knew that you could do it.

I'm sorry that it had to come down to this. Vahn I know that it takes a strong woman to pull herself from the confusion you must be going through in order to get the job done. I have no doubt you'll be able to follow through. I want you to know that the cities best detectives are right here in this precinct and your safety is something that you don't need to be concerned about.

I've seen your stats, I now that with the shot you have this guy doesn't stand a chance, but if you get lonely or scared in there while you're waiting, I want you to have confidence in us and confidence in the fact that we won't let anything happen to you."

"Thank you Captain, I appreciate that."

"Okay then, go home with Chase, or to a friend's house, wherever you need to go, but I don't want you going home tonight. Even though he said tomorrow night I wouldn't want him to get an opportunity and us not be ready. I know you probably won't be able to sleep which is understandable, but at least get some rest and I'll see you here in the morning."

"Thanks Captain," Vahn said as she stood up and leaned over his desk to shake his hand that he had extended.

As she stepped back his nameplate snagged her shirt. She picked it up and freed the fabric from its corner. She read it as she set it back down on his desk. 'Captain Raynor Reese'. As many times as she had been in his office, she wondered why she had never noticed it before.

CHAPTER THIRTEEN

During the three hours they stayed at Chase's apartment neither of them said more than a few words to each other. They simply lay in Chase's bed holding one another. Vahn could not remember a time when she had ever felt so scared, yet lying in his arms she felt as if she drew strength from him, which gave her courage.

At five a.m. they returned to the precinct where their whole department was swarming around making phone calls, preparing for battle. It was reassuring to have so many people on their side. She thought about all the helpless victims who had not had the advantage that he had given her. And why had he? That was a question that she was too scared to ponder.

Walking through her house with Chase that afternoon, she felt as if there was someone hiding in every closet, every cabinet, and under her bed. Both Zane and Zeke could sense that something was wrong with her and it made them uneasy. Dropping them off at the kennel was one of the hardest things she had to do. She knew that it was the best thing. It would be selfish to not want to do everything possible to try to trap the killer. With the dogs still at her house there was a chance that he would not try to enter. Though if he knew where she lived he would have to know she had them and he obviously was not swayed by that fact.

Though he always used a knife with his victims, he would surely bring along a gun to take care of her dogs. It felt awkward knowing that she had bought them to protect her, as well as to be her companions, yet in her most desperate time of need, they would be unable to protect her.

Raynor walked into his office and shut the door. He had closed all of his blinds earlier to hide the smile he could not keep from his face. He loved nothing more than a well thought out, methodical plan. There was simply nothing more perfect. He supposed the funniest part was the fact that everything that they had thought was their idea to help them trap him was actually his ideas on how to take the best advantage of the situation.

Having Vahn put the dogs in the kennel was of course the first priority. Though he was a quick shot, he knew better than to underestimate the training of two police K-9's. Though her dogs weren't in the field, they had the training none the less, and tangling with two of them was not something he intended to do.

The way they set up the team's positions were precisely the way he wanted. Each person would be able to be taken out individually without the other team members seeing. He had advised them to keep radio silence except on sight of the killer, whom they would never see. His excuse for this was that the killer might be monitoring the radio waves.

The icing on the cake had to be the evacuation of the surrounding neighbors. Distractions were what he hated most when he was at work. Having to worry about witnesses and such would only ruin the moment.

He had watched Vahn intently throughout the day. She moved with such grace and poise. She was beautiful. She was part of him. Only someone of his caliber could handle the situation she was in as well as she was. She had no clue what was happening to her. There was no possible way that she could even begin to understand, yet she acted as if this was just another day at the office. He admired her for that.

He also felt proud of the fact that he knew it was partly due to him. She was supposed to draw strength from him. He knew that if he wouldn't have been around her while all this was happening, then she would be falling to pieces. Ultimately, she felt at ease with simply his presence. He wondered if she knew that he was the reason for her strength.

Whether she was conscious of this fact, he did not know. But the anticipation of being able to hold her and tell her everything he had longed to tell her was almost more than he could bear.

—ooo—¦O¦—ooo—

By five o'clock that evening, the team was taking their positions in their assigned areas. The families that had been evacuated from their homes were more cooperative than had been expected. They had been willing to give the detectives access to their cars as well as their houses. This being in the event that the killer had cased out her neighborhood well enough to know what the surrounding neighbors drove. They were only crossing their fingers that he didn't know the neighbors by their faces.

Each officer moved into position individually about fifteen minutes apart from one another. They hoped that this would look more natural in the event that the killer was watching their activities.

After Harper was set across the street from Vahn's house, the Captain and the detective that was to accompany him in the alley were to make a quick sweep of her house. She had given the Captain her spare key that afternoon. They then were to take position in washer and dryer boxes that were set beside of the dumpster in the alley. Chase was then supposed to enter the house across the street through the back and join Harper as Vahn entered into her house and set up for the evening.

As they sat in Vahn's 4-Runner three blocks away waiting for their Captain to give the green light, Chase leaned over and kissed Vahn deeply. She lost herself in that kiss. Though it lasted only a moment it reminded her that she had something to live for. That this was perhaps more than just about doing her job, more than simple good versus evil. This was about her passion for life.

"When this is all over, do you think I could take you to dinner?" Chase asked stroking her hair and looking deep into her eyes.

"If I ever regain my appetite I would love for you to take me to dinner."

"I was thinking that maybe we could make reservations for Portland Place."

Vahn's vision blurred as she felt tears fill her eyes. He didn't need to say anything more. She knew what he was saying and she couldn't think of anything she wanted more.

"Unit one to unit four," they heard the Captain break in over the radio.

Vahn picked up her radio and responded, "Unit four, go."

"You're clear to take position."

"Copy that," responded Vahn.

"All units, radio silence from here out," stated their Captain.

Looking at each other, they knew that there was no way they would let this be their final good bye.

"I lost you once Vahn. I promise it won't happen again." He kissed her on the forehead, got out, closed the door, and walked away.

Putting her vehicle in drive and pulling away from him was almost unbearable. But she had to have faith in him, and in herself. Vahn turned right onto her street and began frantically looking around the street for any sign of the killer. She knew that her team had given her the okay, which meant that there was no possibility of the killer being anywhere near, yet she felt as if he was a lingering presence over her.

Pulling up into the driveway she turned off the ignition. She grabbed her purse out of the backseat and proceeded to the doorway. Once at the front door she had to steady her right hand with her left just to get the key in the lock. As she pushed open the front door her throat closed and she felt like she was unable to breathe.

There was an eerie silence that blanketed the entire house. She was so used to hearing the sound of eight feet hitting the floor running towards her as she entered the house. Now there was nothing, except silence and fear.

After realizing that she had been standing frozen in the doorway, Vahn swallowed and slowly walked into the house, shutting the door behind her. Her legs felt like weights. It took every ounce of energy she had just to put her purse and coat down next to the door and walk over to her couch. She stood there at the back of her couch trembling. She was desperately trying to remember what the hell she was supposed to be doing.

Vahn pulled her gun out of her shoulder holster and checked the clip. It was loaded. Seeing the gun shake as her hands trembled, Vahn quickly chambered the gun. She debated whether or not to even put the safety on. Looking down the hallway, she decided that she would take a quick sweep of the house. She knew that her Captain had checked it once already, but she had to ease her own mind. What the hell else was she going to do anyway?

Vahn walked slowly down the hallway, checking the spare bedrooms, and the bathroom, finally coming to a stop in her bedroom doorway. Was this it? Was this where she was going to blow this bastard's head off? Here in the doorway of her bedroom. She hoped that he didn't make it that far. The minute he entered the house everyone in position was to swarm the house and take him. Alive if possible, dead was even better.

Though for a reason which she could not understand, she knew that it would come down to her and him. She could see herself sitting up in her own bed, holding the gun at the place in which she now stood, staring at the face of death.

He had chosen her for reasons which were unknown. He probably had just been following the media and knew that she was the female detective on the case, happened to be a brunette, and he thought what the hell. Why not fuck with the cops. He had been so sloppy on his last victim that he was probably beginning to crack up. His demented mind had gone from the sly meticulous killer he started out as, to the crazed maniac that he actually was. And now he was signing his death warrant.

He would know without a doubt that there would be surveillance set up around her house, yet he chose to warn her regardless. She could not understand that. Was he trying to keep them busy while he committed more murders around the city that night? As fast as the question entered her mind, she knew the answer. He would be there. This was not meant to be a diversion. This was meant to get their attention. This was meant for him to be the puppeteer and them to be the puppets. Just as he puppeteered his victims as he staged their deaths, so was he doing to her. Being a homicide detective was her life and killing her during the stakeout was killing her in a way that mirrored her life.

She was without a doubt, a targeted victim.

Realizing that she was still standing in the doorway to her bedroom, Vahn quickly scanned the closet and the master bathroom, then returned to the living room. She turned on the TV and sat down on the couch.

Picking up the remote, she muted the TV and sat in silence, gun in hand. Deciding that she would stay on the couch until it turned dark, she looked down at the safety, left it off, and sat listening.

CHAPTER FOURTEEN

As darkness fell Vahn began to tremble with anxiety. She rose from her place on the couch, switching off the TV. She looked around the room and decided to leave on one of the lamps. She looked around again, then nervously walked to her bedroom.

When they had first suggested that she pretend to be asleep in her bed she thought they had lost their minds. She wanted to be parked on the couch with her 9mm in one hand and two shotguns at her feet. Yet the Captain had insisted that they needed it to appear that she had dismissed the threat and was simply living life as normal. This would allow the killer to comfortably slip his way into her house so that they could trap him.

Entering her bedroom she felt her knees begin to shake. She set her gun down on her nightstand then went into her closet. She changed into a pair of sweats and a T-shirt. She looked down at her feet. She was wearing socks. For some reason this made her feel extremely vulnerable. Though she was supposed to look like she was asleep in bed, the thought of lying there in her pajamas was unnerving. She wanted to be prepared. Why she thought having shoes on would make her prepared she didn't know.

Grabbing a pair of Nikes off of one of the shelves, she pulled them on. Looking down at her feet once again, she laughed at herself. She had no idea why having a pair of tennis shoes on helped her confidence, but it did. She felt powerful when she ran. That's the only thing she did that let her feel free.

Vahn bent over and took her radio off the belt of the pants she had just taken off, then walked to her bed and crawled under the covers keeping her radio under the comforter with her. She looked at her nightstand and picked up her gun. She then reached over and turned off her lamp leaving the faint yellow glow of the night light that they had placed in her room earlier that day. Vahn looked toward the window. The blinds were open at a downward angle so that the sniper on the roof across the street would have a good view of her room.

Vahn laid her head back and stared at the ceiling. She could not get comfortable. She sat up and stacked her pillows so that she would be at a slight incline and laid her head down again. She looked at the huge lump her tennis shoes were making under her comforter.

She remembered when they had first realized that he had targeted his victims from running in the park. Again she felt a wave of anxiety wash over her as she imagined the killer watching her run. Had he watched her? Did he know anything more about her than what she did for a living and where she lived?

Vahn became enraged at the thought that he had disgraced the only two things she held sacred. Her home and her love of running. She wondered if she would ever be able to run again and not think of these events. It infuriated her that with victims of any kind, what can physically happen to a human being in a matter of minutes, can torment that person's mind for the rest of their life. What was one person's momentary sick pleasure, was another's eternal agony.

As Vahn lay there with waves of emotions passing over her, she also felt a wave of guilt. Guilt because at that moment all she was concerned with was living through the night. She tried to imagine what the other victims had gone through. The last victim's severed head lying two feet away from her body. What had she gone through? And could the victims see her now? Before she was in their position, they were simply case files to her. Should she have been more emotional? Were they perhaps satisfied that she might now go through what they had?

Vahn sat up and put her face in her hands trying to stop the questions. She was beginning to think irrationally. What the hell was she doing? She needed to focus. She needed to focus on nothing other than blowing the muther fucker's head off the minute it came into view.

She lay back down and turned over on her side keeping her back to the window and her face towards the bedroom door. She felt comfort knowing Chase was across the street watching through the window. As soon as the asshole appeared they would click the radio as a heads up to let her know he was coming.

As hard as she tried to keep her mind free, it was impossible. She began to relive finding the note attached to her door. She had been so paranoid with just the thought of the letter being there, she had not contemplated what it had said. It had a picture of a boy holding a baby and she thought it had said something about missing her. She definitely remembered that it said he was coming for her and that she had until tonight, but what the hell did the first part mean?

Thinking about it now, she vaguely remembered Chase asking her if she knew what it had meant. She couldn't remember if she had even answered him. She had been in a daze from the moment she pulled it off the door to the moment they pulled up to the precinct.

Now she began to panic as her mind raced. She felt a wave of nausea as she heard Shirley's voice in her head, "...you were adopted...sold as a baby...had a brother who was twelve years of age...happened in Oregon..."

Raynor could hardly contain his excitement. He laughed to himself thinking of all the men in position watching and waiting for him. He was wearing the same black clothing he had worn when he had visited his first three victims. In the side pockets of his fatigues he had several items which he would need later. He had his knife strapped to the calf of his right leg, and his .44 was in a holster in the center of his back, which he had attached to his belt. He didn't want to wear his shoulder holster tonight just incase some of his men became aggressive when he went to take them out. The shoulder holster might restrict his movement slightly.

Raynor was sitting cross-legged in the washing machine box, looking through the holes they had made for visibility, at the back of Vahn's fence. Raynor could hear the breathing of the detective next to him. It had been dark for nearly three hours. He knew that as soon as night fell the men would be on their toes. He had wanted to wait a few hours so that their adrenaline would be a little slower. He looked at his watch and smiled to himself. It was time.

Slowly standing, Raynor raised the box up and over his head. He quietly put it down beside of him then stood up and stretched. He took out his gloves that he had made for his third victim and put them on. He then looked up at the moon. It was full, and the man in the moon was smiling at him.

Raynor bent over and pulled his pant leg up then pulled his knife out. He stared at it in the moonlight, kissed the blade, then turned to the box the detective was hiding in. He hadn't seen Raynor because his visibility holes were in the front and to the left of him. His peripheral vision to the right was blinded because they had made no visibility holes on that side, due to the fact that Raynor's box would have been blocking them.

"Evans," whispered Raynor.

"Yes Captain?"

"Come on, I think we've been made."

As detective Evans stood up and pulled the box from over top of him, Raynor pointed down the alley.

"I heard footsteps then they stopped about ten feet shy of us, then I heard running back down the alley that way. I want you to go that way and try to pick him up while I get the others."

As Evans began to walk past him to head down the alley, Raynor stepped behind him, took a fistful of Evans hair with his left hand almost lifting him off his feet, then quickly slit his throat deep enough to keep him from making any sounds. Evan's body instantly began to go limp and Raynor drug him behind the dumpster then threw the two boxes on top of him.

He then turned and headed into the backyard of Vahn's next door neighbor's house. There were two detectives in position there. Raynor walked through the back gate, which had been left open for him and Evans in the event they needed to get in, and walked up to the back of the house. He looked inside and didn't see anyone. There was supposed to be one detective watching the front and one watching the back.

This house as well as the houses across the street were to have minimal lighting. This was so that they could see out, yet the killer was unable to see in. Of course the actual reason was so Raynor could have the ability to be close to his men without them seeing any blood that may be on him.

Opening the backdoor Raynor entered into the kitchen of the house. He walked through to the living room and found both detectives looking out the front window in the darkness.

"What do you have out there?" Asked Raynor holding his knife behind his back.

"Damn, you scared the shit out of me," said Weaver as he jumped at the sound of Raynor's voice.

"There's a car that's driven by twice now. I don't know if it's our guy or if he's just lost," said Travis, the other detective.

"Evans and I thought we heard someone in the alley. Travis, you stay here. Weaver come with me."

Both men nodded as Weaver stood and began walking towards Raynor. Standing to the side, he let Weaver walk in front of him. They walked back through the dining room, then through the kitchen to the backdoor. As they walked into the backyard, Raynor grabbed Weaver by the back of his collar and pulled him backwards as he shoved his knife up into his back puncturing his lung. He twisted the knife and heard a gurgling sound come from Weaver as blood filled his lung. Twisting the knife back and pulling it out of his back, Weaver's body made a loud thump as it hit the ground. Raynor reached down and grabbed Weaver's gun, then tossed it across the lawn.

He then turned around and went back into the house. He wanted to kill Travis as he faced looking out the window but he still had two detectives directly across the street, as well as Harper and Chase right across from Vahn and a sniper on the roof of that house. Raynor stood in the kitchen with his back against the wall next to the doorway that Travis would be coming through.

"Travis, we're going to need your help out here!" Yelled Raynor.

He heard Travis's footsteps pounding toward him and he smiled. He held his knife up and waited. As Travis flew past him toward the backdoor Raynor jumped out behind him, locked his arm around

Travis's eyes and forehead and buried his knife in his neck. He quickly pulled back as he felt the blade against his own chest. It was sticking about two inches out of the back of Travis's neck.

Letting him fall to the floor, Raynor calmly turned around to the sink and washed his knife off. He was almost disappointed that this was so easy. Drying the knife with a hand towel, he walked back into the living room and looked across the street at his next stop. He could not see the two detectives that were positioned there, but he knew they were waiting in the darkness.

Throwing the hand towel on the floor he turned and headed out the back. He would have to go to the end of the alley, cross the main street at the end, and go down the alley behind the houses across the street. If he tried to cross over here they would see him. Regardless of whether or not they recognized him, they would know something was up, and they would be ready.

Chase stared across the street at Vahn's bedroom window. Damn it he hated this. He was terrified that something would happen and he wouldn't be able to get to her in time. If the killer made it in the house, Vahn would have to take care of him herself until they could get in to help her. But what if she couldn't. What if for some reason something happened to where she was unable to get a shot off.

He tried to tell himself that he was being paranoid and that everything would be okay. They couldn't have the area more covered. Yet for some reason he felt uneasy. Once he thought about it, that was exactly why he felt uneasy. Everything seemed too perfect. What if the asshole was setting them up? He wasn't sure what exactly was going to happen, but he knew that something just felt wrong.

Raynor counted the houses back to himself as he made his way up the alley. When he reached the house with Parker and Keller, he stopped at the fence line. This house had a chain link fence instead of a wooden one, which made it easier to see what was going on. He watched the set of sliding glass doors and waited to see if he could tell whether or not one of the detectives was positioned there where he was supposed to be. After a few moments he saw the flicker of a lighter, which answered his question.

Looking to the right at the next house, which was directly across from Vahn's, he could see the sniper on the roof. He had a black tarp over him that was supposed to keep him hidden from "the killer". Since the tarp was not flat against the roof, Raynor knew he was still in position. Another advantage for Raynor having the sniper use the tarp, was that the sniper could not see behind him. Raynor was unable to tell if Harper was watching the adjacent backyard because they had a wooden fence that was obstructing his view.

The men on this side of the street would not be expecting him to possibly be coming through the gate as they had on the other side, so he wasn't about to walk up to this house as he had the other. He knew that he couldn't get to this backdoor without being seen, yet he didn't want to use the radio, and he also didn't want to get shot on sight, and it happened to be dark as hell in that backyard.

After contemplating it for a few minutes, Raynor put his knife back in its holder and took his badge out. Standing up he held his radio in one hand and his badge in the other. He held his arms up over his head.

Though it was dark the detective would be able to see the antenna of the radio and the shape of his badge.

As he walked through the gate toward the house he saw the amber burning of the cigarette rise. He knew the detective had stood up and was checking him out.

The door slid open and a gun pointed out.

"It's Captain Reese," he whispered hoping it was loud enough for only this detective to hear.

Stepping out of the backdoor, Parker lowered his gun. "Captain you had me going there. I thought I was about to cap our killer."

"Sorry, I didn't mean to sneak up on you but I didn't want to use the radio. Everything is covered pretty tight over there. I wanted to see how you were holding up on this side," said Raynor clipping his radio back on his pants and putting his badge back in his pocket.

"We're good. Did you see that car drive by twice? We used the phone and called to run the plates. It comes back okay. Registered to a woman; not stolen. She lives on the north side of the city. We couldn't tell if it was a guy driving past or if the woman just has short hair."

"Let me go in and talk to Keller real quick, then I'll go next door."

"No problem Captain."

Raynor motioned for him to go first, then quickly bent down and pulled the knife from his calf. He wanted to wait until he knew that Keller wasn't watching them from the darkness before he did anything.

Stepping inside the house Parker called out, "Keller, the Captain's here to check us out."

As the words came from his mouth, Raynor stepped forward, grabbed his hair, pulled him backward and quickly slit his throat as deep as he could. Raynor quickly dropped him to the floor as he heard Keller coming towards them. As Keller entered the doorway in front of him, his eyes widened as he saw Parker on the floor. He quickly looked back up at Raynor's face in shock. Raynor smiled, shrugged his shoulders and buried his knife up under Keller's chin.

Holding Keller up and watching his eyes rapidly roll back and forth, Raynor waited until they were still, then pulled his knife out dropping Keller to the floor. Again he stepped to the sink and washed off his knife before heading next door.

Vahn laid in her bed with sweat pouring down her face. It wasn't so much that she was hot, it was that she was nervous as hell. She knew that they were supposed to keep the radio channels clear in case the killer was monitoring them, but she desperately wanted to hear someone's voice. Knowing that she was surrounded by detectives watching and ready to help her out was comforting for about the first hour. Now she felt terribly alone and all she could do was wait.

Staring into the empty hallway she wondered what his face would look like. She hadn't taken a good look at the picture on the note that was left on her door. Besides the fact that the boy's face was almost unrecognizable since the picture that was scanned had been so old.

What terrified her more than anything was not that he would look like a crazed psychopath. It was the thought that he may look like her. What would it be like to look in the mirror after this day? What would she see? Who would she see?

She had been lying there trying to repeat Chase's words over and over in her mind so that she would not drive herself insane with her thoughts, "…this is what he gets off on…don't let him get to you". She was so pissed off at herself for letting him do just that. That was exactly why the killer had warned her. He knew she'd be so fucked up in the head by the time he arrived that she wouldn't be able to function against him.

Vahn took in a deep breath then exhaled slowly. She felt her gun under her hand. "You better hope I can't function this, you fuck," she said. She knew that all she needed was a chance at one shot and her 9mm would do the rest. She just needed to stay calm and wait.

Raynor stood at the back of the fence and debated. He didn't want to enter this fence holding up his badge and radio. Harper was very trigger-happy and would love to get the credit for being the one to take him out. Harper would no doubt shoot first, investigate later.

Pulling out his cell phone Raynor dialed Chase's number.

"Hawk," answered Chase.

"Hey Hawk, this is Reese."

"What's going on Captain?"

"Well, everything is good on Vahn's side of the street. I wanted to make a quick sweep over here and make sure everyone was okay on this side."

"Yeah, we're good here Captain."

"Yell at Harper for me and let him know I'll be coming in the back so he doesn't let loose on me, could you."

Laughing Chase answered, "sure Captain, no problem."

After waiting a few minutes Raynor went through the back gate and saw Harper standing in the kitchen doorway.

"Thanks for calling first Captain. I can't see dick out here," said Harper as Raynor walked toward him.

"I knew better than to take my chances with you."

"Yeah well, what can I say. I am a good shot," said Harper laughing and assuming that Raynor had meant it as a compliment.

"I need to get up and talk to the sniper for a few. Where's the ladder at?" Asked Raynor.

"It's around the side of the house. Let me get it real quick."

When he returned they extended the ladder so that Raynor could get to the roof of the house.

"All right, thanks. I'll be down in a few," said Raynor as he climbed the ladder.

Raynor was excited about taking out the sniper. He wasn't from their squad of course, they had borrowed him from SWAT. If he didn't fully trust Raynor and if he wasn't lying on his stomach, he would be a hard one to take out, but unfortunately for the sniper, this would be all too easy.

"Jackson, it's Captain Reese," said Raynor as he stepped onto the roof. Jackson still could not see him because of the tarp that was draped over his body.

"Captain." He acknowledged.

Raynor crawled up the roof and lay on his stomach to the left side of Jackson and pulled the tarp back slightly so that he could see his face. The only advantage that Raynor would have was that he knew a sniper from SWAT would never take his eyes off his target. That was going to be the only thing that would allow Raynor to take him out.

"See anything yet?" Asked Raynor.

"Not a damn thing," answered Jackson not taking his eyes from the scope.

"How's your view into Vahn's bedroom?"

"Still perfect. She hasn't touched a thing."

"Have you seen her at all? Is she in position in the bedroom?"

"Yeah, she's been in there since nightfall. Either she's asleep or she's scared solid because the girl hasn't moved a muscle in the past two hours."

"She's not asleep. If I know anything about Carver, she's wide-awake and tuned into everything."

"I was told that you might not need me if she gets a crack at him."

"That's more than true. I'm sure she could take his ass out with her eyes closed."

"Maybe we'll have to take her from you and stick her ass up on some roofs now and then," laughed Jackson.

"She'd make the mark, that's for damn sure," said Raynor. As he continued he reached down and slowly began to pull his knife out of its holder. "Listen, just incase she's a little on the edge, there's been a slight change in plans."

"What's that?"

"If the bastard is brave enough to enter through her front door, I want you to drop him." Raynor pulled the knife up close to his body and wrapped his fist around the handle gripping it as tightly as he could.

"Drop him permanently?" Asked Jackson.

"No. Not a fatal shot, just get him where we can figure out what the hell is going on with him. Drop him enough so that he won't get up, but that should do it."

"No problem Captain."

As the words left Jackson's lips Raynor quickly pulled the knife up and buried it into Jackson's left temple with all his strength. Jackson's body immediately went limp. Raynor pulled his knife out and wiped it clean on Jackson's sleeve then put it back in its holder. Raynor then took the rifle from in front of Jackson and slid it to the left past himself so that he could pull Jackson's body up onto the middle of the roof so that he wouldn't slide down.

Taking the rifle off of its tripod and putting it over his shoulder with its strap, Raynor made his way back towards the ladder. He looked over the edge hoping that Harper wasn't still standing there, and was pleased to see that he had went back inside the house. Raynor descended the ladder as quickly and quietly as he could.

Reaching the door to the kitchen, Raynor put the rifle down on the ground and leaned it against the house. He entered the kitchen, and not seeing Harper headed toward the living room. Harper and Chase were staring out the window together, both sitting in chairs they had pulled from the kitchen table.

"Harper, come out with me and lock the fence back behind me would you?" Asked Raynor.

"Sure no problem Captain."

"Hawk, I'll see you in a few," said Raynor as they nodded heads at each other.

Raynor again stood to the side and let Harper lead the way. As they reached the backdoor and Harper stepped out into the grass, Raynor picked up the rifle and fell in step behind him.

"Harper wait a minute," he said pulling the butt of the rifle up.

"What is…" As Harper turned around, Raynor buried the butt of the rifle in his face knocking him out. When Harper hit the ground Raynor set down the rifle long enough to pull out his knife and quickly slit Harper's throat. He then wiped his knife off, replaced it in its holder, picked up the rifle, and headed back towards the house.

CHAPTER FIFTEEN

Chase stared out the window at Vahn's house completely pissed the hell off. What the fuck was the Captain doing on this side of the street? He was supposed to be watching the back of Vahn's house. They didn't know whether the killer would try to enter from the front or the rear, but hell, four detectives and a sniper covered the front of the house. Two men in boxes covered the rear of her house and he leaves only one person there so he could come and check on this side of the street. What kind of stupid shit was that?

Not ten minutes earlier he had called Chase on his cell phone and asked him to tell Harper that he was coming in the back. Why couldn't he have stayed put in his fucking box and made a few phone calls instead of leaving the back of her house open like that. If he had something to say to the sniper, either him or Harper could have went on the roof and relayed the message.

Even though the Captain was running the show, he had just as much responsibility on his post as they did on theirs. For him to leave it, just because he was a damn control freak that had to do everything himself, pissed Chase off so bad he could hardly see straight.

Taking a deep breath and trying to calm down, Chase heard Harper shut the kitchen door. He continued to scan the street as he heard Harper entering into the living room and said, "Can you believe that shit? Is he taking his ass back where it needs to be or what?"

"No quite yet."

Chase froze as he recognized the Captain's voice and quickly swung his view around. He turned just in time to see the butt of a rifle slamming down between his eyes.

Vahn was beginning to get terrified. The time did not seem to be going by slowly, it seemed to be going by too quickly now. She was staring at the clock trying to get time to stand still. She wasn't ready. She wasn't ready at all. Everything felt wrong. She didn't know why but everything felt all wrong.

It wasn't even midnight yet, and she knew from the first three victims' time of death that he usually came after midnight, but she didn't think she could handle the situation. What if she froze up? What if the sight of this man made her unable to move?

Being on the streets as a cop she had never felt this way, but she knew that was because it was never personal. She never had to deal with a murderer stalking her in her own home before. Her emotions went through violent mood swings about every five minutes.

She thought about Chase staring at her window from across the street. What was he feeling right now? Was he confident that they had things covered? She hoped so. Because right then she wasn't feeling like everything was covered. She felt like she had never been more vulnerable in her entire life.

Chase felt a sharp sting in his nostrils as he threw his head back trying to get away from it. He heard laughter behind him and realized that the sting in his nostrils was from a smelling salt. He blinked trying to focus. Slowly his surroundings came into view. His face was about three inches away from the window he had been looking out and he could see Vahn's house across the street.

Immediately he remembered being hit with the gun and tried to jump up to defend himself but he could not. His arms and legs would not move. He shook his head again trying to get his bearings and looked at his arms. They were spread eagle in front of the window. They were both strapped with zip-ties to hardware that had been drilled into the wall. On each side there were metal plates that had been attached to the wall. Each plate had a metal ring. His hands were strapped to the metal rings with zip-ties so tightly that his fingers were already blue and he had blood on his wrists where his weight had pulled his skin down making the zip-ties slice into his skin. He was standing on his knees and his feet were behind him.

"So you're pissed off that I left the back of the house open? Don't worry. The killer won't be going in the back."

Chase could hear his Captain's voice and he was furious. What the fuck was going on?

"You see, he's going to go right in the front door. Or I guess I should say, I'm going right in the front door," said Raynor as he let out a wicked laugh.

Chase was confused, and terrified. Was their Captain the murderer they had been investigating? How could that be? Not saying anything, Chase tried to move his legs again. His knees were together and he couldn't see his ankles but he knew they had to be strapped together with zip-ties as well. He was unable to move any part of his body other than his head, and his face was so close to the window that his peripheral vision was next to nothing. He could only stare out the window in front of him.

"What the fuck is going on?" Yelled Chase.

"Well, what's going on is that you have a front row seat, my friend."

"What the fuck is that supposed to mean?"

"Well, that means that I was going to kill you, like I did everyone else, so that I could be alone with Vahn when she and I reunite. But then I thought about it. For the last couple of years I had to withstand the agony of seeing the two of you together. It ripped my heart out. That's my sweet Vahn over there and you violated her. The thought of you touching her made me sick. I wanted to cut your hands off, peel the skin off of your fingers and crush your bones. But, then I thought about it, and I thought, why not return the favor? I had to put up with watching the two of you together, now I'm going to let you watch Vahn and I as we come together as one."

"Don't you fucking touch her!" Screamed Chase.

"Or what, my friend?"

Chase pulled at his arms and winced as pain shot down them.

"I really don't think you're in a position to be making threats. I was going to be nice and let you watch, but if you're not willing to cooperate and relax and enjoy the show, then I can take care of you now if you'd like."

Chase heard the Captain walking up beside of him. He leaned over and said, "What's it going to be Chase? Would you like to watch? I figure you for a man who likes to watch, but then again, only if you can join in later."

"Go fuck yourself," said Chase. He knew that his only chance would be to hope that the Captain would leave so that he could try to find a way out before he got to Vahn.

Standing back up and pacing the room his Captain said, "I'll let you in on a little secret." He laughed out loud before he continued, "I really liked watching you giving poor Kyle the rough tactics that day in the interrogation room. It's funny that though he was your only lead to possibly being the killer, you didn't give a shit about the damn condoms. All you cared about was how he knew Vahn and why he posed as her husband in Portland Place."

Laughing again, he pulled up a chair and sat down beside Chase. "You see, as your Captain, I was very disappointed in the focus of your questioning, but as the man who hired Kyle to pose as Vahn's husband, I was delighted to see that it fucked you up so bad," he laughed as he poked Chase in the side of his head twice.

Chase felt himself begin to tremble as the words passed over his ears. The man that had ruined his life and intended to destroy it completely had been right beside of him for months. Though he couldn't have possibly known before this moment, he shook with rage.

"See the funny thing about the Witness Protection program is that you go from being a criminal's target, to being an errand boy for the cops. If you want anything done, all you have to do is find some sorry asshole that bought into the whole charade that being in the Witness Protection program is the safest thing to do. The safest thing to do, is to move to Europe to a cold ass country where nobody would look for your sorry ass. Staying in the United States is like signing your own death certificate. Ignorant right? But why would we tell the sorry crooked bastards things like that? It wouldn't benefit us any." Slapping Chase on the back he laughed and continued, "see, all I did was threaten to make a phone call to Florida if he didn't do what he was asked. It was that simple. I thought he did quite well, what do you think?"

Chase clenched his teeth together and said nothing.

"Well, anyway, the two of you were getting a little too close, so what can I say? Vahn is meant to be mine, and mine alone. We are bound by destiny, and destiny is not something that can be stopped." Looking at his watch, he said, "I think Vahn is probably tired of waiting, don't you? I better head over there and get started."

The Captain stood up, shoved back his chair and picked up the rifle. "It's been nice knowing you Chase, I hope you enjoy this as much as I'm going to. I just wonder if you're going to off yourself when this is all over. Will you be able to live with the fact that the woman you love was killed while you watched? Well, have a nice evening," he said as he walked to the front door. He opened it and laughed as he walked through slamming it behind him.

Chase choked back bile and shook violently as he watched the Captain walking across the street to Vahn's house. He pulled desperately on his arms and yelled, as the pain was almost unbearable. The sharp plastic edges of the zip-ties were slicing away at his skin.

"You son of a bitch!" Screamed Chase as loud as he could as he watched the Captain casually walking toward Vahn's house as if he was simply going over for a visit. Hearing Chase's voice through the window he turned around, smiled and waved, then continued on.

Lying in her bed Vahn gripped her gun as she listened intently. She thought that she heard someone trying to get in her front door but she wasn't sure. Through the hours that had passed she had thought that she heard someone trying to get in about every fifteen minutes.

Slightly lifting her head, she strained to listen. She hadn't heard any type of banging sounds only the sound of metal clinking as if maybe someone was trying to pick the lock. Now she heard nothing. She laid her head back down and exhaled. This was insane.

Suddenly she heard her front door open, and her heart instantly began to pound. Oh fuck. What was she going to do? Though she knew she had already chambered her gun she now began to doubt everything.

She cursed herself for not double and triple checking it. She quickly looked at it. The safety was off. She was ready. She tried to steady her breathing and listen.

She heard the door shut and footsteps walking toward the hallway. She felt her body begin to tremble as she gripped her gun tighter. She planned on keeping the gun under the covers and letting off rounds as soon as he came into view.

"Carver, it's Captain Reese. Hold your fire."

Vahn felt a wave of relief as she recognized her Captain's voice. "What's going on?" She asked waiting for him to give her good news.

"We got him, everything's okay, come on out." Vahn threw back the covers and jumped out of bed. She quickly clicked the safety back on and put her gun down the back of her waistline. She went down the hall towards the living room and saw her Captain standing there. He was smiling.

"Where is he?" Asked Vahn as she walked up toward him looking toward the front door anxious to see Chase and to see the man that had tormented her mind.

"Right here," he said.

As quickly as the words came from his mouth, Vahn looked toward him and saw his fist flying toward her. As it upper cut to her chin she felt her head snap backward and she flew back and hit the wall. She felt the drywall cave in she had hit it so hard, and tried to hold on to consciousness as blackness surrounded her.

Chase trembled with fear and cursed under his breath. He had seen the Captain enter Vahn's house and had seen her flying out of bed toward the hallway, but he also saw her put her gun in her waistline. He knew it was up to him now. The bastard had made her put her guard down long enough to overpower her, no doubt.

Chase had been hoping that the asshole would be bold enough to walk down the hall straight into her room and begin to intimidate her just for a second. Just long enough for Vahn to squeeze off one round. But, obviously he was smart enough to stay calm and play the game. The minute he saw her tuck her gun away, Chase knew she would die if he did not free himself. Vahn was a good shot, but her self-defense was not good enough to go up against someone like their Captain. Not when he had the element of surprise on his side. She wouldn't be expecting anything and that was his window of opportunity.

Chase looked again at how his wrists were bound. The hardware that he was strapped to was not there before. The Captain must have had the hardware, the zip-ties, and either a screwdriver or a small drill so that he could install them. That son of a bitch! The whole time they had been planning their strategy in the precinct he had been planning his own. The bastard had an inside line the whole time. Chase knew this setup was almost too good. He could only imagine what the Captain had done to his own men to get this far. He was sick.

Chase's wrists were beginning to bleed freely now. There were small trails of blood running down his arms. At this point he didn't give a fuck if he lost both of his hands, he was not going to sit there and watch Vahn die. Trying to get his feet to come around was impossible. He was strapped so closely to the wall that he had no room to lean back to try to get his feet in front of him.

He looked again at his wrists. There were four screws in the hardware that was attached to the wall. Looking at the head of the screws they looked to be fairly big, maybe inch and a half screws. He wondered whether or not he could pull them out of the wall. Being right beside of a window frame, he looked at the sky and prayed that they were not screwed into studs in the wall. If they were strictly screwed into the drywall, he may have a chance.

Looking back up at Vahn's house he could see the Captain dragging Vahn into her bedroom. He felt his throat choke and hot tears sting his eyes. No! Fuck no! This was not going to happen! He didn't care what he had to do, he was not going to watch her die.

The tops of Chase's feet were flush with the floor with the souls of his shoes pointing up. He needed to try to get his toes up under his feet to give him leverage to try to stand. Chase struggled, he pushed his feet over onto their sides and rocked his body until he could get his toes up under his feet.

Again he looked up and saw the Captain binding Vahn's wrists in front of her with zip-ties. Panicking, Chase tried to use the leverage of his toes to push himself upwards. He had no room to move around. His knees were already almost flush with the wall. As he pushed he pulled down with his wrists. He yelled out against the pain as he felt the muscles in his thighs trying to pull him up and the pain in his wrists as his flesh was being cut.

Raynor hummed out loud as he bound Vahn's wrists together. He was ecstatic. This was the moment he had been waiting his whole life for. He knew Vahn was going to regain consciousness at any second. He knew she would be upset at first, but he also knew that he could get her to come around eventually.

Looking out her window he could not see Chase through the window across the street, but he knew that he would not be able to. Raynor knew that if he left a light on so that he could see Chase, then the glare would keep Chase from seeing him and Vahn. He wanted Chase to see everything. He wanted it to be burned into his memory forever. He smiled at Chase, knowing that he was surely staring straight at him, then turned back to Vahn.

She was beginning to move her head from side to side. Opening her eyes, she sat straight up and looked at him with fear and confusion in her eyes. He was leaning against the wall across from her and smiled reassuringly.

"What is this?" Asked Vahn. Her voice was cracking and she looked down at her wrists trying to get them apart.

"This is our reunion." He said with a smile on his face. He was so proud. This was so much better than he thought it would be.

Tears welled up in her eyes. He knew it was not because she was disappointed, but only because she was confused.

"I don't understand," she said glaring at him.

"I know you don't. That's why I'm here to explain it to you." Raynor walked towards her to sit on the bed with her. She began to try to back up across the bed and he quickly sat down and grabbed her by her hands.

"Listen Vahn. I promise you, you don't have to be scared anymore. I'm not going to hurt you."

"So you're who we've been tracking? You're the serial killer we've been looking for?" Vahn asked as her face was distorted in disbelief.

"Well, yes Vahn. But this goes way beyond that. I will try to help you understand that but first you have to believe that I'm not here to hurt you."

"Right. Just like you didn't cut that woman's head off."

"Well, that was different. She wasn't family. You are."

Vahn began to tremble. He wanted to hold her and comfort her, but he knew that he had to explain more things to her first.

"Do you believe in Destiny Vahn?"

"No," she said avoiding his eyes.

"Look at me Vahn, it is very important that you look at me while I'm explaining this to you."

"I don't think so," she snapped as she kept her gaze at her hands.

Grabbing a fist full of her hair and pulling her face up towards him so that she would look at him, he smiled. "You know, this doesn't have to be unpleasant. But I get slightly upset when things don't go my way. I have been planning this moment for over two years now. Drop your gaze from me again, and I will cut your eyes out and let you hold them in your hand until I'm done talking. I've been told that blind people have better hearing ability than people with sight."

Blood ran down Vahn's chin. She had bitten her lip hard enough to draw blood. She had to feel the blood, yet her gaze did not leave his eyes, and she did not attempt to wipe it away. Smiling, feeling very proud of her, he reached up and wiped it from her chin before he continued.

∘∘∘🔘∘∘∘

Trying to push himself up had been impossible. Chase was too close to the wall. He rested his head on the glass and tried to keep his mind straight. Looking up he saw the Captain grabbing Vahn by the hair and yanking her toward him. Chase felt his heart fall to his knees. He could not let this happen.

He began to frantically throw his body from one side to the other yanking his wrists as hard as he could. He closed his eyes and thought about Vahn trying to block out the pain. He wondered if the Captain had told her that he was strapped to the window watching them. He could not let her down. She must feel helpless.

Chase opened his eyes and looked at his left wrist. The two screws on the left side of the hardware were sticking out of their slots slightly. Chase shook his arm. He felt a rush of adrenaline flow through his body as he noticed that the hardware was beginning to come loose. He looked at his right wrist and noticed that it too was slightly working itself free.

The zip-ties binding his wrists were hardly visible now that they were covered in blood. The pain was so great that his wrists and hands were almost numb now. Chase looked back across the street at Vahn. "Hold on baby. I'm coming for you. I promise." And again he began throwing his body from side to side desperately trying to rip the hardware from the wall.

Vahn felt as if she were in a dream. How could this be reality? What kind of a sick cruel joke was her life? She could not believe that all of the strange and perverse things coming from his mouth had been what had welcomed her into the world, and what was also going to take her from the world.

Vahn hadn't asked what had happened to the other men. She knew. Though the lighting in her house had not been that bright, and the clothes he was wearing were black, they were also wet, and it damn sure wasn't raining outside. She knew he had killed the others.

She felt numb knowing that Chase was dead. Her life was about to end, and she didn't care. She had nothing to live for. Besides the fact that there was no way in hell that she could get out of the situation she was in, why should she? All the fight she may have thought she had, it was gone.

The sick, twisted individual sitting next to her was of her own flesh and blood. He was a mass murderer, and was now getting ready to commit a murder suicide and was acting like he was there to save the day. How could she have the same blood flowing through her veins and be normal. If she were to live, would she reach a point where she snapped and became as he was? If that was the case she was more than happy to let him do his thing.

He had told her that he no longer wanted her to think of him as her Captain, but as her brother. And he wanted her to call him by his first name, Raynor. Looking into his eyes, she saw nothing. They were cold, and they were empty.

Vahn had listened as he had told her about their mother. The junky that she was. He assured her that being sold as an infant was what saved her life. It had been his idea. Otherwise their mother and her friends were going to use her as a human sacrifice. They believed it would bring them more power and wealth.

Raynor had been smart enough to wait until his mother had no cash and was going through withdrawal. She was on the kitchen floor shaking and vomiting, lying in her own vomit. He had told her that she could make quick cash by selling Vahn to a couple that would keep those kinds of things under wraps.

Before Vahn had left, he had taken her out into the shed and performed a ritual on her, which was supposed to keep them spiritually connected. He described it in detail, and acted as if that was what had brought them together at that moment. Obviously she thought that he was full of shit, but as he began to describe things, she felt chills go up her spine.

The words coming out of his mouth were beginning to make sense to her. He said that Destiny has a mind of its own. It cannot be timed and it was not predictable. He said that though it took over twenty years to happen, he had been shown the sign that he had longed for. And it was so strange, that he hadn't quite understood it himself at first.

He told her that he had been standing in the shower almost three years ago, and his shower had transformed into a street. He had been shot in the thigh and had felt his leg burning as he looked at it and touched it. But his hand had not been his own, it had been her hand. He then was looking underneath of a car and saw feet running. He watched as his hand came into view, holding a gun, and pulled the trigger.

Again, this was not his hand, but hers.

He asked her if she remembered this at all. At first she simply thought his words were the ramblings of a mad man. Yet, when she thought about it, she remembered the dream she had the night she had left Johnny. That was it. She had awoken from that dream and had found Johnny in the living room with another girl. Then she left.

That was not the first time she had found Johnny with another girl in their own apartment, but by then she thought of him more as a roommate than anything else. She never cared. So why, after waking from that dream, did she set out and change the path of her life?

She felt cold chills flow over her.

He then began to describe what he had seen that led him to her. He described the prostitute being shot down in the street by her pimp across from the hotel that Vahn had been staying at. She could not believe her ears. She relived the moment as he described standing in his bathroom, then suddenly seeing the events unfolding through the glass of a car door that Vahn had been crouched behind. He had seen her face in the side mirror of the car.

She remembered that like it was yesterday. Watching the pimp pump round after round into the woman's body. And he had been watching it too. She listened as he continued to tell her how he had watched her run to the manager's office and dial the police. He had written down the number printed on the phone, then tracked her there. Raynor told her that he knew they were on the same path when he later saw her applying for the Police Academy.

"You see, Destiny is something that just happens. It led me to you, and in turn, it led you to me," he said still staring deep into Vahn's eyes. "You were a waitress in a diner and had been for years before the night you had that dream. Yet the next day you read in the paper about the Police Department hiring and you went and applied. This being where I already had a substantial career built. Do you think that you would have applied for that position if we hadn't connected that night?"

Vahn shook as his words hit her as if they were boulders. She distinctly remembered that by the time she read the ad in the paper there were only a few days left to apply. It had been posted in the paper for a while, yet she had never noticed it before that day. What did this mean? Was he right? Was she a Homicide Detective simply because fate had drawn her towards him?

Raynor continued on, telling her how he had watched her closely through her time at the academy. He told her how he had Kyle Weathers continually keeping tabs on her and Chase. He explained to her that he needed Kyle to keep them apart so that she would have a place of residency where she lived alone so that they could be together as they were now.

Smiling proudly he talked of his initial conversation with her lieutenant when she first requested that she be transferred to Homicide. He said that he had been so proud of her, yet wanted to put up enough resistance to keep in line with his reputation. He did not like women being in his department. There were several rumors as to why that was, but the truth of the matter was simple. He thought women were scandalous. He viewed them as walking piles of lust and deceit.

He refused to let his department be full of sluts that would fuck their partners in the back seats of their cars. Breaking up happy homes and keeping the men from having their mind on their cases. He wouldn't have it. Women had been transferred in, just to keep people off his back, but they quickly transferred out when he gave them the hardest cases and told them they didn't have what it takes.

Then he began to describe the most recent time that he had a vision. He described in detail, her making love to Chase on the couch in her living room. She felt her face flush as she began to feel embarrassed and manipulated. He smiled seeing that it was affecting her in that way.

After telling her what she had been doing, he began to describe to her what he had been doing. In detail he talked of how he had arranged the third victims garage. How they had spent so much time making sure that everything was perfect. Then, she had done it. Vahn had succumbed to her sinful desires, and he had seen it, and it had enraged him.

He described destroying the woman's face yet seeing Chase as he was doing it.

Vahn felt tears stream down her face as she visualized the woman's mangled head and body. She remembered the tracks of blood marking the ceiling, floor, and walls, showing how violently he had been swinging his arm as he stabbed her.

Raynor picked up on her reaction and stated, "yes Vahn, it was your fault that she was killed that violently. I had originally planned on simply slitting her throat and lying her down softly. It would have been perfect. The piece was to be entitled Desperation.

Catching don't you think?"

Vahn felt an overwhelming urge to vomit, as she realized that he was right. It had been her fault. She knew he wasn't lying. That had been the night that she and Chase had been together.

Raynor then told her of his original plan to have six victims and leave his mark on the city. It was cut short because he felt he couldn't control himself anymore, and he was selfish. He couldn't wait to be with her.

And now they were together at last.

Pulling out his .44 he showed it to her, and explained that they would both be gliding swiftly from this life to the next. This life was tainted with unspeakable things, yet in the next, they would take care of each other forever. He promised that it would be swift, and that she would not feel a thing.

As Chase continually threw his body weight from one side to the next with as much force as possible, he could feel that he was almost there. The two outside screws on each side were already free from the drywall. He just needed to keep going.

Stopping for a split second to look across to Vahn he saw that they were still sitting on the bed talking, but he knew he was almost out of time. Again he threw himself to the left as hard as he could, and felt his wrist almost pull the hardware free from the wall. He then threw all of his body weight to the right with everything he had, and finally the hardware holding his left hand broke free from the wall.

Chase's hand fell hard to the floor. He was looking at his blood soaked arm as if it weren't even his own. His arm was so numb he could barely move it. Quickly he brought his feet around in front of him and looked at them. They were bound with three zip-ties, and he could hardly feel his legs. Using the ledge of the window to pull himself up, he stood and put his body close to the wall where his right hand was still attached. Using his full body weight to help him, he yanked his right hand free from the wall.

Feeling an overwhelming source of energy, and knowing that every second counted, Chase fell to the ground and used his elbows to crawl into the kitchen. Reaching the kitchen sink, he reached up and pulled himself to his feet. He pulled open the drawer to the right of the sink and was looking at the silver wear tray. He pulled open the drawer next to that, revealing potholders.

Frustrated he quickly looked around the room and saw a knife set sitting next to the stove. He jumped over to it, reached up and clicked on the light above the stove then grabbed a knife from the wooden stand. He was having a hard time holding the knife because he could not feel his fingers.

He laid his left arm down on the stove, then had to actually set the knife back down in order to dig the ziptie out from under his skin with his fingers before he could cut his wrist loose. He quickly did the same with his right hand, then reached down and cut his legs free.

He knew that he had lost a lot of blood. He didn't want to run out of energy right when he reached Vahn. He was going to need to have enough in him to rip that muther fucker's head off. Chase ran to the drawer that the potholders were in and quickly threw them on the floor until he came to a hand towel. He ripped it in half, and tied the halves around his wrists to try to stop the bleeding.

His gun and shoulder holster were missing and he did not have time to look for them. He knew Harper's body had to be in the backyard. As fast as the Captain had come back inside, he didn't have time to go any further. Running to the backdoor, Chase could see a body lying in the grass. He practically flung the door off its hinges as he opened it and ran to the body. Harper's gun was still in his holster. Chase grabbed it, and sprinted toward the front of the house.

———∘∘∘▶◀∘∘∘———

"Before we go, do you want to say goodbye?" Asked Raynor.

Vahn did not understand what he was talking about. Say goodbye to who?

Standing up and pulling her to her feet, Raynor led Vahn to the window. He grabbed the string to her blinds and pulled them up to the top of the window so that they could see out.

"Well, your partner happens to be watching us. I told him that since I had to endure watching the two of you, then he could sit through the anguish of watching the two of us."

Vahn's heart began to race. She had assumed he was dead. She looked deep into the darkness and couldn't see him. She knew that he would be hard to see because the house was pitch black, but she was desperately searching, trying to see him. She knew that there was a possibility that Raynor could be lying, but still, it gave her strength.

As she stood there staring out the window, with her arms bound in front of her, and Raynor standing at her back, she saw something that caught her eye. It was her reflection. She could see Raynor's reflection as well, his smug smile splashed across his face.

Looking back at herself, she realized one thing. Whether Chase was alive or not, she could not die this way. The bastard was going to kill her regardless of whether or not she put up a fight. She didn't know what the outcome was going to be, but in that moment, she knew that she was not going to be the submissive sister he wanted her to be. He had mind fucked her until she had almost welcomed death. Now it was time to fuck him.

Locking her fingers together, Vahn closed them as tightly as she could. She looked at her reflection once more, then in one swift motion, moved slightly to the right, stepped back between his legs, and brought her left elbow straight into his groin.

She quickly spun around as he bent over and elbowed him in the eye as hard as she could. She took a step forward toward the door then whirled around, and kicked him in the face with her right foot. His body went flying against the wall then hit the floor. She turned back around and ran for the door. She was running as fast as she could but she seemed to be going nowhere.

Vahn could hear him rising from the floor and she felt her feet falter. Right as she reached the doorway she tripped and saw the carpet flying toward her face. As she hit the ground she heard a thump and looked up at the wall above her head in the hallway. A huge knife was vibrating back and forth where it had buried itself.

Jumping to her feet, Vahn ran to the knife and yanked it out of the wall. She turned and could see him holding his gun, coming towards her. She ran halfway down the hall and turned around. With her hands still bound, she turned the knife around so that she was holding the blade. She held it up next to her ear and waited for him to come into view.

As Raynor stepped into the hallway, Vahn threw the knife as hard as she could. It went sailing toward him. With not even a blink of his eye, he swiftly turned his body to the side, and the knife buried itself in the wall behind him. The look on his face had changed. He no longer looked as if he wanted to be with her eternally. He now looked as if he intended to annihilate her.

As his footsteps came bounding down the hall after her, Vahn turned and was scrambling, trying to run. Her mind raced. She didn't know which way to go. There were more knives in the kitchen. She could try to run out the back, she could try to run out the front. All she could think about was that his .44 was going to blow her back out at any second.

Then she saw it. Sitting on the back of her couch was her 9mm. Apparently he had taken it from her waist when he had knocked her out and had tossed it on the back of her couch. It was only six feet away. She tried to bring her knees up farther, and pump her legs faster. Five feet, she could hear him screaming her name; four feet, she held her hands out and reached towards the gun; three feet, she heard him pull back the hammer; two feet...

Vahn fell to the floor as she heard the boom of a gun. As her head hit the floor she heard two more shots bellow out. As the shots rang out in her ears, she felt nothing. She brought her hands up in front of her and pushed herself up. She whipped around to see Chase standing in her doorway, holding a gun and Raynor lying face down on the floor.

Turning to look at her, Chase had tears in his eyes. He ran towards her and picked her up off the floor.

"Are you hurt?" He asked.

She could say nothing. She fell limp in his arms and stared at Raynor. She could hear Chase's voice asking her again if she was hurt, but she could not answer him. As she shook with fear, she looked up into his face, then pulled the gun out of his hands.

"Vahn what are you doing?"

She heard him ask the question over and over as she walked up to Raynor's body.

He was facing towards the kitchen. She walked around him and stared at his face.

She remembered only hours earlier how she had laid in bed, fearful that if she lived through this night, that she would see his face for the rest of her life. She was going to make sure there was nothing to remember. Holding the gun up, she emptied the clip into his face.

PROLOGUE

It was Thanksgiving. Vahn had her toboggan pulled down over her ears and had her heavy coat on. She was watching as Chase and his brother were the last two contenders in the shooting contest they were having. Her in-laws had taken a vote and she was not allowed to participate in this activity. After winning at every family gathering for a year straight, they thought her reign had lasted long enough.

Vahn had plenty of practice at work anyway. She was now the shooting instructor at the Police Academy. Chase was still a Homicide Detective. Occasionally she helped out at the Kile Shelter. A women's shelter that Ricki had set up in the city.

"Vahn honey, you're wanted in here," yelled Chase's mom from their back porch.

Vahn turned and walked up the steps to their backdoor and pulled her hat off as she stepped inside.

"Mommy!" Yelled her little strawberry-blonde, blue eyed man, running towards her with his arms out.

As she picked him up and kissed him, she smiled. The funny thing about Destiny, is that though it can't be stopped, it's always open to suggestions."

ABOUT THE AUTHOR

Renee Lear is a native of Texas and currently lives in Colorado. She is an author of both fiction and non-fiction novels, screenplays, and children's books.